IN AND OUT OF
NEVER-NEVER LAND
22 STORIES

Maeve Brennan

IN AND OUT OF
NEVER-NEVER LAND

22 Stories

Charles Scribner's Sons
New York

For the Bolgers of Coolnaboy, Oylegate

ANASTASIA JAMES JOHN
ELIZABETH ELLEN WALTER

CONTENTS

Contents

TWO PEOPLE

BLUEBELL

The Door on West Tenth Street

Bluebell the old black Labrador retriever is going to have a holiday from the city. She is going to Katonah, a distant suburb of New York, where she will have trees, grass, hedges, night-smells of earth, and, at a distance, a road to watch, and passing cars. She will have a house of her own, to guard. There is a field in Katonah where she can run as hard as she likes, and, not far away, a lake where she will swim, holding her head high, pouring herself through the water while her big, heavy old body feels light again and her legs stretch themselves. In the lake in Katonah, Bluebell's short, thick, powerful sea legs will stretch themselves until all the dull constriction of city sidewalks and city streets crumbles away from her webbed paws and from inside her muscles. Her legs will become sleek again and they will do what they like, sending her through the water at exquisite speed, so that the people watching her think, Why would anybody want to go faster than Bluebell, and how can anybody bear to go more slowly than she goes when she swims?

Bluebell is a changeling, anxious to please, but water is her element, and when she swims she becomes herself, a solitary reveller with a big, serious, courageous head and a store of indifference that make it seem sometimes that she might never come back to land. She always comes back, shaking herself so that the water springs off

3

her and her fur stands up in spikes. And after shaking she stands for a minute, staring about her with the mad cousinly friendliness of her true cousin, the dolphin. She is ready for anything. At that moment, wet and rakish from her swim, Bluebell seems to have travelled to earth from a far distance—from the bottom of the sea, twenty thousand fathoms down, where the Fish King has his court. The Fish King never speaks, not even to say "Now" or "At once." His words are made of thunder and they reverberate at his will. Great sounds issue from him—sounds of wrath, sounds of mirth, and sounds of hunger. But he never speaks. He sits in oceanic silence under an immense floating canopy that is really an upturned lake of fresh clear water, and in its blue depths and shallows small green flowers and silver goldfish play games with the sunlight that was trapped in the water on the day the lake was stolen—a Monday in Norway, centuries ago. Bluebell has seen the Fish King and his canopy, and she knows his palace guard of dignified young whales, and the thousand sequined mermaids who are his dancing girls. She was at home with them, and she is at home with us. She has seen everything. It is written in her face, in her sad, bright eyes. There is hardly anything she does not know, except when to stop eating. Her true memories are ancestral—they haunt her sleep. In daily life, the compromise she makes is wholehearted, but there is nothing in it of acquiescence. Housebound, she remains herself. She is a dog.

But today Bluebell is going to the country. She is going to Katonah, where her big, hungry nose will find something to smell besides concrete and stone and lampposts, and gutters that seem interesting but that always prove unresponsive in the end. Bluebell does not know that her leash is going to be put away for a month. To her, this is an ordinary day, and it starts as usual in her Greenwich Village apartment. She rouses from her sleep on the bedroom floor, on a dark, flowery carpet that is thin and worn to pale string in spots—a length salvaged from the acres of carpeting that once covered the lobbies and stairs of one of those majestic old New York hotels that disappeared last year, or the year before, or the year before that. The carpet smells of Bluebell's sleep and of the cats' sleep and of the vacuum cleaner, but that is all. There are no memories in it, no echoes of country grass and leaves and earth, no bits of sand, no woodsmoke, no pine needles, nothing of the house by the ocean in East Hampton, where Bluebell lived for most of her life. This is an apartment carpet, anonymous, warm, comfortable, and dull. No field mice ever ran across it, flying for their lives from the cats; no field mice, no moles, no chipmunks, no baby rabbits. Once a regiment of tiny black city ants marched across it and disappeared into the wall. And once an enormous black water bug hurried out of the bathroom and across the carpet in the direction of the kitchen. And a soft, pale-green caterpillar, a visitor from nowhere, crawled timidly about in the dark foliage of the old carpet for a little while before he curled up to die. But that is all. It is a poor, boring carpet, and Bluebell yawns when she wakes up, ignoring it. She stands and stretches and looks about her, showing she is ready for her walk.

Bluebell's walk takes her around Washington Square, and as she passes the doorman of the big apartment house on the corner he grins and says, as he does every morning, "Hello, Old-Timer." Bluebell is nearly eleven years old, and her young, original, shining black face is disguised by a dusty mask of gray hairs, gray eyebrows, gray muzzle, and long gray jaws. The mask makes her comical, and people smile when they see her and say, "Oh, my, that's an old dog." People walking behind her smile, too, because, although her thick, heavy tail is still coal black, her behind is gray and it waggles importantly as she goes along. But however she goes, trotting, cantering, plodding, or simply dawdling, she always looks what she is—a dog out of water, not at ease in the city but

5

putting up with it very well. She is amiable, although not particularly obedient, and she accepts her leash and makes her way, leading with her strong, wide-set shoulders and getting all she can out of this strange world where she has to behave like a clockwork dog who can go only in squares, circles, and straight lines. And she searches. She keeps looking for a black door in a little white house on West Tenth Street. Twice on her walks she happened on that door and refused to pass it, struggling to get into the house and even barking once, but for weeks now, for months, she has not seen it.

The house belongs to a man who took Bluebell to Montauk for six weeks last summer, and when she sees the door on West Tenth Street she knows what lies behind it—a cliff dropping into the Atlantic Ocean. Bluebell loves that cliff, which gave her a wild dash to her morning swim and, on her way back, countless difficult crannies to dig and burrow into. The house on West Tenth Street looks like a real house, and no one passing it would dream that all of Montauk lies behind it—the cliff, the sand, and the ocean. Everything worthwhile is there behind that door, which Bluebell knows is closed only to hide the sea from dogs who are not going there. She has not seen that door for a long time now, but she has not lost hope. She watches for it. She looks for it everywhere, on all the streets east and west of Fifth Avenue, and along Fifth Avenue, and along University Place, and on Fourth Avenue, and on Seventh Avenue, and on little Gay Street and on Cornelia Street and even on Bleecker Street, behind the stalls of vegetables and fruit, but she is never confused into thinking that a strange door is the door she wants. There is only one door on West Tenth Street and she will know it when she sees it again.

Even in the city, Bluebell had adventures. As she walked around Washington Square Park one morning, she came alongside a very, very old man sitting alone on one of the benches that line the paths around the grass. He was more than old, he was ancient, and although it was a glowing day, Indian summer, he was warmly dressed in an overcoat and a muffler and a crumpled gray hat, and he wore laced boots, and his hands were clasped together on his walking stick, and his eyes were closed. Bluebell passed very close to him, and he may have heard her dramatic breathing as she pressed on in her pursuit of the Atlantic Ocean (hiding behind that door on West Tenth Street, so near, but where?), because he opened his eyes and saw her. He didn't smile, but he looked at her. "Hello, Snowball," he said, thoughtfully. "How are you doing, Snowball?" Then he closed his eyes again and went on sitting by himself in the warm sun.

Another time Bluebell found a dead sparrow lying at a grass corner in the center of the Square, where the fountain is. (Where the fountain *was*. It has been dry for a long time.) The sparrow, no bigger than a withered leaf, lay on his side, with his wings folded and his legs close together. He was a very neat little dead body. A wild bird, his fate was strange anyway—to share a shabby city park with hungry, watchful pigeons, big fellows. How old had he been when he learned to dash in among them and grab his crumb? He must have been strong and clever to survive to his full size. His cleverness was finished now, and the story of his life was not even history—it was a big mystery that he had never known anything about, and that was wrapped about him now as he lay by the grass. He lay there, with the secret of his nature in open sight for anybody to look at; but only to look at, not to touch, not really to see, never to understand. He was a sparrow, whatever that is. Samuel Butler said life is more a matter of being frightened than of being hurt. And the sparrow might have replied, "But Mr. Butler, being frightened hurts."

Bluebell looked at the sparrow, and then she sat down and

7

began to contemplate him. There was nothing to smell, but the light breeze blowing from the south, from Sullivan Street, touched a loose feather and it stood up and waved, a tiny flag the color of dust. That was all. It was quite otherwise with the mighty pheasant, an emperor pheasant, Bluebell found dead on the beach in East Hampton one autumn morning, her third autumn by the ocean, years ago. That was an unearthly morning—one mislaid at the beginning of the world and recovered in East Hampton under a high and massive sky of Mediterranean blue. An Italian sky, a young and delighted ocean, a blazing sun; and far away on the white sand something crimson that caught the wind. The wind was so new that it blew cold, in its first rush across the world, but the air was soft. The pheasant's head and body were almost buried in the powdery sand, but he had fallen with his wings wide open, and one of them slanted up to make a wedge of color in the air.

That autumn morning was early in November—the time of year when millions of small stones appeared in flattened wind formations at intervals along the lower part of the beach, where the sand is hard and flat near the water's edge. Some of the stones are as big as walnuts and some are as small as grains of rice, and they lie tightly packed, a harsh sea fabric, while their faint colors—ivory, green, silver, coral—are always vague, almost vanishing, always about to dissolve into the stone. Bluebell used to race along the beach until she was almost out of sight, and at that distance, far away, she became a big black insect with four waving legs and a waving tail and wings that were either transparent or folded. Because it was impossible that a creature who skimmed so confidently and at such speed across the sand and in and out of the water and along the top of the dunes should not also be able to fly up and away and out to sea, with the sea gulls. The sea gulls detested Bluebell and flew off screeching with irritation whenever they saw her hurrying toward them. They stood in a long single line, staring at

8

the water, and waited until she came close to them before they took flight. Their feet left a delicate tracery of pointed marks, a Chinese pattern, in the clean wet sand. Bluebell's big paws made untidy holes in the sand, and sometimes troughs, and even when she did make a recognizable paw mark it was indistinct and awkward, not to be compared with the delicate sea gull imprint. She had attacks of wanting to dig in the sand, and then she dug as frantically as a dervish looking for a place to whirl. She loved to chase her ball into the ocean. She had a succession of balls—red, green, blue, and white, and sometimes striped, but one by one they drifted out to sea while Bluebell stood at attention on the shore and watched them go. She knew the power of the big waves, and how they hurled themselves so far down into the sand that they were able to drag it out from around her legs.

After Christmas, when the storms began, the beach was whipped and beaten into bleak terraces—long ranges of sharp sand cliffs descending from the dunes to a struggling, lead-colored sea that foamed into mountains against the sad sky, while the sea gulls screamed their warnings all day long. One day in January, Bluebell received a present from the grocery shop of an enormous bone, a bone of prehistoric size and weight, a monumental thighbone with great bulging knobs at each end. She took hold of the bone at its narrowest place, in the middle, but even so she had to open her big jaws to their widest and her head was pulled forward by the bone's weight. She straightened up and carried the bone from the kitchen to the lawn in front of the house, where she placed it on the frozen grass and looked it over tenderly before she started to attack it. Two sea gulls appeared out of the fog and circled about not far above her, watching for a chance at the bone, and the day was so strange that the sea gulls seemed to speak as natural claimants for the fog that was taking possession of the house. It was a dark-white day under a lightless sky and the view was ghostly. The small grove of trees at

9

the end of the driveway had become a dim outpost, and to the left of the house, toward the ocean, there was nothing to be seen except shapes formed by the fog. Outside the house only the two sea gulls and Bluebell with her bone had substance. The fog reached the windows as the afternoon wore on, and night came to find the house shrouded, lost, hidden, invisible, abandoned except by the ocean, which filled each room with the sound of eternity, great waves gathering themselves for the clash with earth and darkness. Bluebell had been in and out of the house all day. About seven in the evening she cried to be let in, but when the door was opened to her she backed away from the light and was immediately lost except for her face, a thin gray mask with imploring eyes looking out of the fog. Her eyes were pleading, not for permission to come in but for permission to bring her bone into the house. She vanished and reappeared a minute later, a transparent dog face that held in its ghostly jaws the great bone, which glowed phosphorescent, while beyond it four round diamonds flamed suddenly—two of the cats returning from their usual night-watch. There was no moon that night; no moon, no stars, no clouds, no sky, no real world—only the little house settling slowly into its place in safest memory, guarded by the silence that poured out of the voices of the waves.

The lawn in front of the house belonged to Bluebell. In the summer she stretched herself out on it to bake, and in the winter when the snow was very deep she played boisterously in it, rocking and leaping and plunging, a dolphin again. The lawn was separated from the emerald acres of a famous golf course only by a thin line of trees, and from her place near the house Bluebell could see the public road and the cars passing along there, going south to the beach or north to the village. Sometimes a car turned into her driveway and then she ran forward to welcome it. During her early days in the city she was surprised to find so many cars and all so close to her, parked along the sides of all the streets where she walked, and at first she thought they were all friends and she used to notice each car, and smell it, and look to see if there was a place in it for her. She soon discovered that in the city cars had no connection with her, and she stopped expecting anything from them, although it made her very restless to see a dog looking out of a car window, because she could not help hoping that somebody would offer her a ride, even a short ride, anywhere. Away from home, that is where Bluebell dreamed of being, when she saw dogs in cars, and when she watched for the house on West Tenth Street. Away from home, that is where Bluebell wanted to be.

One afternoon, just before the start of her holiday in Katonah, her walk took her a long way west, to Hudson Street and the walled garden of St. Luke's Chapel. It was a cool afternoon, with thin sunlight, and a complicated country fragrance drifted across the walls of the old garden and through the bars of the garden gate. Bluebell put her nose to the gate and smelled. She could see the big, old-fashioned garden, fading in autumn, and she smelled leaves, grass, and earth. Bluebell smelled fresh earth. Somebody in the garden was digging.

In secret places in the neighborhood of her house in East Hampton Bluebell used to bury her best bones. They were her treasures, and she knew they were still where she had left them, safely hidden, waiting for her. She smelled earth now, the same old earth, but she could not get into the garden because the gate was closed, and locked. There was a lady in the garden, walking near the gate, and Bluebell wagged her tail, but the lady didn't see her, or didn't want to see her. Bluebell stopped wagging, and two or three minutes later she turned from the gate and went around the corner onto Christopher Street. And there, as she walked west on Christopher Street, Bluebell saw a vision. She saw the public road that cuts through the golf course in East Hampton, with the cars passing each other, going north and south, just as they always did. She was looking at the West Side Highway, which is cut out of the air around it just as the road in East Hampton is cut out of the green golf course. All she really saw was cars moving *in the distance*. It was months since Bluebell had seen cars at a distance, and the distance between where she was on Christopher Street and the elevated highway was much the same as the distance between her old lawn in East Hampton and her old view of the golf course. Everything was happening at once. Her head was still full of the smell of new earth, and she was seeing her view again, and now she smelled, very close to her, the Hudson River. The river did not smell like the Atlantic Ocean, but Bluebell knew she was walking toward water, big water. Perhaps she was going to have a swim. Her ears went up and she began to hurry, pulling on her leash. But then she turned another corner and found herself back in the same old concrete quadrangle, walking her geometrical city-dog walk, with only miserable lampposts to tease her starving nose. In her disappointment Bluebell lost her temper and charged furiously across the sidewalk to threaten a five-pound nuisance, a miniature white poodle who yapped rudely at her, and who stood like a hero on his four tiny paws and glared up at her until she was dragged away, seventy pounds of raging disgrace.

Poor Bluebell. She is being made foolish in her old age. She would like to go swimming, show them all what she can do. She would like to go swimming, show them all what she really is. She would like to dig up a bone. She would like to go for a ride in a car. She would like to find that door on West Tenth Street. Most of all, she would like to get away from Home. Yes, she would very much like to get away from Home, who now marches along behind her, holding her leash.

Home speaks: "Good Bluebell. Good Dog. Nice Walk. Good Bluebell."

Home's voice is consoling, but Bluebell can't be bothered to

The Door on West Tenth Street

listen. Bluebell is sick of Home, who holds her on a leash and won't let her go anywhere or do any of the things she wants to do.

"Good Bluebell," Home says.

Bluebell begins to go faster and now it is Home's turn to be dragged along, hanging onto the leash. Home protests angrily.

"Stop it, Bluebell," Home says. "Bad Bluebell. Bad Dog. *Bad.*"

Bluebell doesn't care. She begins to speed.

Home shouts, *"Bad, bad!"*

Bluebell is pulling so hard that her chain collar hurts her throat but she only goes faster and faster. Disappointment and boredom have turned her into a fiend, and all she wants is to get as far as she can from Home.

But that was several days ago. Today, Bluebell is going to Katonah for a holiday in the country. The car comes at twelve, as it promised to do. Bluebell is led out of her apartment house on her leash, just as though she was going for her ordinary walk. But then the car door is opened and Bluebell leaps into the back seat. She is mad with joy. She tumbles over herself and tries to tumble into the front seat, but as soon as the car starts off she quiets down and sits looking out through the window at the streets she is leaving. She is trembling with happiness. She makes no sound, but her eyes are shining with adoration for everything she sees—for the streets, and for the car she is in, and for the driver of the car, and for Home, who sits beside her in the back seat. Yes, Bluebell is going away from Home, and Home is going with her. Bluebell turns her head from the window and looks at Home, who is smoking a cigarette and smiling. "Good Bluebell," Home says, and Bluebell stretches herself out on the seat and puts her head in Home's lap. "Good Bluebell," Home says. Bluebell sighs and half closes her eyes. Her tongue comes out and she licks her lips. She settles herself for a long ride. The wheels of the car go round and round and they sound as though they might keep going forever.

A Large Bee

A large bee, carried by the wind to the edge of the Atlantic Ocean, lay on his back and struggled to free himself from the wet sand. As the wind continued to blow, more sand drifted over him and packed itself around him, and by the time Mary Ann Whitty came along, walking with her dog, there was nothing to be seen of him but a tiny coffin of sand with his black legs waving feebly out of it.

This was on the strand in Amagansett last April, and at first she thought she was looking at some kind of a sea insect, something that lived in the sand. There was no color or shape to show that a bee was there, no evidence that the creature had wings, only the black legs to show that something was alive and wanted to stay alive. With a big shell she scooped this *something* up and carried it back to the high dry sand and tried to turn it right side up, so that it could find its feet, or free its wings and balance itself, or fly away, or burrow down, or do whatever it had to do. But it could not stand, and kept tumbling over on its back, and after a minute the wind picked it up and blew it right back to the edge of the water. The tide was coming in. Mary Ann had a silk scarf in her pocket and she took that and went after the bee—she still did not know the creature was a bee—and scooped him up again and placed him in the middle of the scarf, which she then tied into a bag by its four corners.

A Large Bee

Her dog, Bluebell, a black Labrador retriever, rather fat, had been amusing herself while Mary Ann was rescuing the bee. Bluebell had raced to a distant line of sea gulls who were standing sentinel at the edge of the water, a long way off, and had destroyed their afternoon by making them all fly up into the air. Now she came racing back to Mary Ann and they continued to walk until they came to the opening between the dunes that put them on the path to their house. As she walked along the sandy path, Mary Ann looked into the silk bag to find out if the insect was ready to be set free, and it was then she saw that she was carrying a bee and that he was still half covered with sand, and she thought, I will take him home and let him dry out and see what he wants to do next.

Halfway along the path, she saw what she expected to see—from the undergrowth at the edge of the woods the cats were coming out to meet her. They came out slowly, stretching at intervals, down the bank, onto the road, and then they all sat down heavily and watched, yawning. When she came close to them, they stood up and waited for recognition, which she gave each of them separately. Then Bluebell offered to recognize them and they backed away in disgust, because she was wet and salty from the sea. The cats all began to run for home, running like rocking horses, with their tails arched. Bluebell was tired from her swimming and content to waggle along beside Mary Ann. The bee made no weight in the scarf. It might as well have been empty. There were woods on both sides of the road for a little way, and then woods on one side only, because on the right a clearing had been made, and there the house in which she lived stood, but it stood up on a height, and from it there was a clear view across the tops of the trees to the dunes and across the dunes to the ocean. There were wide, irregular steps cut into the side of the bank that sloped from the road to the house, and in front of the house was a wooden deck. She went in and laid the scarf on the table. She lighted the fire. She poured milk for the cats and lured them with it to the deck and then shut the door on them, shutting them out. Then she untied the scarf and looked at the bee. He was still moving his legs feebly and the sand was falling off of him. She left him there and went to sit by the fire. Bluebell lay down with her head on the hearth and closed her eyes. Mary Ann was always afraid her brain would boil when she did that, but she spoke to Bluebell and Bluebell opened one calm eye and then shut it again.

Bluebell almost never barked, but when she had been waiting outside the house for too long, when she began to lose patience and feared that the door would never be opened, she summoned from some point at the top of her head a sound that was at first so thin and unearthly that it might be called ethereal—an ethereal note from far away. This sound dropped quickly into a vulgar, insistent whine, which dropped without delay into the most shameful manifestation of her impatience, fear, and anger—a sustained squeal so penetrating that no one who heard it ever wanted to hear it twice. Now as Mary Ann sat by the fire waiting for the bee to revive or not revive, she knew that something had been whining at the back of her head, and as she listened the whine gave voice, and what she heard was not a squeal but a harangue that was familiar to her because it sounded at intervals from the side of her brain where the random insights that other people had had about her grew and flourished and multiplied themselves, like the weeds that they were. They had a weedy strength, a weedy tenacity, a weedy life, and their own weedy truth, and she supported them, and she allowed them to live and to express themselves, because she could afford them. At the time that they took root in her mind she could not afford them, but she accepted them, after a struggle—by that I mean that she made room for them. There are some natures that can expand to include anything, even the things that ought to be thrown away.

A Large Bee

Mary Ann was hearing the voice of her conscience, which, of course, was familiar to her, although it bore no more resemblance to her own voice than Bluebell's unpleasant squeal did to her ordinary gentle silence.

The bee would have been dead by now. Why do you bother all these creatures? Why not leave them alone? The field mouse the cats brought in this morning has been living in the box you arranged for it in the bedroom all day, waiting for the darkness, when you will put it out again, and the cats will probably catch it again, and in any case it has nothing ahead of it but fear and the search for food. It was dead when they brought it in, but you would bring it back to life. Why don't you let these animals alone? The same with the baby rabbits and the chipmunk and the rest. Nothing but egotism. Why not let things be? Let everything alone. Stop interfering. Nature must take her course. . . .

At that moment a great excitement started in the room and Bluebell jumped up as though she had been stung. No, she had not been stung. But the bee had collected all his force and had come to vigorous life and had come out fighting. He raced around the room, making a very loud noise, and tried to get out through the back windows, which looked over a green space that had a few trees and, at the far side, a bed where daffodils were in bloom. Mary Ann opened the window and he flew out. He was so big that she could follow his flight for a good distance. He seemed all right, and he seemed to know what he was doing. *That bee will be swept right back to the ocean with the first wind,* the voice said. *You did him no good. He must be stupid or he would never have been blown down there in the first place. . . .*

She went into the kitchen to put the kettle on for tea. All true, she said to herself. No doubt about it, everything you say is true.

The Children Are Very Quiet
When They Are Away

It is a winter-afternoon sky, very dark, and lowering itself now to thicken the heavy mist that is gathering over the dunes. The Atlantic Ocean, hidden by the fading dunes, is thundering today. The line of the dunes is growing dimmer, and the huge house that stands up there over the sea is becoming ghostly. It is an enormously clumsy house, with hundreds of diamond-paned windows and a massive front door that has flights of stone steps going up to it. Inside, there must be at least eighty or ninety rooms, all of different shapes and some with balconies. In clear weather, some of the balconies can be seen from here.

"Here" is a small lawn that stretches its little length with modest satisfaction in front of a fat, romantic cottage that is very closely related to the amiable monstrosity on the dunes. The cottage might have been baked from a bit of dough left over after the giant's place on the dunes was made. They are alike, and the cottage has its own massive doorway and its diamond-paned windows and its big beams and its gingerbread roof.

The giant house is inhabited in the summertime by seven children, and the cottage is the home of a black Labrador retriever and five handsome mongrel cats. The retriever's name is Bluebell and she is almost six years old. On a bleak day like today, the cats stay indoors. They are asleep around the house, or they are at the windows, attentive to nothing. But at the edge of the driveway that separates the small lawn from the great one leading to the dunes, Bluebell lies on guard, with a large hollow bone between her front paws and her head turned toward the big house away up there in the distance. Bluebell must wonder why the children do not appear. They were always appearing, from all directions, and descending on her, when she did not reach them first. They used to swoop down from their house and across the lawn in a flight of white shorts and white shirts, and Bluebell never crossed the driveway to trespass on their grass until she was certain they were coming to her. They used to call her name as they ran for her, and as their breath shortened and their voices came closer, her name sounded louder, and the sound of it filled her with a joy that could only increase, because there was no limit to the children's energy or to their affection for her. "Bluebell. *Good* Bluebell. Good *Bluebell.*" There had never been so many voices calling her all at once, or so many legs to charge at and then avoid, or so many admiring faces to watch and please. Please them all, always please, that was her duty, her only duty, and she had never before seen it so plain, or felt it to be so simple, or so interesting, or felt herself so valuable. She was a dog and she performed like a dog. She forgot her middle age and her extra weight and her gray muzzle, and she frolicked like a puppy, and like a mustang, and like a kitten.

She found a treasure in the short grass and then, after smelling it importantly, she tormented it for a few seconds with her paws before she pranced away and left it as it was, invisible. She entertained like a dog. She lay stretched on her back with her huge chest heaving dramatically. Upside down she is grotesque, a vulnerable monster. She might be a sacrifice, on the lawn, in the sunlight. Her front paws hang in the air empty and aimless, and the big, soft ears that make her look demure and mournful fall away, inside out, and leave her face exposed and wild. And her eyes are wild; they look at nothing. The children are astonished to see their familiar turn mysterious, and they make a circle around her. They are embarrassed, because she is shameless, and they try to clear the air with their laughter. "Look at Bluebell. She is *funny*." Who is Bluebell now, and what is she? She is not herself. The smallest girl decides that Bluebell is a bench, and she sits heavily down on the softest place, the stomach. Bluebell springs rudely up and resumes her proper shape. Now she is a dog again, and she stands on four legs again. The children welcome her return by telling her her name: Bluebell, Bluebell, Bluebell. Bluebell brandishes her heavy tail and challenges the eyes that watch her with her eyes, and then she races away and they all race after her. She has never been so pursued. She has never been so famous or so celebrated. Her name is on every lip. She has come into her own. She is the only dog in the world.

But here it is winter, with the cold winter weather that is so good for playing in, and she has been waiting for hours, ever since last summer, and the children have not appeared. If she watches faithfully they will appear. They generally come out around this time. Whenever they come out is this time. Bluebell moves the old bone over to the middle of the driveway and then she resumes her dignified attitude, with her paws precisely arranged, as though she were lying in wait on her own tomb. Her head is turned to the house on the dunes. It is lost in the mist. The house is gone. There is no sound except the pounding of the sea in the distance, and that sound means nothing to Bluebell. What use to plunge into the sea and brave the waves when she has no witnesses? The lawn is empty, shrinking away into the mist, and the air has turned to silence. No voice is calling from up there on the dunes. There is no Bluebell. Her name is lost. She was the only dog in the world, but now she is only a dog. It is all the children's fault, all this absence. It

The Children Are Very Quiet When They Are Away

is all their fault. They are too quiet. All this silence can be blamed on them, and all this waste. Bluebell takes her eyes from the dunes and puts her chin on the empty bone between her paws. She drowses. It is all the children's fault. Everything is too quiet. It is all their fault. The children are quiet because they are away. But what is away, and then, what is here? Bluebell is here. Bluebell sleeps. Now Bluebell is away where the children are who are so quiet here.

In and Out of Never-Never Land

In East Hampton, it was the Fourth of July, the hour just before dawn—very early-morning teatime. Mary Ann Whitty looked into the brown eyes of her dog, Bluebell, and she thought, The dog is kind and good, but the cats have style. . . . She was sitting in her living room, which was remarkable to her because it was hers alone, and because it contained her furniture, her books, her dog, and her cats. The furniture was shabby, the books were worn and showed the signs of long storage, the cats all wore mixed furs, and Bluebell, the black Labrador retriever, was not as serene as a dog of her age and nature ought to be. Bluebell had spent too much time in too many different kennels.

Mary Ann did not care that her household was a trifle bedraggled. What mattered to her was that all her possessions were collected together in one place. She admired the room she had made for herself, and she admired everything in it. She was so pleased with herself and her possessions and arrangements that she even admired the lacks in her house. For example, a simple example, she had no dining-room table. She knew she should have a proper table, a proper place for eating, and that without it her life was makeshift, but she thought that makeshift ways were very well suited to this strange little house, which wore such a temporary air that the first time she walked into it she said to herself that it was not a real house but an impossibility, not a house at all, and that she must rent it immediately, because it might very well not be there when she looked for it again. Not that the house looked as though it might fall down or be blown away. It had a solid look; there was nothing at all fragile about it. But it did not look as though it belonged where it was, by the edge of the sea.

Mary Ann had a friend who rejoiced when he first saw it. "This is not a house by the sea," he said. "It is certainly not a house in East Hampton. It is somewhere else. It is a town house. No, it is a house in the middle of a forest. The Black Forest, I think. It is a *folie*. Whatever it is, it is not real—not a real house, at any rate. And why did they put it sideways?"

Instead of facing the ocean, which was so close that the waves made themselves heard all day and all night, the little house faced its lawn—really only a strip cut from the huge lawn that swept down from the great house on the dunes where the seven children lived, all of them Bluebell's friends. Alongside Mary Ann's house, hidden from her by a tall hedge, there was a lovely, simple flower garden that slanted away from a small apple orchard and into a field of long grass. Bluebell wandered among the apple trees without permission, and without permission the cats had taken the wild field for their hunting ground. On Mary Ann's side of the hedge the flower bed that stretched the length of her lawn was strikingly neglected, but the daffodils and roses and hollyhocks that had been planted there long ago still bloomed at their appointed times, as if to show what they once had been and still might be if somebody would give them a little help.

Sometimes Mary Ann walked from her front door to the grove of pine trees that separated her lawn from the golf course, and as she walked she inspected the tangle of weeds and withered vines that smothered the beds, and she thought, It is a disgrace. But the word disgrace came tranquilly into her mind and caused no uneasiness there. She excused herself from gardening as she did from sewing, simply by announcing she had not the gift for it. She was inclined to be mulish about the things she did not do—not drive a car, not garden, not sew—and it was in something of the same spirit that she congratulated herself as sincerely on what her house lacked as she did on what it held. But in spite of all it lacked, and for all its temporary air, the little house had an air of gaiety about it, and even of welcome. It is the high ceiling, Mary Ann thought, and the books, and the big fireplace, and the mauve rug casts a cheerful light. And in any case, she thought, the house, like me, is good-hearted in spite of itself.

It was absurd, the little house with its baronial front door and its towering diamond-paned windows that had more wood than glass in them, and its lofty black beams that were not very old and not at all necessary, and its scalloped black-iron hasps, and handles, and hinges on all the doors—even on the bathroom door. The hinges were always flying off the doors and landing at Mary Ann's feet with a noisy clank, and she was constantly on her hands and knees searching for the long black spikes that would hold them back on the door until the next fit of humor took them, but she did not mind. The house was always losing bits of itself, and she spent hours trying to find lost pieces of paper—letters, bills, lists, old checkbooks that might tell her where the money had gone, but she persevered just as the house did, and she thought, As long as nobody asks me any questions, everything will come out all right.

Her house was closely related to the house on the dunes where the seven children lived. The children's house was really enormous —hundreds of rooms pressed into the shape of a cottage and covered with a deep shingled roof. It had been put up shortly after the First World War, and at the foot of its majestic lawn its miniature, Mary Ann's house, had been built for the caretaker. Th' people who had lived in the big house and employed a caretak' had all gone away long ago, and the seven children had been in possession there for years now.

Mary Ann, the newcomer, did not know exactly when Bluebell and the children had discovered each other. She imagined Bluebell on the grass in the sun one morning, or one afternoon, raising her big head to see a pair of bare legs, several pairs of bare legs, standing at a safe distance and on their own side of the driveway that separated them from Bluebell's private ground. The children must have been on their toes, ready to fly if the strange dog turned fierce. Bluebell was very black, and her ample body was covered with shining flat fur, a handsome coat of it, but her muzzle was gray, and she had a comical look. Comical or not, she had long sharp teeth and great paws that could hold her prey to the ground if she chose to find prey. The children must have wondered about her. Bluebell would not have bothered to wonder. What she saw was what she always saw—not children or birds or cats or mice but interesting new manifestations of the friendliness she believed existed for her in all that lived. If it lived, it moved, and whether it moved by creeping or running or walking or flying or hopping or simply by blowing like torn paper about the lawn, Bluebell wanted it. This new apparition, so near to her and quite unknown, must have struck her with joy. Fourteen legs, seven faces, and a variety of voices, all there just waiting to be claimed. She would have begun her campaign at once, beating a vigorous overture on the ground with her heavy tail.

Mary Ann could only imagine all that. What was certain was that Bluebell no longer decorated the front of the house for hours in the morning and during the afternoon. Now she was always away, off somewhere, following the children into their house and out of it again, and travelling with them along the beach and over the golf course and even into the village. Bluebell had another secret now to y on top of the eternal secret that was guarded, or imprisoned, by her animal silence. She had a new world of her own that was free of the cats and free of Mary Ann, but she showed her independence of them only at the moment of her departure from the house and the moment of her return to it. These days, when she went out in the morning, she was purposeful, and her eyes turned at once to the house on the dunes to see if anyone was out and about. And when she came back and her own door was opened to her, she burst in, breathless, and threw herself on the floor, unable to speak for exhaustion and importance. While she panted, her tail hammered on the floor and her eyes roved wildly around the room, reclaiming everything she saw, but most of all reclaiming Mary Ann. "I choose you," Bluebell's eyes said to Mary Ann, "you, you," and her gaze turned fervently to the kitchen, where her dinner waited.

The cats showed a faint, lazy interest in all this commotion. The biggest of them, the bright orange, sat up and then stood up and stretched, and lay down again, wrapping himself up in his own coat. "I am ignoring you," each cat said, opening its eyes just enough to show a gleam of light, and then, closing its eyes again, each cat said, as always, "I choose myself."

But the moment had arrived when East Hampton, with its waves and sand and its wide golf course and its ponds of wild water birds and its fine main street and its hilly green graveyard, was about to be revealed all over again by the new light. Mary Ann heard the first birds, the smallest ones, who sing suddenly at the end of darkness. She listened to their sweet voices, and then she stood up and went to open the front door. It was still night out, but the darkness had retreated into the bushes and trees. She could see the sky shifting. It was the moment she liked, because it proved she was right and that nothing was real. It was also the moment when the cats went out to kill. She looked around the room and saw the big orange, the little black favorite, the longhaired wild one, and the quiet calico. Only Tom, the secret hunter, was absent. Tom hunted alone and far away and never, thank God, brought his little victims into the house. Mary Ann walked through the empty blue-floored room that led to her small kitchen and heated a saucepan of milk and gave it to the cats, hoping to lull them back to sleep and sloth. She turned out the light in the kitchen and saw the dim blue world outside. It was nearly time for the sea gulls to start their march inland. She would have liked to go outside to watch them, but the one morning she had gone out, her long white robe had startled them, and they had risen up in outrage and gone away screeching that their day was ruined.

She went upstairs and stood at her bedroom window, which faced the sea. The sea gulls were just appearing, coming in from the beach and lining up along the top of the long rise that banked the road going down to the sea. They began to walk at once, taking their usual path, which brought them at an angle across the golf course and down the children's lawn to Mary Ann's house. Now the golf course was ghostly with them, and they continued to advance, white birds that whitened and grew bigger as they drew closer. They all walked. The few that flew up descended to the ground at once and started walking again. Some sailed while they walked, showing their wings. They came this way every morning, sometimes more of them and sometimes fewer, and the leaders always stopped at the far edge of the narrow driveway that separated her lawn from the children's. A few steps more would have brought the sea gulls to the walls of her house, but they never took the last few steps, and no matter how close they came they always seemed to be very far away. They walked like emperors, or like jockeys, or like stoics. They knew the ocean, and kept vigil by it in regimental rows, and they screamed against patience, and walked for their health on expensive grass, and Mary Ann thought they knew themselves and she was baffled by them. They were indomitable. There was no need to fear for them or pity them. In her imagination they were living stones that had found wings to save themselves during some long and drastic fall in forgotten times.

Now the leaders reached the edge of the driveway, the limit of their walk, and paused, and there was a general pause all the way back across the lawn and the golf course, and then they all rose up and flew back to the sea. To watch the sea gulls go was like watching the snow stop falling. You couldn't say when the last flake fell, and you could not mark the last sea gull. Mary Ann turned from the window and looked at her bed, which was very large and took up most of the room. She had closed the bedroom door after her, but Bluebell had slipped in with her and was now curled humbly on a corner of the pink quilt. "All right, Bluebell," Mary Ann said, "as long as you're here," and she lay down and pulled the quilt over her and fell asleep, knowing unrepentantly that the sun had risen.

Late in the morning, wide awake and dressed at last, she heard the children on her front lawn, and she went out to wish them a happy Fourth of July. The children were going to the big fireworks display in the evening. Mary Ann was not going. The children teased Bluebell while they talked to Mary Ann, and as they talked they straggled irresolutely toward the driveway. They were on their way to the pond to take a boat out, but they were delaying. They were taking their time. Like Mary Ann, they had all the time in the world today. It was the Fourth of July, and the hours were turning in slow motion. There was nothing to do that had to be done, except wait for the fireworks to begin, and the children were finding time for long farewells to Bluebell, who could not go in the boat with them because she was too heavy. "Too heavy and too slippery," the eldest boy said. One time they had taken her in the boat, and she rocked them all around the pond.

The youngest girl, Linnet, spoke up. "Bluebell might have drowned us all," she said.

Linnet was only six. When the others walked, she dawdled

behind them or ran after them, and when they stood as they were standing now, she stood in front of them, or at the side, apart from them. She was kneeling at the moment, in the grass beside Bluebell, who sat with her front feet apart and her gaze fixed worshipfully on the eldest boy, the leader in everything but particularly in this boating expedition from which she understood she was to be excluded. She had heard the ban (Bluebell is to *stay*), and she was determined to shame him into changing his mind. But the eldest boy was looking at Linnet, who had announced that Bluebell might have drowned them all. "Listen to her," he said scornfully. "She wasn't even there."

The second boy came out of the reverie in which he spent most of his time. "She's talking through her hat," he said with finality.

Linnet's elder sister, Alice, who was eight and very responsible, looked tolerantly at Linnet. "She wasn't even there," Alice said. "I wasn't there, either," she added sensibly.

"I only said *might* have," Linnet said, and went on stroking Bluebell's anxious, unresponsive neck.

Mary Ann looked at Bluebell, who might have been a murderess. "Bluebell only wanted to drown you so that she could save you," she said.

The second boy emerged from his reverie for the second time, this time in a seizure of decisiveness. "Let's go," he said, so abruptly that Mary Ann thought they would all start running, but they still delayed, moving their feet in anticipation.

Bluebell accepted her fate with dignity. She sank to the ground, composed her paws, and began to gaze coldly past the children's legs at something they couldn't see even if they tried.

Linnet stood up. "I wish it was time to go to the fireworks now," she said. "I have matches. I found them in the road." She put her hand into the pocket of her dress and took out a battered white match folder.

Mary Ann took it from her and opened it. The heads of the

matches were crumbling, they had been rained on, and they were quite useless. She handed the folder back to Linnet, who returned it carefully to her pocket. "I hope your mother knows you have those matches, Linnet," Mary Ann said. "You know matches are forbidden."

"But they're for the fireworks," Linnet said, and her face took on the dull expression of one who remembers this argument from other times, and the frustration of it, and sees more frustration ahead.

The boys were moving off, laughing unkindly. "She thinks they're going to run out of matches at the fireworks," the eldest boy said, and the youngest boy doubled up in noisy mirth.

Even Alice, who was so serious, had to smile. "Linnet, you know those matches were run over by a car and *everything,*" she said.

Linnet's faith in her matches was evident in the bitter look she gave them all. But she had her triumph in her pocket, and she was stubborn. She could afford to wait for vindication, and enjoy the last laugh.

The boys set off backwards and gradually turned until they were really walking off. "See you later," they called to Mary Ann.

One of them called, "Goodbye, Bluebell," and poor Bluebell betrayed herself, starting to attention and staring after them, so tense and ready that for an instant she looked like the royal hunting dog she might have been and sometimes thought she was, in her sleep, when she stirred and seemed to run, while her gruff baying showed the course and splendor of her dreams.

"Stay, Bluebell, good dog," Mary Ann said.

"Come on, Linnet," Alice said, and ran off after her brothers.

"No, wait a minute, Linnet," Mary Ann said. She wanted to tell Linnet the truth, that the matches were no good, and to prove to her that they were no good, but instead she said feebly, "You know, you shouldn't have those matches, Linnet."

In and Out of Never-Never Land

"But I found them on the road," Linnet said.

"All right, well, I hope you have a nice boat ride."

"I will," Linnet said, keeping her hand in her precious pocket. "Goodbye, Miss Whitty," she said politely, and she ran off.

Mary Ann watched her running, going more and more slowly as she drew near to the little group waiting impatiently for her by the edge of the road. The road was busy with cars driving down to the beach and driving away from it. The golf course was dotted with figures that moved gravely and then stood still, gravely considering the next move. It is not a very funny game, Mary Ann thought. She wished she had had the courage to show Linnet that her hopes were not only all false but all wrong, considering that they were based on matches that were strictly forbidden. I should have told her, Mary Ann thought sadly. No matter how you look at it, I should have made her see. I don't think they light fireworks with matches, and even if they do they won't run out of them, and even if they run out, Linnet will be much too far out in the crowd to help and even if she got a chance to offer the matches, the matches are no good. One way or another, she is going to be disappointed. But false hope feels the same as real hope, and she is going to have a nice day dreaming. She's not going to have a chance at the fireworks, but that doesn't alter the fact that I should have given her a lecture on obedience and a demonstration of what happens to matches that have been lying out on the road in the rain.

Mary Ann went into her house and let the screen door bang behind her. Bluebell dreamed of rescuing people from drowning, and Linnet dreamed of saving the fireworks extravaganza from disaster, and Mary Ann dreamed of being able to persuade a proud six-year-old girl that when the choice must be made between being a heroine and being a good child, one always chooses to be a good child. Well, I'll see Linnet again before the display, Mary Ann

31

thought, and I'll tell her about the matches. She'll be so excited by that time that she won't care. I'll make a point of seeing her. But I should have told her. I should never have let her go off like that. Linnet and the matches went out of her mind. What came into her mind was the house she stood in, which seemed now like a beached ship, stuck in the middle of the summer weather that only Bluebell was really at home in. The little house was very quiet. Buttoned up in its diamonds, with its shingled roof pulled down about its ears and its left shoulder turned to the ocean, the house seemed to enjoy the summer sun cautiously, as though it knew it wasn't a summer house, and not a seaside house, and, in fact, not a real house. And it wasn't a real house. It wasn't a bit real. The living room, where Mary Ann stood, had been copied from the set of some opera or operetta—*Hansel and Gretel,* Mary Ann had heard, although she would have guessed *Lilac Time.* Whatever it was, and operetta or not, the performance must have depended on a good deal of coming and going, people appearing and disappearing and hurrying through from right to left and from left to right, or looking in, talking, perhaps singing, through the enormous windows in the back wall. A small flight of steps led up and off to the right and another small flight to the left. The living room had five ways out—five exits. Eight, if you counted the diamond-paned windows, which were big enough for two people to vault, scramble, or leap through at one time. Nine exits, if you allowed the fireplace, which was roomy enough to walk around in and had a chimney that was as big around as a barrel and went straight up through the roof like a tunnel. Mary Ann thought the chimney probably *was* a tunnel, mislaid from another stage set in another house someplace else. *Journey's End?* As a chimney the tunnel did very well. She had no complaints about the fireplace. As a matter of fact, she had no complaints at all, but she could not help wondering what had been going on in the mind of the architect when he made his scale drawing for this room. He had got in all that the action of the operetta called for. There never was so much big detail in a room. Doors and windows and fireplace all stood out in their full theatrical size, all surrounded with big frames of blackened wood, so that you could see from a mile away what you were looking at. Only, there was no room left for walls. The architect forgot about the walls.

Mary Ann didn't care. It didn't matter. The room pleased her. She had grown fond of it. It was improbable and impermanent, and anyway it was only a stage designed for dialogue and gestures, with two small rooms right and left that were also full of doors and windows, and that were good only for lingering in, because they were anterooms, and as anterooms they resisted furniture the way a cat will resist a collar. Mary Ann had tried several arrangements, but at the moment both rooms were empty. The room with the mauve floor was empty, and the one with the shining dark-blue floor that led to the kitchen was empty. Anterooms were new in Mary Ann's life, and she wanted to have them always. She had not known that rooms could be so content with themselves. But she wondered what the original caretaker had thought when he first stepped into his brand-new living room, with its operatic humility and its need to be explained and its obvious falseness and its meager fate; because it did not even represent a dream but was only the echo of somebody's memory of romantic escape—to a hunting lodge, a mountain hideaway in Austria, or a secret place in Switzerland. It was a wistful conceit, and it stood here only because this site had presented itself and a house was needed here, for the caretaker. Someone must have thought, Since I cannot have that place at all, I might as well have it here, where I can at least look at it. The little house was not real. It was only a façade that stood at the end of somebody's lawn, and Mary Ann thought it did wonderfully for a person who wanted to live by the Atlantic Ocean but who only wanted to live there for a while.

In and Out of Never-Never Land

Late in the afternoon, Mary Ann went upstairs to sleep for a half hour, and she slept so late that she was awakened by the first of the explosions from the fireworks display. It was dusk outside her window, and a few minutes later, standing on the high ground of the children's lawn, where she had a good view of the aerial lights, she felt that the night was cold. A cool, quick wind blew in from the sea. She would build herself a fire when she went back into the house. Bluebell, dutiful, sat beside her, and stared as she did into the distance, where they saw the sky brighten after explosions they heard but could not see, and then they saw shooting stars, streams of brilliance, and dazzling ribbons of color that turned into balloons and garlands and cornucopias as they ascended, to hang for an instant at their highest point and then vanish in glory.

Nearer to Mary Ann, on the beach below the children's house, some people were having a private display, a very minor one. A few arrows of light shot up, and then again, more arrows. Someone was walking on the beach, throwing sparklers as he went. Lawbreakers, Mary Ann thought, disobedient people; everyone is committing sins today.

It had grown very dark, and she had had enough of the fireworks, the legal ones and the illegal ones. Time to go home and make a fire, but instead she went inside and made a Martini. She tasted it. It was delicious, but she had made it too soon, and she left it in the freezing compartment while she virtuously washed stringbeans and lettuce and turned up the heat in the oven. All the time she was working, she enjoyed the attention of six pairs of animal eyes, five pairs solemn and the sixth pair, Bluebell's, devotional. Every night, Mary Ann gave her cooking demonstration, providing the cats and Bluebell with their favorite entertainment, and every night, as she chopped and peeled and arranged her saucepans on top of the stove, she wondered if it was better to go to a restaurant and have a plate of food brought to you and know that the vegetables will be dreadful or to cook for yourself. While making up her mind, she had become an expert in very small plain dinners, and it was with some complacency that she left her work in progress, retrieved her Martini, and returned through her blue-floored anteroom to her living room, where she proceeded to build a big fire. The flames blazed up, filling the room with shadows, and as she stood back to watch them she heard the fire alarm sound far away. Somebody's house going up, she thought; it always happens on the Fourth of July.

She was quite wrong. It was not *somebody's* house that the alarm was sounding for but the seven children's house, and if Mary Ann had left her front door open, as she often did, even in the winter time, she would have seen the air outside filled with smoke that was billowing down in great clouds from the big house on the dunes. Great excitement was gathering at her windows, and she missed it all. She missed seeing the first engine come hurtling across the flat green and watery landscaped land that stretched from her right all the way back to the sky. On a dark night like this, with all its lights going, the engine must have been a wonderful sight. All lighted up, racing to the rescue, and followed by a second engine and then by a third. Mary Ann missed it all, and she missed seeing the swarm of small cars that flew after the engines and turned with them into her narrow driveway, which was full of holes and long deep ruts like trenches, so that they were all slowed up, coming along one after the other so close together that they might have been sections of a caterpillar. It was a very long, narrow driveway. At the best of times there was room only for one ordinary car. The driveway turned at a right angle from the road that led to the sea and came straight through the golf course and between the lawns to Mary Ann's house, where it made a sharp right turn and disappeared between two dense walls of trees and bushes that led up to the children's house and the sea. Those trees were full of pheasants, and if you walked up that dark curving avenue on a summer night, the wild beating of indignant wings drowned out the sound of the waves that beat out their slower measure on the beach below the children's house. What the pheasants must have thought on this night on the Fourth of July was unimaginable. First they were enveloped in clouds of thick smoke, and then came the invasion by heavy machinery. And all Mary Ann was thinking about was whether or not to put the screen back in front of the fire she had made, or leave the fireplace open and risk sparks on the rug. She was putting the screen back when she heard the first of the engines come lurching and rumbling past her house, and she thought, What a big oil truck. But then came more rumbling and grinding, and she thought, Armored cars.

She ran to the door and opened it and ran out on her lawn, to find that the lawn had vanished. She was hostess to a long line of cars that had pulled in and parked in a neat row with their noses turned toward the big house, and the driveway was so jammed with firefighting cars and apparatus that she could not have crossed over to the children's lawn even if she had wanted to. The smoke was thick, but the children's house was visible, standing up against the night sky with all its lights on. If the lights are on, perhaps things are not so bad, Mary Ann thought, and she saw the miles of floor boards up there, and the deep shingled roof that would blaze up like a torch if a spark caught it. The smoke now seemed to be coming from behind the house. Perhaps it was only a grass fire.

She walked over to the nearest of the cars that were parked by her house and said foolishly, "What's going on?"

The driver glanced at her and then looked back at the house. "Fire up there," he said. The car was full of children, and they all stared out at Mary Ann. She walked away from them, and called Bluebell to follow her. She thought, There is that man has driven in here, tripping up the Fire Department, and now he's trapped here with all those children, and they may not get out until morning.

The avenue of trees that hid the approach to the big house ended just short of the house and to the side of it and out from the shadows up there a small fire car appeared and careered wildly down the children's lawn and across the golf course and was gone. It was followed immediately by another, and then Mary Ann saw that her driveway had been cleared from the pine grove back to the sea road and that the cars lined up in front of her were starting, tentatively, to edge their way back, going out backwards. A tall man in a helmet appeared and ordered the cars parked on Mary Ann's lawn to leave. He was very short with them and she was very glad. She would say to him, "But I live here," she thought, and then she wondered if he would order her to go into her house. Would he be within his rights, ordering her into the house? She began to worry about what she would do if he pointed to her house and said to her, "You get in there and shut that door." She had the right to stand on her own lawn, she knew that, but on the other hand it was hardly the moment to have an argument with a fireman. His colleagues on wheels were making desperate attempts to extricate themselves from the driveway and from one another. Backwards and forwards they went, and none of them moved. It was all the fault of the cars that had joined them for fun, and tied them up. Mary Ann thought of the confusion that must exist on the shrouded avenue leading up to the house. Then, away up at the house, one of the big engines appeared and tore down the lawn and away. The fire was really over. But the cars nearest to her were still stuck, and she thought that in a minute they would all start barking in frustration. The man in the helmet had cleared her lawn and he did not appear to have seen her. All the same, taking no chances, Mary Ann spoke to Bluebell and they both retreated into the house and shut the door. Then Mary Ann looked out through the smallest diamond-paned window. What with the thickness of the window frame and the darkness outside and the angle she was looking from, she couldn't see much, but she had already seen enough to know what was going on. Another big engine shot into sight and out again, vanishing on the far side of the pine grove. A little more to the left and he would have gone down in one of those deep sand craters on the golf course. He could have struggled all night without getting out. The other cars were getting out as best they could, and then they were all gone, but disorder still hung in the air. Over the well-cut lawns that surrounded the golf course, and over the polite undulations of the course itself, and over the clubhouse that sat in wary hospitality on its eminence high above the dunes—over all of these particular human arrangements, Chaos stirred, and smiled, and went back to sleep. What a Fourth of July, Mary Ann thought, and wondered why the firemen had cut their sirens off.

In the morning she was awakened by the sea gulls, who were making more noise than usual because, she thought, they were coming closer to the house than usual. But when she got to the window she saw that they had already turned and were flying back to the sea, protesting all the way against everything. There was mist out and they vanished into it. It had rained in the night, and the holes in the driveway were filled with silver water. Last night the fire engines had bumped in and out of those holes, today the birds would bathe in them. She wondered if the lawns had been much damaged by the traffic. There were car marks on her lawn, nothing serious, and the children's lawn, when she got downstairs, looked all right. The house looked all right, too, and there was Linnet, in her white nightgown, running wildly down the lawn. "Linnet," Mary Ann said, "come into the house at once. Put this shawl around you. Do you know what time it is? It's not six o'clock yet. I saw the fire engines. Was there much damage to the house?"

In and Out of Never-Never Land

"I called them," Linnet said. "I was the only one that thought of the telephone."

"That's wonderful, Linnet."

"It was only a grass fire," Linnet said.

"Even so," Mary Ann said. "You saved the house. That is really marvelous. That's wonderful, Linnet."

Linnet had been first to the telephone. While the rest of the family stood transfixed with horror, staring at the grass, she had rushed to the phone and called the fire brigade. What had happened was that something, perhaps a spark from the stray fireworks Mary Ann had seen, had caught the brush below the house and suddenly it had all flared up. They had just arrived home from the fireworks, and they had all gone onto their terrace overlooking the sea, and while the others stared at the sheet of flame that suddenly rose up and became a wall and rose higher as they watched it, Linnet called for help. "Then you saved the house," Mary Ann said. Linnet nodded modestly. "And now you're going to have a glass of milk," Mary Ann said, "and you're going to go straight home and back to bed, before your mother finds out that you're gone. You must go home at once."

"Bluebell has nice paws," Linnet said.

"I know," Mary Ann said. "Now don't sit down, Linnet. You really must come outside, and I'll watch you up to the house. Go in the front door, so that I can see you safely home. Keep the shawl around you."

When they were outside, Mary Ann said, "That's wonderful that you saved the house, Linnet. It's really great." The hem of her robe was wet from the wet grass, and there was Linnet in her bare feet. "Now you *must* hurry home," she said.

"May I come back to see you?" Linnet asked.

Mary Ann looked at her. Linnet was small and friendly, and Mary Ann, who feared trustfulness, had often rebuffed her, but now she put her hands out and tightened the shawl around the little shoulders. "Yes," she said, "but right now, this minute, you must run home. Your mother will be frightened if she finds you not in your bed. Then come back later and tell me everything about the fire. I'll have questions ready. All right?"

"All right," Linnet said, and she started off. When she had crossed to her own lawn, she turned and waved, and Mary Ann waved back. She watched the child running and walking and then running again. It was a long way up that lawn. Mary Ann thought, I had a chance to do the right thing yesterday and I am very glad I failed, and I hope the same chance does not come my way again for a long time. She thought of a joke. "Never put off till tomorrow what you should have done yesterday," she said to herself, and she went placidly into the house to put on the water for her coffee.

The Children Are There,
Trying Not to Laugh

Far out on Long Island, beside the Atlantic Ocean, there is a famous golf course that stretches for miles alongside the dunes, edging up to them and at some points eddying into them. The golf course has its own turreted clubhouse, which stands up high, a flimsy play-fortress, between the ocean and the sky. Some distance to the east, also high on the dunes, the clubhouse has its nearest big neighbor, a giant's mansion that sits contentedly on its roomy eminence, facing the waves. The mansion has a soft, comfortable outline, like a gingerbread cottage. Its deep, shingled roof is pulled down low over the tops of its walls, and it has hundreds of diamond-paned windows that keep their own dark secretive shimmer even when all the lights go on inside and the house comes to life from end to end and from attic to cellar, when the seven children who live there are all at home. The children are not secretive, but they are secret—seven open secrets that can never be unravelled or deciphered or described, any more than you could unravel or decipher or describe a wave in its passage from the distant horizon to the familiar sandy beach, or find it, once the sand had caught it. The children are restless and inquisitive and remorseless in their pursuit of questions and answers, and they never stop talking, but they change by the minute. You can see time racing away in their

The Children Are There, Trying Not to Laugh

friendly, impatient eyes. *What? Where? How? When? Who?*
They ask questions. And *Why? Why? Why?* They ask more questions. You might as easily stick pins into the wind as try to keep up
with them, but to remain silent, and try to watch them, is just as
difficult.

One Saturday afternoon in January, several Januarys ago, the
snow began falling, and it continued through the night, falling
thickly until about midnight, when there was a brief clear interlude,
with moonlight. The moon remained hidden, but her light flowed
calmly in all directions, revealing an untenanted fairyland beside a
flickering, wandering ocean. The thin line of wind-bent trees that
separates the lawn of the giant's mansion from the golf course cast
spidery shadows in the moonlight, and, nearer the dunes, the fragment of hedge where pink and white beach roses bloom in summer
was a little bundle of darkness in the quiet expanse of snow. Only
one light showed in the turreted clubhouse—it was their night-light
—and the giant's mansion was dark. The children were all asleep,
and there was no one to notice when the moon withdrew her light
and the snow began falling again, not to stop this time until after
dawn.

About nine o'clock in the morning, the entrance door of the
giant's mansion opened and the seven children hurried carefully
down their broad, snow-laden stone steps, between their two tame
stone lions, and began racing about the pure and glowing surface of
the lawn, which seemed even larger white. It was a big world, in the
snow. The children tried to fill it, calling to one another, but their
voices sounded thin and small, the way the trees looked, even with
a round line of snow along each branch and twig. The snowy
universe looked eternal, as though it might remain as it was forever,
sea, sky, and snow, but the whirling children appeared and vanished
and reappeared and vanished again, in a dazzling jigsaw of hands

The Children Are There, Trying Not to Laugh

and feet and faces and arms and eyes and legs and bodies, running and falling and rolling and tumbling, catching at the air and at the snow, every movement separate and sudden and disconnected, and yet every movement part of one continuous movement, as though they had been playing that game for centuries. It was a Chinese battle, white on white, with porcelain dunes in the background. The children were snow children, except for their red faces and dark hair, and their cries were less fierce than the sea gulls'. They tore about, breaking their lawn into large slabs and then ruffling the slabs into a plowed field of white. The snow yielded softly, here, there, and everywhere, and the battle ended at the finish line, where the driveway was that separated the big lawn from a much smaller lawn, the modest territory of a fat, solitary cottage that has its own deep, shingled roof and its own five or six diamond-paned windows. The cottage faced north, keeping its left shoulder to the ocean, and the lawn in front of it was perfectly white and untouched, except for a narrow trench that ran diagonally from the front door to the pine trees that stood halfway down the lawn, where the bird feeder was. And straight across the middle of the lawn, running to their food, the pheasants had left their prints—a frieze of claws. And around the base of the bird feeder, under the biggest pine, thousands of other tiny footmarks had beaten the snow into a great, shallow earthenware bowl of brown, black, and white, streaked with seed. The little black cat who liked to sit under the bird feeder, staring up, waiting for a chance at murder, and who often fled from the feeder with seeds, like retribution, glittering wickedly from the inside corners of her eyes, was not in her place this morning. She was asleep somewhere inside the cottage, and so were the other cats who lived there asleep, and the house itself seemed to sleep soundly, as though the snow had claimed and sealed it, just for the day.

The children crossed the driveway and paused to survey the small lawn and to consult together. At least, they put their heads together, although the eldest boy did all the talking, and when the talking was over he took the first step. He was wearing huge-footed boots of dull black rubber, and he planted his right foot deeply into the fresh snow of the small lawn and then planted his left foot firmly in front of his right, and proceeded to walk like that, wobbling a little, until he was a good distance across the lawn. Then he turned smartly to face the cottage, and stood at attention with his arms at his sides, and fell backward his full length and lay there stiffly, grinning and calling to the eldest girl, who was next in line, to follow him. She was already making her way, even more unsteadily than he, along his track, and when she was a couple of feet from him she stopped and turned and dropped back as he had done. As she fell, without his athletic confidence, she tumbled, but the snow bed she made for herself was just as neat as his, and she lay stiffly, as he did. The second boy followed and dropped back into his place, in his turn, and very soon all seven children were lying in a row, giggling with excitement and constraint, and raising their heads awkwardly to see if anybody was watching them from the cottage.

The front door of the cottage opened and a black Labrador retriever charged out, looking joyful, because her mouth was open. She was Bluebell, and she was growing old, but she wore her gray hairs very lightly, and nothing could dim her determination to be wherever the people were. She stood beside the eldest boy and stared expectantly along the line of bodies, wagging her tail and waiting for them all to get up. When they didn't get up, she began washing the eldest boy's face with her large pink tongue. The eldest boy squealed and moaned and wriggled but did not break the mold he lay in, and Bluebell moved from him to the eldest girl, who shrieked while she was being washed but did not wriggle. The second boy was rolling his eyes, and when he saw Bluebell's big face coming close to him he yelled and jumped up and ran out into the

44

driveway, and the others all followed him. But not one mold was broken. The seven molds remained clear and clean in the snow, and the children stood in the driveway and screamed with laughter and looked at the lawn they had conquered without doing it any mischief. Then they turned and raced away up their own rumpled lawn. Since there were seven children, Bluebell transformed herself into seven dogs and ran among them like a lunatic, upsetting them all. When she had made them dodge as much as she pleased, she raced for the big house and flew up the front steps and was at the door before any of them. The smallest girl, who had begun the rush up the lawn, was soon left behind, and so she stopped running and dawdled carelessly along to show that she was last on purpose and that she was in no hurry to get home. But she too reached the house in her own good time, and climbed the steps and walked inside, and the heavy front door closed behind her. The game was all over.

The following morning a thaw had set in, and the outlines left by the children's bodies had begun to blur. The children drove off in their car to their house in the city, not to return till spring, they said. But even before they were out of sight, smiling and waving, as excited to be leaving as they had been to arrive, the place had taken on an aloof, deserted look. The snow was in disgraceful wet rags. The trees looked sad and lonely, and the seagulls circled and swooped and screamed with exasperation at the sameness of it all. "Every year," the sea gulls screamed, *"every year."* By afternoon the country had turned to marshland. Wet, driving snow fell haphazard, slapped to and fro by a confused, angry wind. The narrow driveway ran with water like a river, and there was only the long bleak line of the horizon, straight and sharp as a ruler, to show the separate slate-blue darknesses of sea and sky. The children's outlines sank slowly away into the soaking grass, showing almost to the last that there had been seven places of different lengths. Except in a few

The Children Are There, Trying Not to Laugh

stubbornly frozen corners, the snow was gone. The children had made their mark, only just in time, but forever. They never came back, not really, not as they were, but their marks remain. In the buried city of a past winter the marks endure, clear as day in that year's snow—seven bodies, raging with life, seven faces, seven ages, seven weights, and seven measurements. The children are there, trying not to laugh. You can see them again, if you have the patience to watch. You have to wait until the snow falls, and then it is simply a matter of waiting for the snow to settle.

I See You, Bianca

My friend Nicholas is about the only person I know who has no particular quarrel with the city as it is these days. He thinks New York is all right. It isn't that he is any better off than the rest of us. His neighborhood, like all our neighborhoods, is falling apart, with too many buildings half up and half down, and too many temporary sidewalks, and too many doomed houses with big Xs on their windows. The city has been like that for years now, uneasy and not very reasonable, but in all the shakiness Nicholas has managed to keep a fair balance. He was born here, in a house on 114th Street, within sight of the East River, and he trusts the city. He believes anyone with determination and patience can find a nice place to live and have the kind of life he wants here. His own apartment would look much as it does whether he lived in Rome or Brussels or Manchester. He has a floor through—two rooms made into one long room with big windows at each end, in a very modest brownstone, a little pre-Civil War house on East Twelfth Street near Fourth Avenue. His room is a spacious oblong of shadow and light—he made it like that, cavernous and hospitable—and it looks as though not two but ten or twenty rooms had contributed their best angles and their best corners and their best-kept secrets of depths and mood to it. Sometimes it seems to be the anteroom to many other rooms, and sometimes it seems to be the extension of many other

rooms. It is like a telescope and at the same time it is like what you
see through a telescope. What it is like, more than anything, is a
private room hidden backstage in a very busy theatre where the
season is in full swing. The ceiling, mysteriously, is covered in
stamped tin. At night the patterned ceiling seems to move with the
flickering shadows, and in the daytime an occasional shadow drifts
slowly across the tin as though it was searching for a permanent
refuge. But there is no permanence here—there is only the valiant
illusion of a permanence that is hardly more substantial than the
shadow that touches it. The house is to be torn down. Nicholas has
his apartment by the month, no lease and no assurance that he will
still be here a year or even three months from now. Sometimes the
furnace breaks down in the dead of winter, and then there is a very
cold spell for a few days until the furnace is repaired—the landlord
is too sensible to buy a new furnace for a house that may vanish
overnight. When anything gets out of order inside the apartment,
Nicholas repairs it himself. (He thinks about the low rent he pays
and not about the reason for the low rent.) When a wall or a
ceiling has to be painted, he paints it. When the books begin to pile
up on the floor, he puts up more shelves to join the shelves that now
cover most of one long wall from the floor to the ceiling. He builds
a cabinet to hide a bad spot in the end wall. The two old rooms, his
one room, never had such attention as they are getting in their last
days.

The house looks north and Nicholas has the second floor, with
windows looking north onto Twelfth Street and south onto back
yards and the backs and sides of other houses and buildings. The
neighborhood is a kind of no man's land, bleak in the daytime and
forbidding at night, very near to the Village but not part of the
Village, and not a part, either, of the lower East Side. Twelfth Street
at that point is very narrow and noisy. Elderly buildings that are not
going to last much longer stand side by side with the enormous,

blank façades of nearly new apartment houses, and there is a constant caravan of quarrelsome, cumbersome traffic moving toward the comparative freedom of Fourth Avenue. To his right Nicholas looks across the wide, stunted expanse of Fourth Avenue, where the traffic rolls steadily uptown. Like many exceedingly ugly parts of the city, Fourth Avenue is at its best in the rain, especially in the rain at night, when the whole scene, buildings, cars, and street, streams with such a black and garish intensity that it is beautiful, as long as one is safe from it—very safe, with both feet on the familiar floor of a familiar room filled with books, records, living plants, pictures and drawings, a tiny piano, chairs and tables and mirrors, and a long desk and a bed. All that is familiar is inside, and all the discontent is outside, and Nicholas can stand at his windows and look out on the noise and confusion with the cheerful interest of one who contemplates a puzzle he did not create and is not going to be called upon to solve. From the top of a tall filing cabinet near him, Bianca, his small white cat, also gazes at the street. It is afternoon now, and the sun is shining, and Bianca is there on the cabinet, looking out, only to be near Nicholas and to see what he sees. But she sees nothing.

What is that out there?

That is a view, Bianca.

And what is a view?

A view is where we are not. Where we are is never a view.

Bianca is interested only in where she is, and what she can see and hope to touch with her nose and paws. She looks down at the floor. She knows it well—the polished wood and the small rugs that are arranged here and there. She knows the floor—how safe it is, always there to catch her when she jumps down, and always very solid and familiar under her paws when she is getting ready to jump up. She likes to fly through the air, from a bookcase on one side of the room to a table on the other side, flying across the room

49

without even looking at the floor and without making a sound. But whether she looks at it or not, she knows the floor is always there, the dependable floor, all over the apartment. Even in the bathroom, under the old-fashioned bathtub, and even under the bed, and under the lowest shelf in the kitchen, Bianca finds the well-known floor that has been her ground—her playground and her proving ground—during all of her three years of life.

Nicholas has been standing and staring at rowdy Twelfth Street for a long time now, and Bianca, rising, stretching, and yawning on top of the filing cabinet, looks down at the floor and sees a patch of sunlight there. She jumps down and walks over to the patch of sun and sits in it. Very nice in the sun, and Bianca sinks slowly down until she is lying full length in the warmth. The hot strong light makes her fur whiter and denser. She is drowsy now. The sun that draws the color from her eyes, making them empty and bright, has also drawn all resistance from her bones, and she grows limp and flattens out into sleep. She is very flat there on the shining floor —flat and blurred—a thin cat with soft white fur and a blunt, patient Egyptian head. She sleeps peacefully on her side, with her front paws crossed and her back paws placed neatly one behind the other, and from time to time her tail twitches impatiently in her dream. But the dream is too frail to hold her, and she sinks through it and continues to sink until she lies motionless in the abyss of deepest sleep. There is glittering dust in the broad ray that shines on her, and now Bianca is dust-colored, paler and purer than white, and so weightless that she seems about to vanish, as though she were made of the radiance that pours down on her and must go when it goes.

Bianca is sleeping not far from Nicholas's bed, which is wide and low and stands sidewise against the wall. Behind the wall at that point is a long-lost fireplace, hidden away years before Nicholas took the apartment. But he has a second fireplace in the back part of the long room, and although it stopped working years ago, it was left open, and Nicholas has made a garden in it, a conservatory. The plants stand in tiers in the fireplace and on the floor close around it, and they flourish in the perpetual illumination of an electric bulb hidden in the chimney. Something is always in bloom. There are an ivy geranium, a rose geranium, and plain geraniums in pink and white. Then there are begonias, and feathery ferns, and a white violet, and several unnamed infant plants starting their lives in tiny pots. The jug for watering them all stands on the floor beside them, and it is kept full because Bianca likes to drink from it and occasionally to play with it, dipping in first one paw and then the other. She disturbs the water so that she can peer down into it and see the strange new depths she has created. She taps the leaves of the plants and then sits watching them. Perhaps she hopes they will hit back.

Also in this back half is Nicholas's kitchen, which is complete and well furnished, and separated from the rest of the room by a high counter. The kitchen gets the full light of one of the two windows that give him his back view. When he looks directly across, he sees the blank side wall of an old warehouse and, above, the sky. Looking straight down, he sees a neglected patch, a tiny wasteland that was once the garden of this house. It is a pathetic little spot of ground, hidden and forgotten and closed in and nearly sunless, but there is still enough strength in the earth to receive and nourish a stray ailanthus tree that sprouted there and grew unnoticed until it reached Nicholas's window. Nobody saw the little tree grow past the basement and the first floor because nobody lives down there, but once it touched the sill of Nicholas's room he welcomed it as though it was home at last after having delayed much too long on the way. He loved the tree and carried on about it as though he had been given the key to his inheritance, or a vision of it. He leaned out of the window and touched the leaves, and then he got out on the fire escape and hung over it, making sure it was healthy. He photographed it, and took a leaf, to make a drawing of it. And the little ailanthus, New York's hardship tree, changed at his touch from an overgrown weed to a giant fern of extraordinary importance. From the kitchen counter, Bianca watched, purring speculatively. Her paws were folded under her chest and her tail was curled around her. She was content. Watching Nicholas at the ailanthus was almost as good as watching him at the stove. When he climbed back into the room she continued to watch the few leaves that were high enough to appear, trembling, at the edge of the sill. Nicholas stood and looked at her, but she ignored him. As she stared toward the light her eyes grew paler, and as they grew paler they grew more definite. She looked very alert, but still she ignored him. He wanted to annoy her. He shouted at her. "Bianca!" he shouted. "I see you!" Bianca narrowed her eyes. "I see you!" Nicholas yelled. "I see you, Bianca. I *see* you, Bianca. I see you. I see you. I SEE you!" Then he was silent, and after a minute Bianca turned her head and looked at him, but only to show there was no contest—her will was stronger, why did he bother?—and then she looked away. She had won. She always did.

In the summer it rains—sudden summer rain that hammers against the windowpanes and causes the ailanthus to stagger and shiver in gratitude for having enough water for once in its life. What a change in the weather, as the heavy breathless summer lifts to reveal a new world of freedom—free air, free movement, clean streets and clean roofs and easy sleep. Bianca stares at the rain as it streams down the glass of the window. One drop survives the battering and rolls, all in one piece, down the pane. Bianca jumps for it, and through the glass she catches it, flattening it with her paw so that she can no longer see it. Then she looks at her chilled paw and, finding it empty, she begins to wash it, chewing irritably at it. But one paw leads to another and she has four of them. She washes industriously. She takes very good care of her only coat. She is never idle, with her grooming to do, and her journeys to take, and then she attends on Nicholas. He is in and out of the apartment a good deal, and she often waits for him at the head of the stairs, so that he will see her first thing when he opens the door from the outside. When he is in the apartment she stays near him. If she happens to be on one of her journeys when he gets home, she appears at the window almost before he has taken off his coat. She goes out a good deal, up and down the fire escape and up and down the inside stairs that lead to the upper apartment and the roof. She wanders. Nicholas knows about it. He likes to think that she is free.

Bianca and the ailanthus provide Nicholas with the extra dimension all apartment dwellers long for. People who have no terraces and no gardens long to escape from their own four walls, but not to wander far. They only want to step outside for a minute. They stand outside their apartment houses on summer nights and during summer days. They stand around in groups or they sit together on the front steps of their buildings, taking the air and looking around at the street. Sometimes they carry a chair out, so that an old person can have a little outing. They lean out of their windows, with their elbows on the sills, and look into the faces of their neighbors at their windows on the other side of the street, all of them escaping from the rooms they live in and that they are glad to have but not to be closed up in. It should not be a problem, to have shelter without being shut away. The window sills are safety hatches into the open, and so are the fire escapes and the roofs and the front stoops. Bianca and the ailanthus make Nicholas's life infinitely spacious. The ailanthus casts its new green light into his room, and Bianca draws a thread of his life all around the outside of the house and all around the inside, up and down the stairs. Where else does she go? Nobody knows. She has never been seen to stray from the walls of the house. Nicholas points out to his friends that it is possible to keep a cat in an apartment and still not make a prisoner of her. He says disaster comes only to those who attract it. He says Bianca is very smart, and that no harm will come to her.

She likes to sit on the window sills of the upper-floor tenants, but she never visits any of them unless they invite her in. She also likes to sit in the ruins of the garden Nicholas once kept on the roof. She watched him make the garden there. It was a real garden and grew well, until the top-floor tenant began to complain bitterly about his leaking ceiling. Even plants hardy enough to thrive in a thin bed of city dust and soot need watering. Nicholas still climbs to the roof, not to mourn his garden—it was an experiment, and he does not regret it—but to look about at the Gulliver world he lives in: the new buildings too tall for the streets they stand in and the older, smaller buildings out of proportion to everything except the past that will soon absorb them. From the street, or from any window, the city often seems like a place thrown up without regard for reason, and haunted by chaos. But from any rooftop the city comes into focus. The roof is in proportion to the building beneath it, and from any roof it can easily be seen that all the other roofs, and their walls, are in proportion to each other and to the city. The buildings are tightly packed together, without regard to size or height, and light and shadow strike across them so that the scene changes every minute. The struggle for space in Manhattan creates an oceanic uproar in the air above the streets, and every roof turns into a magic carpet just as soon as someone is standing on it.

Nicholas climbs to the roof by his fire escape, but when he leaves the roof to go back to his apartment he goes down through the house, down three flights to his own landing, or all the way down to the street floor. He likes the house and he likes to walk around in it. Bianca follows him. She likes to be taken for a walk. She likes to walk around the downstairs hall, where the door is that gives onto the street. It is an old hall, old and cramped, the natural entrance to the family place this house once was. To the left as you enter from the street there are two doors opening into what were once the sitting room and the dining room. The doors are always locked now—there are no tenants there. The hall is narrow, and it is cut in half by the stairs leading up to Nicholas's landing. Under the stairs, beside the door that leads down into the basement, there is a mysterious cubbyhole, big enough for galoshes, or wine bottles, or for a very small suitcase. Nobody knows what the cubbyhole was made for, but Bianca took it for one of her hiding places, and it was there Nicholas first looked for her when he realized he had not seen her all day—which is to say for about ten hours. He was certain she was in the cubbyhole, and that she wanted to be coaxed out. He called her from the landing, and then he went downstairs, calling her, and then he knelt down and peered into the dark little recess. Bianca was not there, and she was not on the roof, or under the bed, or down at the foot of the ailanthus trying to climb up, and she was not anywhere. Bianca was gone. She was nowhere to be found. She was nowhere.

There is no end to Bianca's story because nobody knows what happened to her. She has been gone for several months now. Nicholas has given up putting advertisements in the paper, and he took down all the little cards he put up in the cleaner's and in the grocery store and in the drugstore and the flower shop and the shoeshine parlor. He has stopped watching for her in the street. At first he walked through the street whispering her name, and then one night he found himself yelling for her. He was furious with her. He said to himself that if she turned up at that moment he would kill her. He would certainly not be glad to see her. All he wanted was, one way or another, to know whether she was alive or dead. But there was no word from Bianca, and no word from anyone with actual news of her, although the phone rang constantly with people who thought they had seen her, so that he spent a good many hours running around the neighborhood in answer to false reports. It was no good. She was gone. He reminded himself that he hadn't really wanted a cat. He had only taken Bianca because a friend of his, burdened with too many kittens, pleaded with him. He finds himself wondering what happened to Bianca, but he wonders less and less. Now, he tells himself, she has shrunk so that she is little more than an occasional irritation in his mind. He does not really miss her very much. After all, she brought nothing into the apartment with her except her silence. She was very quiet and not especially playful. She liked to roll and turn and paw the air in the moonlight, but otherwise she was almost sedate. But whatever she was, she is gone now, and Nicholas thinks that if he only knew for sure what happened to her he would have forgotten her completely by this time.

48, CHERRYFIELD AVENUE

The Morning After the Big Fire

From the time I was almost five until I was almost eighteen, we lived in a small house in a part of Dublin called Ranelagh. On our street, all of the houses were of red brick and had small back gardens, part cement and part grass, separated from one another by low stone walls over which, when we first moved in, I was unable to peer, although in later years I seem to remember looking over them quite easily, so I suppose they were about five feet high. All of the gardens had a common end wall, which was, of course, very long, since it stretched the whole length of our street. Our street was called an avenue, because it was blind at one end, the farthest end from us. It was a short avenue, twenty-six houses on one side and twenty-six on the other. We were No. 48, and only four houses from the main road, Ranelagh Road, on which trams and buses and all kinds of cars ran, making a good deal of noisy traffic.

Beyond the end wall of our garden lay a large tennis club, and sometimes in the summer, especially when the tournaments were on, my little sister and I used to perch in an upstairs back window and watch the players in their white dresses and white flannels, and hear their voices calling the scores. There was a clubhouse, but we couldn't see it. Our view was partly obstructed by a large garage building that leaned against the end wall of our garden and the four other gardens between us and Ranelagh Road. A number of

59

people who lived on our avenue kept their cars in the garage, and the people who came to play tennis parked their cars there. It was a very busy place, the garage, and I had never been in there, although we bought our groceries in a shop that was connected with it. The shop fronted on Ranelagh Road, and the shop and the garage were the property of a red-faced, gangling man and his fat, pink-haired wife, the McRorys. On summer afternoons, when my sister and I went around to the shop to buy little paper cups of yellow water ice, some of the players would be there, refreshing themselves with ices and also with bottles of lemonade.

Early one summer morning, while it was still dark, I heard my father's voice, sounding very excited, outside the door of the room in which I slept. I was about eight. My little sister slept in the same room with me. "McRorys' is on fire!" my father was saying. He had been awakened by the red glare of the flames against his window. He threw on some clothes and hurried off to see what was going on, and my mother let us look at the fire from a back window, the same window from which we were accustomed to view the tennis matches. It was a really satisfactory fire, with leaping flames, thick, pouring smoke, and a steady roar of destruction, broken by crashes as parts of the roof collapsed. My mother wondered if they had managed to save the cars, and this made us all look at the burning building with new interest and with enormous awe as we imagined the big shining cars being eaten up by the galloping fire. It was very exciting. My mother hurried us back to our front bedroom, but even there the excitement could be felt, with men calling to one another on the street and banging their front doors after them as they raced off to see the fun. Since she had decided there was no danger to our house, my mother tucked us firmly back into bed, but I could not sleep, and as soon as it grew light, I dressed myself and trotted downstairs. My father had many stories to tell. The garage was a ruin, he said, but the shop was safe. Many cars had been destroyed.

The Morning After the Big Fire

No one knew how the fire had started. Some of the fellows connected with the garage had been very brave, dashing in to rescue as many cars as they could reach. The part of the building that overlooked our garden appeared charred, frail, and empty because it no longer had much in the way of a roof and its insides were gone. The air smelled very burnt.

I wandered quietly out onto the avenue, which was deserted because the children had not come out to play and it was still too early for the men to be going to work. I walked up the avenue in the direction of the blind end. The people living there were too far from the garage to have been disturbed by the blaze. A woman whose little boy was a friend of mine came to her door to take in the milk.

"McRorys' was burnt down last night!" I cried to her.

"What's that?" she said, very startled.

"Burnt to the ground," I said. "Hardly a wall left standing. A whole lot of people's cars burnt up, too."

She looked back over her shoulder in the direction of her kitchen, which, since all the houses were identical, was in the same position as our kitchen. "Jim!" she cried. "Do you hear this? McRorys' was burnt down last night. The whole place. Not a stick left. . . . We slept right through it," she said to me, looking as though just the thought of that heavy sleep puzzled and unsettled her.

Her husband hurried out to stand beside her, and I had to tell the whole story again. He said he would run around to McRorys' and take a look, and this enraged me, because I wasn't allowed around there and I knew that when he came back he would be a greater authority than I. However, there was no time to lose. Other people were opening their front doors by now, and I wanted everyone to hear the news from me.

The Morning After the Big Fire

"Did you hear the news?" I shouted, to as many as I could catch up with, and, of course, once I had their ear, they were fascinated by what I had to tell. One or two of the men, hurrying away to work, charged past me with such forbiddingly closed faces that I was afraid to approach them, and they continued in their ignorance down toward Ranelagh Road, causing me dreadful anguish, because I knew that before they could board their tram or their bus, some officious busybody would be sure to treat them to my news. Then one woman, to whom I always afterward felt friendly, called down to me from her front bedroom window. "What's that you were telling Mrs. Pearce?" she asked me, in a loud whisper.

"Oh, just that McRorys' was burnt to the ground last night. Nearly all the cars burnt up, too. Hardly anything left, my father says." By this time I was being very off-hand.

"You don't tell me," she said, making a delighted face, and the next thing I knew, she was opening her front door, more eager for news than anybody.

However, my hour of glory was short. The other children came out—some of them were actually allowed to go around and view the wreckage—and soon the fire was mine no longer, because there were others walking around who knew more about it than I did. I pretended to lose interest, although I was glad when someone—not my father—gave me a lump of twisted, blackened tin off one of the cars.

The tennis clubhouse had been untouched, and that afternoon the players appeared, as bright and immaculate in their snowy flannels and linens as though the smoking garage yard and the lines of charred cars through which they had picked their way to the courts could never interfere with them or impress them. It was nearing tournament time, and a man was painting the platform on which the judge was to sit and from which a lady in a wide hat and a flowered chiffon dress would present cups and medals to the victors among the players. Now, in the sunshine, they lifted their rackets and started to play, and their intent and formal cries mingled with the hoarse shouts of the men at work in the dark shambles of the garage. My little sister and I, watching from our window, could imagine that the rhythmical thud of the ball against the rackets coincided with the unidentifiable sounds we heard from the wreckage, which might have been groans or shrieks as the building, unable to recover from the fire, succumbed under it.

It was not long before the McRorys put up another garage, made of silvery corrugated-metal stuff that looked garish and glaring against our garden wall; it cut off more of our view than the old building had. The new garage looked very hard and lasting, as unlikely to burn as a pot or a kettle. The beautiful green courts that had always seemed from our window to roll comfortably in the direction of the old wooden building now seemed to have turned and to be rolling away into the distance, as though they did not like the unsightly new structure and would have nothing to do with it.

My father said the odds were all against another fire there, but I remembered that fine dark morning, with all the excitement and my own importance, and I longed for another just like it. This time, however, I was determined to discover the blaze before my father did, and I watched the garage closely, as much of it as I could see, for signs that it might be getting ready to go up in flames, but I was disappointed. It stood, and still was standing, ugly as ever, when we left the house years later. Still, for a long time I used to think that if some child should steal around there with a match one night and set it all blazing again, I would never blame her, as long as she let me be the first with the news.

The Old Man of the Sea

One Thursday afternoon, an ancient man selling apples knocked at the door of our house in Dublin. He appeared to me to be about ninety. His hair was thin and white. His back was stooped, his expression was vague and humble, and he held his hat in one of his hands. His other hand rested on the handle of an enormous basket of apples that stood beside him. My mother, who had opened the door at his knock, stood staring at him. I peered out past her. I was nine. The first question that came into my mind was how did that thin old man carry that big basket of apples—because there was no one in the vicinity, as far as I could see, who might have given him a hand. The second question was how far had he come with his burden. I am sure the same dismayed speculations were in my mother's head, but she had no chance to ask him anything, because as soon as the door began to open he began to talk—to describe his apples and to praise them, and to say how cheap they were. After every few words he paused, not so much to catch his breath, it seemed, as to collect his wits, and to assure himself that the door was still open and that we were still listening, and, perhaps, to make certain that he himself was still standing where he thought he was. As soon as my mother could with politeness interrupt him, she said hastily that she would take a dozen apples for eating and a dozen for cooking. She got two large bowls from the kitchen, filled them with apples, and paid the old man. She left me to close the door. I watched him shuffle down the tiny tiled path that led to the sidewalk. He closed our gate carefully behind him, and started to open the gate next door, but I was quick to tell him that our neighbors were away. He nodded without looking at me, and continued on his way. I hurried into the front sitting room. From the window there, I could see what luck he had at the four other houses that remained for him to visit. By the rapidity with which he retreated from each door, and by the abrupt manner in which he pulled the gates to after him, I judged that he had sold no more apples.

I charged off down to the kitchen. My mother was already peeling the cooking apples. My Uncle Matt, my mother's brother, was standing in the door to the garden, smoking a cigarette. My little sister Derry was sitting on a chair and trying to clasp her hands behind its back.

"I suppose you took every apple he had in the basket," my uncle said to my mother.

"Oh, no," I said quickly. "He had most of them left, and he didn't sell any more. We must have been the only people who bought any."

"What did I tell you?" my mother said, not taking her eyes from the apples. "God help him, it would break your heart to see him standing there with his old hat in his hand."

"A half a dozen would have been enough," my uncle said amiably. "Now you've encouraged him, he'll be on your back the rest of your life. Isn't that so, Maeve?"

"Like the Old Man of the Sea," I said, but they paid no attention to me.

"You ought to be ashamed of yourself," my mother said to my uncle, "always thinking the worst of everybody. This is the first time I ever laid eyes on him, and I'd be very much surprised if he

65

ever turns up here again. It's not worth it to him, dragging that big basket around from door to door."

I was thinking of the old man who had attached himself to Sindbad the Sailor. I was thinking how helpless and frail the old man had looked when Sindbad first encountered him, and how, after Sindbad took him on his back to carry him, the old man grew heavier and heavier, and stronger and stronger, until, when it was too late, Sindbad began to hate him. It was a story that had fascinated me, especially the description of the old man's cruel, talon-like hands and the way they dug into Sindbad's shoulders.

On the following Thursday, the old apple man again appeared at our door, at the same time in the afternoon. When my mother opened the door, he was standing as before, with his battered hat in his hand and his thin shoulders stooped and the basket of apples beside him, but this time on top of the basket were balanced two large brown paper bags, full of apples. He bent over painfully, lifted the bags, and offered them to my mother, saying something we did not understand. He had to repeat it twice before we caught it. "A dozen of each," he was saying.

My mother started to speak, but changed her mind, turned away, got the money, paid him, and took the apples. I stood at the door and stared at him, hoping to catch in his faded eyes a glimpse of the villainy that had possessed the old sinner Sindbad found on the beach, but this old man seemed to have no sight at all. Again I watched him from the front sitting-room window, and then I joined my mother in the kitchen.

"He didn't go near any of the other houses," I announced. "I suppose he was afraid they wouldn't buy any."

"I suppose he was," my mother said dismally. "But I didn't want two dozen apples today. The most I would have taken was a half a dozen. And I didn't want to say it the other day with your Uncle Matt here, but he charges more than McRory's." McRory's was the store around the corner, where we bought our groceries. "Oh, well," said my mother, "maybe they're better apples." But she left the bags unopened on the kitchen table.

"He was depending on us," I said.

"Oh, I know that very well," my mother said. "I was a fool in the first place, and now I'll never get rid of him. If he turns up *next* Thursday, I'll take a half a dozen and no more. I'll have the exact money ready."

This resolution cheered her, and she spilled the apples out on the table.

"They are very good apples," she said, "I wonder where he gets them."

"I wonder where he comes from," I said.

"Oh, the poor old Christian," she said. "And he probably has to walk all the way."

"Unless he could find someone to carry him," I said.

"Not with all those apples," she said in surprise.

"He looks very tired," I said, trying to remember if his fingers were talonlike.

"Why wouldn't he look tired?" my mother said. "He's a very old man."

The next Thursday, she had the money ready in her hand when she answered the old man's knock. She hardly had the door open before she spoke.

"I only want a half a dozen apples today," she said clearly, smiling at him. I smiled, too, to show that we meant no harm. He already had the bags in his arms and was lifting them up to her. It was a step down from our front door to the path, so that, although she is a small woman, he appeared smaller than she. She gravely repeated what she had said, and shook her head at the bags.

"Just give me a half a dozen," she said, and I could not have told if she was still smiling, because I was staring at the old man.

The Old Man of the Sea

He seemed about to cry. My mother suddenly reached and took the two bags, and hurried away, calling to me to get the money and pay him.

"Now what'll we do?" I asked her when he had gone.

"Oh, it isn't that I mind the apples so much," she said, "but I don't like feeling I *have* to buy them."

"Did you see that his basket is always full up, except for the apples we take?" I said.

"Oh, I suppose he only goes to the ones he's sure of," she said bitterly, "and you can't blame him for that. He's only trying to get along, like everybody else in the world."

The following few Thursdays, we put up no fight, but I did notice that the old man's fingers were not at all talonlike. They were short and stubby, with bulging knuckles.

Then one Thursday afternoon about three months after we had bought the first, fatal two dozen, my mother decided, everything having gone wrong that day, that she would put her foot down once and for all.

"Now look here," she said, "I'm buying no apples from that old fellow today. Even if I wanted them, I wouldn't buy them. Even if he breaks the door down, I won't answer it."

Derry and I exchanged a glance of anticipation. We were going to pretend we weren't in. We had done that before when unwanted callers came, and we enjoyed it very much. We liked keeping rigidly quiet, listening to the futile knocking at the front door, and we especially enjoyed having our mother at our mercy for those few minutes, because we all felt sure that the least squeak we made, no matter where we were in the house, would betray us to the straining ears outside. Then there was always the sense of triumph when at last we heard our little gate clang shut again and knew that we had defeated our enemy. This time, however, there was an extra suspense that we could not have explained. We were all in the kitchen when the old man's knock came. Our kitchen was separated from our front door only by the length of a small, narrow hall, so we shut the kitchen door. We heard the first knock, and then the second, and then the third. Finally, the old man knocked several times more in rapid succession. Derry and I began to reel around, giggling helplessly, and my mother gave us a reproachful look. She was distressed anyway.

A familiar scratching noise came to our ears, and we gazed at one another, aghast.

"He must have got in somehow," my mother said in a fearful whisper.

I opened the kitchen door very gradually. "He's got his hand in the letter box," I whispered over my shoulder to the others.

In the middle of the front door there was a wide slot, through which the postman pushed letters and papers so that they fell inside on the hall floor. On the outside, the slot was protected by a brass flap, and the old man had lifted this and was trying to peer into the hall. We knew very well that the slot gave only a limited and indistinct view of the hall, but we were unreasonably startled to realize that he had found an opening in the house. Suddenly he began to shout through the slot.

"He's roaring mad!" Derry whispered. "He'll kill us all."

"Can you make out what he's saying?" asked my mother, who was appalled.

"He's saying, 'apple, apple, apple,'" I said.

Derry and I collapsed into hysterical mirth. My mother bundled us out into the garden, and came out herself.

"Have you no heart?" she said. "To laugh at an unfortunate old man who probably never gets enough to eat!"

"Now we're really not in," I said, "because we're out in the garden."

Derry joined me in screeches of laughter.

The Old Man of the Sea

"If I thought he could hear you," my mother said fiercely to us, "I'd murder you both."

"Well, it's too late to answer the door now," she added. "I couldn't face him after this. I'll make it up to him next week."

There was sudden silence—no knocking, no shouting.

"He's gone away," my mother said, in a tone of guilty relief.

At that moment, the tousled head and avid eyes of the woman next door appeared over the wall that separated our garden from hers. "Mrs. Brennan!" she shouted. She had a powerful voice. "There's an old fellow outside with apples for you. He says he's been at your door for a half an hour. He says he comes regularly and he knows you're depending on him. I told him you were in the garden. He must be back around at your door by now. There he is."

There he was. The knocking had started again.

"Oh, God forgive me!" my mother cried. "That old villain! He must have known I was hiding from him."

"What are you hiding for?" our neighbor shrieked. "Do you owe him?"

"Oh, no," my mother said indignantly, "but I don't want any apples."

"Well, why don't you just tell him to go about his business?"

"I will, of course. That's what I'm going to do."

"Just give him a piece of your mind for making a nuisance of himself, and shut the door in his face," commanded our neighbor, with relish.

My mother went into our kitchen, took her purse in her hand, and marched to the door, with Derry and me following. The old man was a pitiful sight. He had forgotten to take off his hat, and his eyes glittered, whether with anguish or with anger it would have been hard to say. He pushed the two bags of apples rudely into my mother's arms without looking at her. She opened her purse to pay him, and gave a cry of distress: "Didn't I go and pay the grocer only an hour ago, and I'm fourpence short!" She handed him the money, and showed him that it left her purse empty. "It's all I have in the house at the minute," she said.

He grabbed the money, counted it, and gave her back a dreadful look of contempt. Then he lifted his enormous basket, which was, as always, full to the brim, and turned his back on us. This time, we all stood in the front sitting-room window, and watched him. He didn't close our gate, and he scuttled slowly off down the street as though he couldn't get away from us fast enough.

"First, he thought we were making fun of him," my mother said, "and now he thinks I was trying to bargain with him. He might have known I'd make it up to him the next time."

She, who never tried to bargain with anybody in her life, was filled with shame.

"Next week, we'll have the door open for him before he knocks," I said.

But the following week there was no sign of the old man, and he never came near us again, although, filled with remorse, we watched for him. One afternoon, my Uncle Matt dropped around to see us, and my mother, in a confiding mood, told him the whole story.

"Well, I could have told you," he said, grinning.

"It wasn't so much the apples, you know," my mother said.

"Oh, no," said my uncle. "You'd have liked him to come to your door and ask straight out for money, like the rest of your beggars."

My mother was noted for her inability to refuse food, clothes, or money to anybody who came to the door.

The Old Man of the Sea

"How many times must I tell you not to call them beggars," she said angrily now to my uncle. "They're just unfortunate, and I wouldn't be so quick to laugh at them if I were you."

"Well, you're well rid of *him*," my uncle said. "And I may as well tell you now that I saw him strolling down O'Connell Street the other morning wearing a suit of clothes that I couldn't afford to buy, and not an apple in sight. There's your poor old man for you."

"Now how did you know it was him?" my mother cried skeptically. "You never saw him at all."

"Wasn't I here the first time he came to the door? I was standing in the middle of the kitchen, and you had the hall door wide open. Of course I saw him."

"Well, you're making all that up about seeing him on O'Connell Street."

"I saw him, and I passed close enough to touch him. He had his married daughter from Drumcondra with him."

"And how do you know she was his married daughter from Drumcondra, may I ask?"

"Oh, you couldn't mistake *her*," my uncle said airily. "I knew her by the way she was wearing her hat."

"That tongue of yours, Matt," my mother said. "I never know whether to believe you or not."

For my part, I believed every word my uncle said.

The Barrel of Rumors

In Dublin, my mother used to take parcels of food to a community of Poor Clare nuns who had their convent a long walk from our house in Ranelagh. Sometimes she used to send my sister and me with the parcels. The Poor Clares are silent. They never speak, to each other or to anyone, and they are a closed order, which means that they never see outsiders and no one ever sees them. These Dublin Poor Clares had no food except what their friends—women, mostly, people like my mother—brought to them. They were forbidden to ask for anything, but we heard that if their food supply got dangerously low, the Reverend Mother was allowed to signal their distress by ringing the bell in the steeple of their chapel. To my regret, our house was too far from the convent to let us hear the bell, but my mother assured me that there was no need to worry; the nuns had never yet been driven to ring for help.

One hall in the convent was open to visitors for a part of every day, and it was there we used to call with our offerings of food. A huge revolving barrel with an open section had been built upright into the narrow end wall that sealed the public hall away from the rest of the convent. We used to place our parcels on the floor of the barrel, and then turn it around so that the open section faced the nun on the other side of the wall. The nun would immediately turn it back to us, always sending us a present of a few holy pictures or some medals.

The Barrel of Rumors

The nun who attended the barrel was named Sister Bridget. She was the only member of the community who had permission to talk to visitors. A tiny square waiting room opened off the hall, and we used to go in there and hold conversations with her through a blind grille in the wall. One of my names is Bridget, and she had the idea that I would someday develop a vocation, and maybe become a Poor Clare like herself. She used to offer many prayers for my vocation, and I enjoyed talking with her about it. I was about twelve then.

I had heard that the Poor Clares slept in their coffins, with stones under their heads. I had been told that they were measured for their coffins the first day they entered the convent, and that they never knew any other bed afterward. My mother liked to throw cold water on this story, but I could not forget it. I used to wonder if they had separate cells for sleeping, with a coffin in each cell, or if they slept in a dormitory, and if they had sheets and blankets and pillowcases, and, if so, how they made their beds in the morning. Also, I wondered, what about the coffin lids? Where were they kept? On the floor alongside the coffin? Or leaning, like hockey sticks and bicycles, against the wall? I knew that the nuns never slept more than a couple of hours at a time and that they arose at intervals during the night, even in the dead of winter, to go to their chapel and pray. It was a picture to dwell upon.

I asked my mother many questions about the nuns, but her answers were never satisfactory. One time that I remember asking her about them, her younger brother, my Uncle Matt, was lounging about the room. We were in the front sitting room, and she was trying to coax one of her precious ferns to twine itself around a long bamboo cane that she had stuck into its pot.

Q—Do the Poor Clare nuns have any other convent besides the one here in Dublin?

74

The Barrel of Rumors

A—I think they have another convent somewhere in Ireland, and I believe they have one in England.

Q—If nobody is allowed to see them, what happens when they're moved from one convent to another?

A—How would I know? I suppose a car, a little van, maybe, backs up to the convent door, and the nun gets in and shuts herself in.

Q—Would she bring her coffin with her?

A—I wish you'd stop all this nonsense about the nuns sleeping in their coffins.

(UNCLE MATT: Of course she'd bring her coffin with her. Doesn't she have to get her sleep, like anybody else? She'd carry it under her arm like a music roll. Do you mean to tell me you've never seen a nun walking along the street with her coffin under her arm?)

Q—What if a Poor Clare gets sick and has to have the doctor?

A—I don't know.

Q—What about if they're dying, and the priest has to come?

A—I don't know. Besides, that would be different. A priest would be different.

Q—What about if they talk in their sleep? Would that be a sin for them?

(UNCLE MATT: Well, of course, it would depend what they said.)

A—That's enough of that, now. I don't want to hear another word out of either of you.

Lentils, dried peas, eggs, and flour were chiefly what my mother used to bring to the nuns. Sometimes she baked a cake for them. Once, she brought salt, and Sister Bridget thanked her particularly, telling her that the community had been without salt for two weeks. Although the walk to the convent was long, it was not lonely. We had to cross at least two busy main streets, full of traffic as we walked along, and the way was very pleasant, with trees lining the sidewalks in front of the houses, and benches to sit on in case we got tired.

The convent and its chapel formed three sides of a square court, which was carefully tended and had a small, smooth grass lawn and bright flower beds. The fourth side of the court was on the public road and was walled off, with an iron gate through which visitors entered. The wall was very high and you couldn't see through the gate. To the right of the gate was the gate lodge, where an old woman lived and attended to visitors who called during off hours.

Although the convent had fixed visiting hours, the chapel was always open, and people could go in there and pray any time. People who lived near the chapel used to attend Mass and Benediction there. It was a beautiful little chapel, the plainest I have ever seen, with a small, almost bare main altar flanked by two tall statues of nuns—Saint Clare on the left as you knelt facing the altar, and Saint Camillus on the right. Both saints wore the brown habit of the Poor Clares. To the right of the altar, a great grille was set into the wall, and through this grille the nuns used to witness Mass and receive Benediction, and through the grille people kneeling in the chapel could hear their voices answering the prayers and singing the Benediction hymns.

One Sunday afternoon, my mother took me to Benediction there. I watched the altar and listened to the voices of the nuns, but my real attention was given to a small old woman kneeling in the seat ahead of me. This old woman, dressed in black, had her head half turned, so that I could see her face, and she was listening to the voices from behind the grille with such concentration that she appeared desperate, her eyes wide open and her mouth working along with the words.

My mother saw me watching her, and as we left the chapel, she said, "That poor old woman comes here every chance she gets. Her daughter has been in there fourteen years, and she's got so she imagines she can hear her daughter's voice out of all the others. We came out together one day, and she told me she can't hear any of the other voices any more, only her daughter's voice. It's like as if her daughter was in there alone, she says. It's sad to see her straining like that, to hear every word."

"Was it her oldest daughter or the youngest?" I asked. Being the middle one, I was concerned with such things.

"I don't know that," my mother said.

"Do you suppose the daughter thinks about her mother out there, and doesn't think of anybody else?" I asked.

"She could hardly help thinking of her," my mother said. "After all, she's still her daughter. But, of course, once they're in there, they're in there," she added, "and they're not supposed to think about what they've left behind. It's hard to know what goes on in their heads. Maybe they try to forget about the outside world altogether."

"Except for our sins," I said. "They have to pray for us."

"That's true," my mother said. "They have to think about all the sins we commit."

If this thought amused her, she gave no sign of it.

One sunny morning late in the summer, my mother called me into the kitchen, where she was packing a parcel for the Poor Clares.

"I was wondering if you would like to take Robert with you," she said. "It's a long walk, but you could go slow. Then you could put him in the barrel and send him around to see the nuns."

"Put Robert in the barrel?" I cried.

Robert, my brother, was at this time about two years old.

"Certainly," my mother said. "Children are allowed in the bar-

rel until they're three years old. After that they're too old. You can
take him if you like. I'll put his blue suit on him."

A few minutes later, I started off, pushing Robert in his pram.
He sat back placidly against his pillow and stared at me. The nun's
parcel made a comfortable prop for his feet. He was very pink and
cheerful. My mother had dressed him in a suit of pale-blue wool
that she had knitted herself and that fitted him very tightly all over
and left his fat legs bare. He wore short white-cotton socks and
brown sandals. His hair, of which he did not have much, was
brushed into a golden crest on top of his head, and he shone with
health, contentment, and cleanliness. I was in a great hurry to get
him into the barrel, and I sped along, almost skating behind the
pram.

When I got to the convent, I rushed into the waiting room and
told Sister Bridget I had brought Robert to see her. She was delighted, and said she would call the other nuns. I didn't know, and
didn't like to ask, whether she meant that she would call all the nuns
or just a few of them. I imagined them, silent and swift, of all ages,
descending upon Robert from every part of the convent. I hoped
none of them would be in the chapel, because surely they would
never be allowed to interrupt their prayers.

I went back to the hall and lifted Robert into the barrel, making sure he had his back against the wall. He sat very solidly where
I placed him, a good deal larger than the parcels I was in the habit
of bringing. As soon as I heard Sister Bridget's voice, I revolved him
out of sight. He didn't seem to mind disappearing. There was
silence on the other side of the barrel. I couldn't hear a rustle—not
even the suspicion of a whisper. Even Robert made no sound. I
stared at the blank side of the barrel and wondered what was going
on on the other side.

After a minute or two, the barrel began to move, and Robert
gradually came into view, sitting exactly as I had placed him, look-

ing very matter-of-fact and friendly. I lifted him out, and put the parcel on the warmed-up spot where he had been sitting. When the barrel came back the second time, Sister Bridget had sent us more presents than usual. There were extra holy pictures and extra medals and a special present for Robert, a holy picture sewn by some nun to a square of white satin and embroidered with white-satin thread. I went back into the conversation room and received Sister Bridget's compliments about Robert, and acknowledged the hopes she expressed for him, which I took to be blessings, considering their source. Then I heard a few words, perfunctory this time, about my vocation, and left.

As I trundled Robert home, I was exasperated to think that he had been where I might never go, and that he didn't even realize his luck. He was in great good humor. He waved his arms and pointed at people and objects that interested him, and even talked a little, but I could make no sense of his language, and anyway none of his remarks seemed to have to do with the barrel, which he had apparently forgotten. He was unable to tell me what he had seen, and by the time he got old enough to express himself, it would all have passed from his memory. Not from him would I ever learn how the nuns looked, if they were young or old, if they were pretty or ugly, if they smiled at him, or nodded to him, or tried to take his hand or stroke his head, as other strangers did. He never would be able to tell me what the inside of the convent looked like. Worst of all, I realized that no matter what I heard, I would never really know for sure if the nuns slept in their coffins, with stones for pillows.

The Day We Got Our Own Back

One afternoon some unfriendly men dressed in civilian clothes and carrying revolvers came to our house searching for my father, or for information about him. This was in Dublin, in 1922. The treaty with England, turning Ireland into the Irish Free State, had just been signed. Those Irish who were in favor of the treaty, the Free Staters, were governing the country. Those who had held out for a republic, like my father, were in revolt. My father was wanted by the new government, and so he had gone into hiding. He was on the run, sleeping one night in one house and the next night in another, and sometimes stealing home to see us. I suppose my mother must have taken us to see him several times, but I only remember visiting him once, and I know I found it very odd to meet him sitting in a strange person's house, and to leave him there when we were ready to go home. Anyway, these men had been sent to find him. They crowded into our narrow little hall, and tramped around the house, upstairs and downstairs, looking everywhere and asking questions. There was no one at home except my mother, my little sister Derry, and me. Emer, my elder sister, and my mother's chief prop, was out doing errands. Derry was upstairs in bed with a cold. I was settled comfortably on a low chair in our front sitting room, threading a necklace. I was five.

After the men had searched the house, they crowded into the

room where I sat, from which they could watch the street. They brought my mother in with them. They camped around the room, talking idly among themselves and waiting. My mother stood against the wall farthest from the windows, watching them. She was very tense. She feared that my father would risk a visit home and that he would be trapped, and that we would see him trapped. One of the men came and stood over me. He pointed out a blue-glass bead for me to add to my necklace, but I explained to him that the bead was too small to slip over my needle and that I had already discarded it. This exchange with this strange man made me feel very clever. He leaned closer to me then.

"Tell us do you know where your Daddy is," he whispered.

I stopped threading and began to think, but my mother flew across the room at him. She is a very small, thin woman with a pointed face and straight brown hair that she has always worn in a bun at the back of her head.

"Aren't you ashamed of yourself?" she cried. "Asking the child questions."

The man drew away from me, and she went back to her place against the wall. At that time, in 1922, she had been through a good many years of trouble and anxiety. All the first years of her marriage were dominated by the preparations for the Rebellion of Easter, 1916, and she had seen my father captured and condemned first to death and then to penal servitude for life. At the time that I was born, he was in jail in England and she was alone in Dublin, not knowing when, if ever, she would see him again. Actually, he was released less than a year later, and in 1921 we moved into our house in Ranelagh, where we now waited to see what was going to happen.

Suddenly my mother, thinking of Derry, alone in the room above, abandoned her wall and darted to the door leading to the stairs, but one of the men was before her, with his revolver raised against her. She stood with both hands against the doorjamb, staring up at him, half smiling. I have often seen her smiling like that when she is agitated.

"You can't open that door," the man said.

"Didn't you see the little one sick upstairs?" my mother said. "She'll be frightened by herself."

"Never mind about that," the man said. "You're not getting out of this room."

Again my mother retreated to her wall, and I returned to my necklace, and the men continued their talk. After a while, they abruptly got up and went away. My mother remained anxious, suspecting that they might be watching the end of the street for my father's arrival. She went upstairs to speak to Derry, and when she came back, I followed her down the three steps into the kitchen, which was small and squarish, with a red-tile floor and a door that gave out onto the garden. She sat down at the kitchen table. I asked her if she would like a cup of tea, and she said yes, she would like a cup. I filled the kettle, splashing water all over the floor, but she wouldn't trust me to light the gas, and in the end she had to make the tea herself. Some time later, Emer came home, and my mother gave her tea, and told her everything that had happened and all that had been said, not forgetting the question that had been put to me. Listening to her, I was once again spellbound with gratitude, excitement, and astonishment that the strange man had included me in the raid.

The only other raid I remember took place about a year after that, and the men were rougher. Again there were in the house only my mother, my little sister, and I. This time, the men came in the morning. My mother was getting along with her housework, and she had an apron tied about her waist. She had shined the brass rods that held our red stair carpet in place, and now she was polishing the oilcloth on the dining-room floor. The men crowded in as before, with their revolvers, but this time they searched in earnest. They pulled all the beds apart, looking for papers and letters, and they took all my father's books out of the shelves and shook them, and they looked in all the drawers and in the wardrobe and in the kitchen stove. There was not an inch of the house they did not touch. They turned every room inside out. The newly polished oilcloth was scarred by their impatient feet, and the bedrooms upstairs were torn apart, with sheets and blankets on the floor, and the mattresses all humped up on the bare beds. In the end, they went back to the kitchen, and they took down the tins of flour and tea and sugar and salt and whatever else there was, and plunged their hands into them, and emptied them on the table and on the floor. They took all the cups and saucers and plates down. Still they had found nothing, but the house looked as though it had suffered an explosion without bursting its walls. At last, they got ready to leave, but as they were on the point of going, one of them, a very keen fellow, rushed over to the fireplace in the front sitting room and put his hands up the chimney and shoved his face as far into the grate as it would go, trying to look up and see what might be there. A great soft shower of soot came down around him, covering his shoulders and his face. He pulled hastily back into the room, with black hands and a black-mottled face. Some of the soot had gone up his sleeves. Some of it was still drifting out over the carpet. He glanced at his companions and pawed at himself, and then they went away.

When they had gone, my mother gazed about her at all the work they had made. It would be a long time before she had the house neat again. We all trailed down into the kitchen and surveyed the mess there. This time, there was no question of making tea, because the tea was on the floor, along with the flour and the sugar.

The Day We Got Our Own Back

We had seldom heard my mother's voice raised in laughter. She has a very quiet, almost secret manner in amusement. Now, however, she began to tremble and to smile.

"Oh," she cried, "to see the look on his face when he came back out of the chimney!"

My little sister and I began to jump around, cackling.

"Oh," cried my mother, "what warned me not to have the chimney cleaned? Oh, thanks be to God I forgot to have the chimney cleaned!"

And with us chattering a delighted, incredulous accompaniment, she laughed as though her heart might break.

The Clever One

Not long ago, I was staying in Washington, D.C., with my younger sister, Deirdre, who is married and has four young children. It was spring. We sat in her large, pleasant living room, with the trees all fresh and green outside on Garfield Street, and the shrubs bursting into bloom—white, pink, blue, yellow—in her garden, where the children were giving themselves wholeheartedly to some raucous game, and we began to speak, as we often do, of the time when we two were small together. There is less than two years between us. Our childhood was spent in Dublin, most of it in a small house in Ranelagh.

"The first time I remember seeing you," I said, "was before we went to live in Ranelagh. It was when we were living in the house on Belgrave Road. You must have been about eighteen months old, I suppose. Someone was holding you in their arms, and you snatched Emer's cap off her head and threw it in the fire, and she cried. It was a new woollen cap she had." Emer is our older sister.

"I don't remember that," Derry said, but she looked pleased at the thought of the burning cap. "I don't remember Belgrave Road at all."

"The next time I have a clear memory of you," I continued, "you must have been about three. We were living in Ranelagh. I went into the front bedroom and found you wandering around in your skin, crying for someone to dress you, and I dressed you."

"I don't remember *that,*" Derry said.

"Well, do you remember when you were six or seven and almost got St. Vitus's dance? You kept shaking, and dropping things all over the house."

"Oh, I remember that, all right," Derry said, smiling.

All the time we were talking, she was hemming a pink-cotton dress for her older daughter. I looked at her hands, so steady and sure with the needle, and I thought of how we had all feared she would lose the use of them.

"You were never able to help with the washing-up," I said, "for fear you'd break all the cups and saucers. When you weren't dropping things, you lay on the bed with your eyes wide open, not able to wake up. You looked awful. You gave Mother a terrible fright. She got the woman from next door in to look at you."

"I *remember* all that," Derry said impatiently.

"But you were asleep," I said.

"I was no more asleep than you are now," she said. "And I was no nearer getting St. Vitus's dance than you are now, either," she added, this time with a touch of defiance.

I stared, or glared, at her. "What do you mean?" I cried.

She looked me straight in the eye, but the color began to rise in her face.

"Do you mean to tell me you were putting it all on?" I cried, sounding almost as thunderstruck as I felt. Derry's delicate health had loomed as importantly in my childhood as the Catholic Church and the fight for Irish freedom. The first word I ever remember hearing about Derry was that she had been underweight when she was born and that her health was precarious. My mother always dressed us exactly alike, and people used to call us Mrs. Brennan's twins, but I was the large, hardy twin and she was the thin, pale one, always with me, and always silent, while I talked endlessly.

Remembering how strongly all this had shaped our childhood, and the way it had determined everything between us and around us, I naturally was aghast to hear her now, more than twenty years later, calmly tearing it all away. I decided that she was joking.

"You're joking, aren't you?" I said.

"I am not," she said.

"But why did you do it?" I asked.

"Well, for one thing, I always got out of doing the washing-up," she said. "And I was always too delicate to go to school much, if you remember."

"All those washing-ups I did," I said. "And do you mean to say you never told anyone at all about it?"

She gave me an exasperated look. "That would have been pretty silly, wouldn't it? The whole point was that no one knew."

"And you've kept it a secret all these years," I said.

"To tell you the truth, I hadn't thought about it for years, till you brought it up just now. Of course, I really did have colds sometimes, and I did have those terrible chilblains in the wintertime." She began to laugh, and so did I, but not very heartily.

Just then, two of her children began a battle under the windows, and she ran out to investigate them, leaving me to think about her duplicity all those years ago, when she was so small and frail it would have taken a strange-minded person to accuse her of the least offense, let alone of keeping the house in an uproar over her health for years on end. I was more admiring than anything else, because I hadn't really minded doing the washing-up alone, since I always received high praise from my mother for doing it, but I was stunned to think that Derry had been capable, so young, of thinking up and carrying through such a black and complicated plot, and of not speaking about it to anyone—not even to me.

It was then I remembered that this was not the first time she had set me back.

The Clever One

The first time it happened, she was not more than seven and I was almost nine. In those years, as I say, I was larger than she was, and I won't say I bullied her, but I did boss her around. All her life, I bossed her unmercifully until the moment of which I am about to speak, and I suppose that even after that things did not really change very much between us. I remember I had a favorite game called "sitting on Derry." I used to make her lie flat on the floor while I sat on her stomach and stared into her face, grimacing in a manner that we both considered terrifying. It was a simple game, but I suppose she must sometimes have grown weary of it.

I felt superior to her, and protective toward her because she was so tiny, and because she hated school and never did well in her lessons, and because she got ugly, painful chilblains in the cold weather and I never did, and most of all because she was shy. As a matter of fact, I never gave her a chance to say a word. People were always told that I had the brains in the family. "Derry has the beauty," they used to say, "but Maeve has all the brains." I believed every word of this. I used to look at Derry and think solemnly about my brains, and about how I never had any trouble in school and always got good marks. In games, I always hammered myself into the lead, while Derry played off by herself somewhere, and I was always first to enter myself in singing competitions, although I had no voice, and in reciting contests, although I had no eloquence. I had even made up my mind to become an actress, but I had not spoken to anyone at school or in the family about my ambition, for fear of being laughed at.

However, one day Derry and I were sitting together in the back garden of our house in Ranelagh. It must have been summertime, because we were sitting on the grass, and there were forget-me-nots and London pride in bloom in my mother's flower beds. We had a bead box on the grass between us, and we were stringing necklaces and enjoying my conversation.

The Clever One

"When I grow up," I said to Derry, "I'm going to be a famous actress. I'll act in the Abbey Theatre, and I'll be in the pictures, and I'll go around to all the schools and teach all the teachers how to recite."

I was about to continue, because I never expected her to have anything to say, but she spoke up, without raising her head from her necklace. "Don't go getting any notions into your head," she said clearly.

I was astounded. Where had little Derry picked up such a remark? I had never said it, and I was not sure I had ever even heard it. Who had said it to her? I was astounded, and I was silent. I had nothing to say. For the first time, it had occurred to me that little Derry had *brains*. More brains than I had, maybe, even?

The Lie

There was a joke between my mother and me about the first time I went to confession. She took me to see the priest herself, but we were late leaving home, and by the time we got to the chapel there were two long rows of women kneeling outside the confession box, waiting to be heard. My mother said later that she could tell by the expression on their faces that they all had a great deal to confess, and that they would take their time about it. She was worried, fearing we had a couple of hours to wait, and knowing that I was only seven, and restless and nervous because this was the first time I was going to get into the box. However, we knelt together at the end of one line, and settled down to wait. The priest had not yet arrived, but when we had been kneeling there a couple of minutes, we saw him hurrying down the aisle from the altar. He was a fat old man, and I stared at him in terror. As he came toward us, he glanced around at all the waiting women, and then he saw me. He stopped and spoke to my mother.

"Is this the first time she's going to confession?" he asked.

When he heard that it was, he took my arm and pulled me gently to my feet and along past all the knees of all the waiting and greatly surprised women, and pushed me into the box ahead of the first woman in line. There I was, kneeling in the dark, when the shutter just above my face was pulled back and I saw the priest's profile.

90

"Start now, child," he said impatiently. "Don't be afraid."

After I had stumbled through the first prayer and come to the telling of the sins, I stopped, because I couldn't remember any sins.

"All right now, child," the priest said, "were you disobedient?"

"Yes, Father."

"And did you lose your temper a couple of times?"

"Yes, Father."

"That's right. For your penance say three Hail Marys. Now make a good Act of Contrition."

A minute later I was again stumbling past all the knees, and all the irritated faces, and my mother took me to the altar rail, where I said my penance, and we left the chapel.

"What penance did he give you?" she asked as we were walking home.

"Three Hail Marys."

"You must have had more sins than I thought," she said, laughing. "Didn't he give that crowd the surprise of their lives! Some of them must have been kneeling there an hour or more."

After that, whenever I went to confession, I got the same penance—three Hail Marys—and my mother always asked me what the priest had given me, and when she heard, she would laugh again, thinking of the angry faces of the women the first time. Sometimes she told other people about it, and I always liked to hear the story. Although everyone knew about it, I still felt it to be a private joke between the two of us, and I loved that. Then one day, some time in my ninth year, I spoiled it all. I saw the little joke die, and I knew that I had killed it.

It happened in a very simple way. My younger sister, Deirdre, had a toy sewing machine that she loved. She was seven then. The machine actually made stitches, and she used to work with it for hours, turning the little handwheel that made it go. I had no interest in sewing, and never touched the machine, but it was her favorite toy.

One day, I wandered into the front sitting room, where I found my mother in her usual chair, with a pile of mending on a table at her side. She was busy with a sock. I hurled myself across the room and into her lap. Under this onslaught, she pricked her finger with the needle, gave a cry of irritation, and pushed me away. I tumbled deliberately down on the floor, and sat there, glaring at her in outrage.

"What's the matter with you?" she cried, putting her punctured finger in her mouth.

"I wanted to sit on your lap."

"Well, you can't. You're too big, for one thing."

"Derry sits on your lap," I said.

"Derry only weighs about a half a pound."

That was true.

"And," continued my mother, "you must weigh almost as much as I do myself."

It was all too true. I rushed upstairs in a fury, and into the room I shared with Derry. There was the little sewing machine, sitting on the window ledge, where she had left it. I took it up and gazed at it in hatred. Then I tugged the little wheel off. After that, I wrestled with the machine until it was ruined. When it was all broken, I regarded it, first with satisfaction and then, very quickly, with dismay and regret. I was very sorry I had broken Derry's toy, and I was afraid of what would happen to me. I did the only thing I could think of. I leaned out of the window and dropped all the pieces down onto the cement path outside our kitchen door. Then I went thundering back down the stairs again.

"Derry, Derry!" I shouted. "I was trying to work your sewing machine, and it fell out through the window, and I'm sure it's all broken."

My mother and Derry came running, and we all dashed into

the garden and surveyed the pitiful remains of the little machine. Derry began to cry. I was very much upset. After all, it was my first murder.

My mother stooped down and gathered up the pieces. "How did it happen to fall out of the window, Maeve?" she asked.

"I don't know, I was only holding it in my hand and out it went. Isn't it a good thing I didn't fall out, too?"

My mother refused to be diverted by the picture of me following the machine down onto the cement.

"Are you sure you did nothing to *make* it fall out, Maeve?"

"Oh, no!" I cried. "No, I didn't!" and tears of real grief filled my eyes, to think that she would believe me capable of such an act.

My mother looked perplexed and sad, but she promised Derry a new machine, and we all went back into the house, where peace soon descended on us. As a matter of fact, Derry got very much interested in the workings of the machine, which had been somewhat mysterious to her till then, and she spent a good deal of time examining the broken parts. I tried to forget about the whole incident, and succeeded until the following Saturday, when I had to go to confession.

I told the priest that I had flown into a bad temper, and he nodded. Then I told him that I had been envious of my younger sister.

"Envy is a serious sin, my child," he said. "You must beware of that."

I told him I had smashed my sister's sewing machine.

"Deliberately?" he asked.

"Yes, Father."

"You broke one of her toys because you were envious of her?"

"Yes, Father."

"That is a very serious matter, to do a thing like that," the priest said. "If you don't learn to curb yourself, you may do something you'll be very sorry for, one of these days. Did you tell her you were sorry?"

"Yes, Father."

I then told him I had lied to my mother.

"You told a lie to your *mother?*" He went on to say that lying is a serious sin in itself, but that one who told a lie to her mother had taken a very bad turn on life's road.

"For a penance," he concluded, "you can say five Our Fathers and five Hail Marys."

Much shaken, I left the confession box, said my penance, and went home, feeling very free and glad it was all over, and full of love and contrition and good resolutions.

I arrived home just as tea was being put on the table, and we all sat down and started to talk.

"And where were you this afternoon?" my father asked me.

"I went to confession, Daddy."

"And what penance did you get this time?"

"Five Our Fathers and five Hail Marys, this time," I said.

"Well," remarked my father, "you're going up in the world. I wonder what you had to tell, to get that size of a penance."

I hardly heard him. The minute the words were out of my mouth, I knew I had made a terrible mistake. Burning with guilt and shame, I stared at my mother. She was looking back at me in a way that confounded me still further, because although her expression was serious, I knew she was not angry. I was very sorry and very sad. I was ready to yell with anguish.

"Oh, Maeve," she said at last, "my poor child, why couldn't you have kept your mouth shut?"

"What's going on around here *now?*" my father asked, bewildered.

He got no answer.

The Devil in Us

I was peacefully approaching the end of my thirteenth year when I was startled out of all placidity by an unanswerable question that still returns sometimes to puzzle my mind. I was at a convent boarding school in Kilcullen, a village in the County Kildare. There were sixty or more girls at the school, and we used to be taken for long crocodile walks into the flat and spiritless countryside that surrounds the village. There were several shops in Kilcullen, but the only building I ever entered there was the church, where we occasionally went to confession. Most of the time, we went to confession in the convent chapel, which we approached on tiptoe through the darkened main hall of the nuns' quarters. We wore navy-blue uniforms, with long black wool stockings and black slippers, and before entering the chapel for confession, or for morning Mass or Sunday-afternoon Benediction, we covered our heads with white-net veils. By the end of my first term, my veil was so full of the chapel's dark and musky fragrance—of incense and flowers and snuffed-out candles—that I was afraid to wash it, for fear of committing sacrilege.

My first year at school went off fairly smoothly. I was not an outstanding success, but neither was I a failure. There was nothing to read, because the tiny school library was kept locked up behind the doors of a tall, glass-fronted bookcase, and I detested hockey and basketball and all the other sports we were expected to practice, but I was a cheerful enough scholar. It was at the beginning of the second year that things began to change, but the change was so gradual that I was never able to decide which day, or even which week, I began to recognize it, and to grow accustomed to it. I did feel, however, that it all started one fine September afternoon in singing class. It was the only class for which the entire school was brought together. We met in the biggest classroom, which had a piano. We used to stand in a great, sweeping semicircle, with the choir girls on the right and the rest of us arranged roughly according to height. I was in the middle of the curve, and felt myself to be directly under Sister Veronica's eye, although actually, of course, I was no more conspicuous than any of the others. And in any case I knew from experience that a girl who tried to remain hidden was often the first one to attract attention to herself.

That afternoon, with all the other girls, I was rendering "The Mountains o'Mourne" at the top of my voice and keeping my eyes fastened on the pale, protruding eyes of Sister Veronica, who kept time for us with one of her long, limp hands. Sister Veronica believed that a girl who can look you straight in the eye is a good girl, and I was hoping she would notice my honest gaze.

The door opened, and Sister Hildegarde, the Sister Superior in charge of the school, walked in, portentous and unsmiling. She was a short, wide woman with a large white face on which moles grew. She and Sister Veronica together ruled us, with the help of three young lay teachers and two or three lesser nuns. We were afraid of the two head nuns. We were afraid of them separately, but our fear increased threefold when they were both present, because they seemed to set each other off, and the decisions they made when their eyes met were always to our disadvantage, and there was no appeal from them. They were unpredictable and deadly in their accusations and in their judgments, and we never knew where we were with them. This time, however, the occasion seemed peaceful enough, and we continued to sing with all our hearts. Sister Hildegarde took up her position behind Sister Veronica and a little to the side, so she could see us all.

When the song was finished, we started in on "Who Is Sylvia?," which we had learned to sing in parts. Halfway through, Sister Veronica, at a word from Sister Hildegarde, waved abruptly to us to stop.

Sister Hildegarde stepped forward. "I have a suspicion that all of the girls are not doing their best," she said. "You know, Sister, that there are certain girls here who are only too glad to let the others do the work for them. If it were not for your work, and Maggie Harrington's voice, I don't know where the choir would be this year."

Maggie Harrington was the star singer of the school. She led the choir in singing for Benediction every Sunday, and she was also head girl. She was eighteen years old, with wiry brown hair that she wore in a queue down her solid back, and a broad red face on which rimless spectacles rode and flashed in triumph. Sister Veronica smiled at Maggie, and at the other members of the choir, who were grouped around her. They were very important girls, although some of them were only twelve, and the rest of us looked at them enviously, because they were in everybody's good graces and always knew the right thing to do.

"I am going to watch very closely this time," Sister Hildegarde said. "I think I know which girls are shirking. I think you know, too, don't you, Sister?"

Sister Veronica agreed that she was pretty sure which girls were holding back their voices, and added meaningfully that it was usually the girls who gave the most trouble, in and out of class, who did the least work. "I've never seen it to fail, Sister," she said, staring us all down. "Laziness and troublemaking go hand in hand. A busy girl is a good girl. The Devil can always find work for idle hands."

Sister Hildegarde nodded agreement. "Give them a note, Sister," she said.

Sister Veronica gave us a very loud note on the piano, not taking her eyes from us. " 'The Spinning Wheel,' " she said.

This was one of my favorite songs. During the chorus, we were supposed to whir like spinning wheels, and I was whirring with every ounce of breath when, to my astonishment and dismay, I saw that Sister Hildegarde was beckoning me to come forward. My conscience was clear. I knew that I had been making a great deal of noise, and the thought went through my mind that perhaps the best girls were now going to be brought forward, to give an example to the rest of the school. I stood in the spot she indicated, facing the piano, and was immediately joined by three others girls who had been summoned from the ranks. We stood together, not singing, until the song was finished.

"Now we know who the culprits are," Sister Hildegarde said.

"I suspected it all along, Sister," Sister Veronica said. "In fact, I think I could have given you the names of these four girls without ever coming into this room."

"Girls, why?" asked Sister Hildegarde intensely. *"Why* are you not singing along with the rest of the school? Do you think you're too good to sing with the other girls? Do you think it's beneath you to take advantage of Sister Veronica's instruction?"

We knew enough not to attempt to answer; in a case like this, to answer meant to answer back, a very grave offense. Also, we kept our eyes on the floor boards; a direct gaze when one is in the wrong is evidence not of goodness but of boldness.

"You see, Sister," said Sister Hildegarde, "they have nothing to say."

"That is how they sounded when they were singing, no doubt," said Sister Veronica.

The Devil in Us

Maggie Harrington gave a musical laugh, and smothered it decorously.

"Well may you laugh, Maggie," Sister Hildegarde said. "Now let's hear what these four can do by themselves. Give them a note, Sister."

We took the note and set up a self-conscious but passable version of "The Spinning Wheel."

"They sound more like Singer sewing machines than spinning wheels," Sister Hildegarde said coldly when we had finished.

"A pity you can't feel inclined to sing like that in class," said Sister Veronica. She turned to Sister Hildegarde. "You see they *have* voices, Sister. It's sheer stubbornness that keeps them from doing their part."

"Now that they know they're being watched, perhaps they'll do a little better," Sister Hildegarde said in a discouraging voice.

A week later, singing class came around again, and this time the four of us got into trouble over "The Rose of Tralee." We grew a little desperate, trying to give the impression that we were singing as loudly as the others, but by now Sister Veronica was convinced that we were defying her, and no matter how red we got in the face, or how hard we breathed, she would not believe that we were not cheating. The others watched us with amusement and some scorn. They wondered why we wouldn't sing or, if we *were* singing, why the nuns insisted we weren't.

That is what puzzled me. I could hear and feel I was singing, and I thought my three companions in guilt could hear and feel they were singing, too. I couldn't ask them, because we had been forbidden to talk to each other, on the theory that we were less harmful to the general tone of the school apart than together, and we were too cowardly to break the rule. The worst of it was that once we had been proclaimed black sheep in singing class, our

The Devil in Us

disgrace gradually spread out and discolored all of our school life. In a short while, everything we did seemed to be wrong. I learned very little that term, because I spent most of the time either standing in banishment outside this or that classroom door or marching around to Sister Hildegarde's office to inform her of some new sin. The three other black sheep were just as badly off. Those three weren't very close friends of mine. As a matter of fact, Sister Hildegarde's mysterious accusation was the first bond we had in common. One of the girls, Sally Lynch, a tiny black-haired girl with a fringe across her forehead, was only twelve. The two others, Mary Anne Rorke and Cecilia Delaney, were fifteen. Cecilia was fat, but Mary Anne was very ordinary in appearance. We were all in different classes. It puzzled me then, and it still puzzles me, to know why we were chosen to play this role. It was an unexciting, quiet school. No great crises arose, and no great crimes were committed. It seems to me now that, far from making trouble, we four simply attracted what little trouble there was, and perhaps it all looked the same to the nuns. After having been judged guilty, of course, we began to look very guilty in our efforts to reinstate ourselves, and that didn't help us at all. Also, I grew quite nervous, partly from importance.

Finally, one Saturday night, Sister Hildegarde walked into the recreation hall during the desultory hour that preceded bed, and raised her hand for silence. "Girls," she said, "you know that a few among you have given us a great deal of anxiety this term. The four to whom I refer have caused a great deal of discontent and bad feeling this term. We call them the Devil's walking sticks. He couldn't get along without them. But now they are going to have a chance to redeem themselves. Tomorrow afternoon, they are going to have a chance to show Our Blessed Lord that they are sorry for their bad behavior and want to make amends. Maggie Harrington and the rest of the choir will not sing for Benediction. Instead, these

four girls will go up into the choir loft and sing the hymns alone.
They have had as much practice as anyone else in the school. If they
don't know the hymns now, they'll never know them."

I had never even imagined such a severe trial. All the girls
looked at us with sympathy. No one smiled. We four went to bed
and had nightmares, and woke next morning to face the worse
nightmare that was waiting for us. When the moment finally arrived, near four o'clock, we ascended the stairs to the choir loft as
though we were mounting the scaffold. We could hear the girls
shifting about down in the well of the chapel, and we could see the
white-veiled heads of the smallest girls, who knelt in the front rows.
Immediately behind the students, the postulants, in their first year
of religious life, would be taking their places, and behind them the
novices, and at the back the black-veiled nuns. To add to our distress,
we knew that five or six pairs of parents had come visiting that
Sunday, and that they were down there, too, waiting for us to begin.
No doubt their daughters had told them that we were up here to
vindicate ourselves.

The priest, Father O'Connor, came in, followed by the altar
boy, and Sister Angela, a very young, pretty nun who taught piano,
and who had been sitting at the organ with her head bent in meditation, struck up the first hymn of the service, the "O Salutaris
Hostia." Staring at her, we opened our mouths to sing, but we could
only caw. Again she began, and again we cawed, this time so piti-
fully that even we were not sure we were making any sound at all.
A third time, smiling wildly to encourage us, she tried, and we gave
up altogether, and made no sound, and stopped looking at her, and
looked at the floor instead. She raised both hands from the organ
and tried to conduct us back into the hymn, without the music,
when suddenly, from below, arose the heroic voice of Maggie Harrington, and she was joined almost at once by all the voices of the
regular choir. They sang the Benediction right through, hymn after

hymn, without faltering, and Sister Angela accompanied them but kept her eyes charitably averted from our faces. Later, we heard that they had begun singing where they knelt, and I have often thought of how they must have looked, kneeling up straight with their hands joined and their white-veiled heads raised to the altar, while they sang and saved the day. We four, far above them, had no courage for anything. We didn't even have the courage to pray.

When the Benediction was over, Sister Angela rose and went swiftly down out of the loft. Almost at once, the terrible face of Sister Veronica appeared at the head of the stairs. "You made a fine show of yourselves," she said calmly. "I hope you're pleased with yourselves. You may come on down now."

We trooped down, relieved that we were not to be abandoned forever in the loft but very unwilling to face the immediate future. Sister Veronica remained on the narrow stairs, and we had to press past her, touching her heavy black robes. At the door of the chapel, Father O'Connor was congratulating the heroines. He was still in his vestments, and he looked over their heads at us with a glance that was incomprehensible to me then, but that now seems to me to have borne a glimmer of amusement.

Nothing happened the rest of that Sunday. We went in to tea along with the rest of the school. I felt mournfully elevated—I did not yet know why—and I ate a great deal of bread and butter, and marked the glances of fearful speculation thrown at me by the other girls at my table. Anything might happen to me now. I might even be expelled.

Several relatively peaceful days went by, and then we had singing class again. Sister Veronica and Sister Hildegarde entered the room together. They nodded to the four of us to come to the front of the room and stand before the school. When we had been isolated in this manner, Sister Hildegarde, whose face was filled with severity and grief, said, "We all heard these girls try to sing last Sunday. We know what a shameful exhibition they made of themselves and of the school. I am not going to punish them and I am not going to scold them. Their case is too grave for that. No only did they let us down but they deliberately let Our Blessed Lord down. I am only going to say that they need all the prayers they can get. Will every girl who is willing to give an extra minute each day to say a prayer for these misguided and stubborn girls raise her hand?"

We four continued to look where we had been looking, at the floor. Cecilia, the fat girl, began to sob. I was relieved to know where we stood. We had been given our chance, and the Devil in us had defeated us. The reason for our guilt was still hidden from us, but in a dim but comforting way we were now convinced of its existence. We had not seen the shape of the Devil, but we had felt his power, in our dry throats and thumping hearts. The thing was now clear to us that had always been clear to the nuns, because we realized as well as they did that if God had been on our side, surely He would have given us the voice to sing His praises.

MRS. BAGOT

The Twelfth Wedding Anniversary

M rs. Bagot had a very short straight scissors for cutting all the flowers except the roses. She had a small knife for the roses. The scissors and the knife were kept together at the end of the narrow shelf over the kitchen sink, beside the door that led out into the garden. The door was thick and heavy, of painted green wood. It often got stuck in its frame, especially at the bottom, but today, in the warm August weather, it stood open, showing a small corner of cement yard enclosed by the sharp right angle of two gray walls.

Bennie, the rough-haired white terrier, lay outside the kitchen doorway with his back firmly pressed against the step. Bennie was getting old. His legs were stretched stiffly in front of him and his eyes were closed, but when Mrs. Bagot stepped over him, stepping from the red tiles of the kitchen floor to the gray cement, his stubby tail began to wag gently and his uppermost eye, at least, opened and followed her until she reached the grass, a few feet away. Then he scrambled up and ran after her. The grass was a neat oblong surrounded on three sides by flower beds. Mrs. Bagot moved very slowly along at the edge of the grass. She had only the scissors with her. She wanted a few flowers to brighten up Martin's room—a few pinks, a few daisies, a few marigolds to fight with the pinks, no roses, no wallflowers, perhaps a sprig of forget-me-not if it looked strong enough not to droop. She kept her neck bent, and looked at the flowers with severity and concern, frowning. She wore a navy-blue skirt and a white blouse and an apron of faded blue cotton. She was very thin to be the mother of three children, one of them dead. Every time she paused, or bent to cut a flower, Bennie sat down at her feet.

Where the cement joined the grass, the garden wall that separated Mrs. Bagot from her neighbor dipped suddenly to a height of only five feet, and along this low part Mrs. Bagot had put up a green wooden trellis. She had extended the trellis to about a foot above the wall, and there she trained ivy, and something she called "the vine," but for politeness' sake she left an open space where the red-haired lady next door, Mrs. Finn, could peer through and make remarks. Mrs. Finn had something to say about everything, and she never waited to hear whether you agreed with her or not. She was good-hearted, in her way, but she was too loud.

Beyond the wall Mrs. Bagot and Mrs. Finn shared, a row of identical walls stretched off into the distance. All the gardens were attached, like all the houses. A grove of trees, forty diminishing walls away, completed the view to the sky. It was a narrow side street, a dead end, in the suburbs of Dublin. There were shops around the corner, on the main road, but none on the street itself. Schoolteachers, shopkeepers, and minor civil servants lived on the street, and a policeman had recently moved into one of the houses with his family. Because it was a dead end the street was safe for the children to play in, although Mrs. Bagot was not yet willing to let her two daughters outside their front garden, they were so small. Lily was six and Margaret was four. They were in the front garden now, sitting on a rug she had laid down on the patch of grass there. She had looped a piece of chain around the spikes of the gate and the railing so that they could not unlatch the gate and walk out and away.

The end wall of Mrs. Bagot's garden was raised too far beyond

The Twelfth Wedding Anniversary

its normal height by the back of the big garage that had been built along there to the length of five houses. Mrs. Bagot hated the garage when it was first put up, because it cut off her view of the open fields, but she had got used to the high end wall now and in any case the fields had been made into tennis courts. It was impossible not to admire the orderly appearance of the courts, and the neat way they were cut out, and the care that was given them, to keep them exactly right, but she missed the peace and simplicity of the fields. There was a sense now of being shut in. To her right and left there were the neighbors' houses, and their gardens. At her end wall there were the garage and the courts, and in front of the house there was the street, with the row of houses opposite. Sometimes in the evening they heard music—dance music from the tennis clubhouse, which everybody called the Pavilion. There was no music at this hour in the afternoon, but she could hear voices from the courts, and the sound of the game.

Mrs. Finn next door had one boy, Willie, ten years old. She was very particular about him. She had had concrete poured down all over her garden, making a hard gray surface where grass and flowers might have grown, so that Willie could play out there without getting mud on his shoes. Willie never went out there anyway. He preferred study to play. He stayed in his room and read his books and did his homework. He always got good marks in school. Mrs. Bagot had heard a good deal about Willie's eternal industry, and she could have believed it all except that she had often seen him standing at the window of his room staring across at the tennis courts and down into her garden. She thought that perhaps the reason he shut himself up in his room so much was to escape from his talkative, bossy mother. He had the big back bedroom for his own, and his mother said he had his books and his desk and his writing materials and his maps all so neatly arranged that his room looked like a little monk's cell.

The Twelfth Wedding Anniversary

There was no sign of Willie at his window today, and Mrs. Bagot thought his absence made the day more quiet. When he was there, she felt his eyes looking down on her, or imagined she did. He looked down at her as well as at everything else, and sometimes she waved up at him, although he never waved back. Once when she waved he put his head on one side, looking at her, and she was so surprised that she dropped her hand and then put it up again, to wave at him, but he turned and vanished behind the thin net curtain that veiled his window. A few feet to the right of Willie Finn's window was the window of the bedroom Lily and Margaret Bagot shared. Lily and Margaret slept together in a big brass bed. What sort of bed Willie Finn had Mrs. Bagot did not know, and she had no idea what his room really looked like. Mrs. Bagot had never been in the Finns' house, and Mrs. Finn had never been in hers. Mrs. Finn and Mrs. Bagot held their conversations across the garden wall and that was the extent of their friendship, except for a greeting when they met occasionally outside their houses or down on the main road that ran past the end of the street on its way in to the heart of Dublin.

They were four-room stone houses that jutted out at the back to give space for a kitchen, and above the kitchen a small extra room with a bathroom next to it. Mrs. Bagot's husband, Martin, slept alone in their small extra room, and she had been standing at the window there looking out at the garden when she had the idea of putting a few flowers in his room to brighten it up. Seen from his window, the garden was a deep oblong filled with shadows, light, flowers, grass, the ivy, the vine, and the laburnum tree that stood over to the right by the trellised wall. The sun made dark shadows but seemed to concentrate all its light in the half naked, yellow circle of grass where the big pot of geraniums had stood until recently, near the corner where she had made the rock garden. The grass at that corner was cut back into a crescent to conform with the shape of the rock garden and to give it more space. Mrs. Bagot had worked very hard to get the crescent right. The yellow circle where the pot of geraniums had stood was so close to the edge of the crescent that it seemed to be revolving on it—an exercise in geometry, or in balance.

A few feet below the window of Martin's room, Sebastian, the big orange cat, lay sleeping on the slanted, corrugated-tin roof of the shed where she kept her gardening things, empty flowerpots, and the shears and the rake and so on, and the dustbin. Sebastian lay on his side, sleeping peacefully. He looked very soft. His front right paw covered his eye and nose. His back paws were crossed and his tail lay neatly alongside them. The corrugated roof was uncomfortable to lie on, but Sebastian was so fat that he flowed into it and may even have imagined he was lying on a flat surface. Mrs. Bagot let the curtain fall into place and turned back into the room, which seemed dull and small after the brightness and life and space outside. The room was so dull it reminded her of Mrs. Finn's gray concrete yard, and it was at that moment she decided to run down and find a few flowers to put on Martin's desk.

When Mrs. Bagot had collected the flowers she wanted, she took them into the kitchen and began to arrange them in a small green bowl. Then she changed her mind. She went up to the dining room, to the glass-fronted cabinet there, and got a cut-glass bowl, a treasure of hers. She took the bowl to the kitchen and started all over again, arranging the flowers quite differently. The glass bowl was particularly well suited to the flowers, and she carried it upstairs proudly and set it on the desk by Martin's window. He got home from work very late, long after they were all asleep, and he would be surprised when he put on the light and saw the flowers waiting for him there beside his books. She was used to his coming home late. He didn't want to disturb her or the children, and then he didn't want to be disturbed by them in the morning when they all got up. It had seemed natural enough at the start, when he first said he'd like to be able to lie down in the little room when he came in very late, and she remembered the pleasure it had given her to arrange the room for him and put some of his shirts and things in here to make it more convenient for him. Now he was beginning to collect his books in here. And yet she was certain that at the beginning he had not known any more than she had that he would prefer this room to the big front room where she slept, or that what he really wanted was to be alone. She was certain now that if she had raised some objection at the beginning he would have thought no more about the little room. Or if the little room had never existed, he would never have had the idea of shutting himself away from her. What an alarming truth it was that if they had had a smaller house they might have been happier. And yet, the house was quite small.

When she went down to get the flowers, Mrs. Bagot had left the window open, and now she wanted to shut it. Sebastian was too lazy even to attempt the leap from the shed roof to this windowsill, but Minnie, the thin black cat, could do it easily, and Mrs. Bagot did not want to risk Martin's coming home tonight and finding Minnie on his bed. Mrs. Bagot did not know for sure whether it was the animals or Martin's hatred of the animals that caused a good many of the complications in the house. She gave in to him on most things, but she wouldn't give up the animals. The children would miss them terribly, and so would she. She would simply have to go on keeping the animals out of Martin's way, and keeping the children away from his door in the morning when he was sleeping. And in the end, all she was really doing was keeping herself out of his way. She couldn't bear to think about it, because what had started out as a simple arrangement for Martin's comfort had gone all out of hand, and now there seemed to be no way of putting an end to it. The situation in the house was unnatural, with no real consideration going for anybody. She found herself getting very nervous about the children when Martin was in the house, and when they were all together she couldn't stop herself from watching the children, as though Martin was there only to pass judgment on them. She was always keyed up, ready to defend them against him, and ready to take any blame on herself for what they did, and ready to snap at them if they showed signs of doing anything that might irritate him.

They were all much happier when he wasn't in the house, and that wasn't right. She wished she knew what to do. She kept remembering Martin the way he used to be, good-natured and always making jokes. Sometimes even now he was like that, but more often than not he seemed to be trying to control himself, as though seeing them all together and being shut up with them was more than he could bear. And on the weekend he went off for walks by himself, long walks that kept him out for hours. There was a lot of strain in the house. She felt constantly anxious, as though something terrible might happen, or as though she had done something terrible and might be found out. And all because of this little room. She was sure it was all because of this little room. It was bewildering to know that you started out helping somebody, agreeing with somebody about an ordinary private matter—a room to lie down in when he came in late—and you ended up building a wall that went on forever and that would never come to an end, because you made it stronger every day, without wanting to and without being able to stop yourself. She was constantly trying to keep her thoughts from going in this direction, because she became lost in their confusion, so that instead of reaching the words she wanted, and instead of being able to find the words that would explain everything she felt to Martin, she felt herself becoming incoherent, and she felt herself beginning to smother with anger, and then all she wanted was to run away and not make any explanations to anybody, and not listen to anybody's explanations. No, Martin was too clever for her. He was always able to shut her up. And yet it wasn't his words she minded so much as his silence. There were times when she thought Martin's clever silence might drive her out of her mind.

There was no use trying to think things out. Her ability to think was destroyed by strong feelings that stopped her easily because they were so much stronger than she was. Mrs. Bagot's feelings towered like ancestors, like reminders of a past that she could not remember but that she must remember if she was to get control of herself. These huge feelings, which appeared shrouded, triumphant, and ugly, were what she must face up to before she could face up to Martin. There was no use trying to speak to him if she was going to start gibbering. She did not know where to start.

She leaned across the desk and closed the window down to within an inch of the bottom, and then she stretched up and opened it an inch down from the top. Even Minnie could never squeeze herself through such narrow spaces. As she stepped back from the desk she looked at the flowers, and she had a moment of despair for herself because she had gone to the trouble to cut them and arrange them and put them there. But they were beautiful, and they improved the room. She would leave them. She put out her hand to touch the biggest marigold, and she imagined she saw her wedding ring reflected in the sharp edges of the cut glass. It was a plain gold ring, the only one she wore. Today was her wedding anniversary, the twelfth. She had been waiting for this day for weeks.

She had not known until this morning how much she had been counting on this day to somehow break the stillness between herself and Martin, but to break it in a natural way as any anniversary, Christmas or Easter or any feast day, will break into life and bring everything to a stop for the time of its celebration. She had been sure in the morning when she took in the breakfast tray that Martin would say something, but he was sitting on the straight chair beside his desk, reading the paper with such concentration that for a minute she thought he hadn't heard her come into the room. When she put the tray on the desk, he said, "Thanks, honey," and she hesitated, still thinking he would surely say something to her, but he said nothing. He had forgotten. And she walked out of the room and closed the door quietly behind her, not knowing if she was angry with him or with herself. She was shaking with anger. She was so upset that she had to hold onto the banister, going down the stairs.

As she looked at the flowers, she thought, I should have spoken up. It's too late now, but I should have spoken up.

There was nothing more for her to do in the room, but still she lingered, and when she finally went out she went very quickly, and closed the door behind her with relief, not realizing that once again she had substituted a prayer for a decision, and that the prayer was not even for certainty but only for an extension of hope.

She was beginning to wonder about the children. They were very quiet out there. She should have taken a look out at them on her way upstairs with the flowers. She wanted to hurry to them, but Bennie was in her way. She had to push him with her foot, because he had gone to sleep on the landing and the landing was very little bigger than he was. When Bennie was up, she hurried down the stairs and into the front sitting room and looked out through the bow window.

The children were all right. She had forgotten about them for a time, and so endangered them, but they were all right. She continued to look at them without speaking to them. They didn't see her. They didn't seem to have moved from the rug since she left them. They were undressing a small rag doll. When the doll was naked they would dress it again. They sat facing the railings so that they could see whatever went on out there on the quiet, narrow road. Far away at the head of the road some children were playing. Mrs. Bagot could hear their voices from the distance. She was pleased at the way her children looked in their short pink dresses. She was leaning across the table of ferns that crowded the window. One of the taller ferns tickled her chin and she stepped back. The ferns were in good condition. The flowered carpet she stood on was well brushed. It looked very nice under her feet. Her shoes were new. She was breaking them in, wearing them around the house, but she shouldn't have worn them into the garden. Fortunately it was a dry day. The shoes were as clean and shining as when she put them on in the early morning. Bennie was there at her feet, of course, looking up at her. Bennie, too, looked very well today. His nose glistened, and his tiny brown eyes were full of life. His coat was snow white and woolly. She had given him a bath yesterday. He looked like a new dog. He opened his mouth, to catch more of her attention, and Mrs. Bagot remarked that he had the strong white teeth of a very young dog.

Bennie was intelligent. He knew why she was at the window, looking out. She was looking at the children. Bennie gave the children patient devotion at all times, but even when he was asleep he watched Mrs. Bagot for every scrap of affection she had to spare for him. The children would grow up, but Bennie would remain the same—the same size, with the same expression. Years from now, Bennie would appear in Mrs. Bagot's memory exactly as he was this minute. There would never be another dog like him, she thought. He was a very unusual mongrel. Tears came into her eyes as she looked down at him, but she smiled. Then she began to hurry. She hurried across the room and along the hall and she opened the front door in a hurry. She wanted to get to the children at once. She wanted to speak to Lily, to praise her for having been a good child, and she wanted to pick Margaret up. She wanted to snatch Margaret up off the rug. She couldn't wait to get her arms around Margaret, to pick her up and hurry with her into the house while she was still small and young enough to be carried close like a baby.

Martin Bagot knew perfectly well it was his wedding anniversary, and the thought of it embarrassed and irritated him. Things were going along well enough, and he wanted no sentimental reminders. He wanted no reminders of any kind. He wanted to be left alone. When Delia hesitated after putting down the breakfast tray, he thought he knew what she was going to say, and he felt panic-stricken. Then when she left the room without speaking he was glad—ashamed of himself but glad anyway.

Lately he had the feeling of putting things off. He only had that feeling when he was at home, or when he was on his way home, and he would have liked to put off coming home indefinitely. He would have liked to have a rest from himself. When he was in the house he was hateful to himself. The feeling of being hateful to himself grew worse every day. He knew it grew worse, because at times he was able to remember his feelings of six months ago, and the feelings that had seemed so painful then were nothing compared with what he felt today.

He wanted time to think. He wanted a chance to separate the hateful picture he had of himself from his real self, so that he could stand back and decide what to do. There was a phrase that kept coming into his mind that filled his eyes with tears of shame: "a wife and family around his neck." That was the phrase, and it kept torturing him. "He has a wife and family around his neck now." It was a common enough phrase, and he couldn't understand why it kept haunting *him,* because it didn't describe his case and didn't describe his attitude to Delia and the children. That was not how he felt about them. His life was not so small that it could be dismissed in a cheap phrase like that. His life had not come to that, because he was not the sort of man who could be reduced like that. He was not an ordinary man. He, Martin Bagot, might be described as having a wife and family "in the background" but never "around his neck." That's why he wanted time to think, so that he could free himself once and for all from the hateful self who behaved like a poor wretch with a wife and family around his neck. He detested the house when he felt like this, because he felt the house transformed him. When he was away from home he was all right, and able to convince himself that Delia was all right. After all, she had the house and the children, and what more did she want. She had a life of her own. That is what he told himself. But then the minute he got home he felt harassed and pursued, as though the house was full of people all waiting for him to say the one word that would make them all happy.

She seemed to have no resources of her own. When she looked at him the expression in her eyes put him on edge. He was always afraid she would say something that would bring the house down around his ears before he had time to decide what he was going to do. And now, on the morning of their anniversary, when she left the room after that significant hesitation, he had a sudden feeling of fondness for her, and of gratitude that she had said nothing to make him uncomfortable. Perhaps, after all, she understood. He didn't pause to wonder about what she understood, what it might be, or anything like that. With her silence still glowing about him he felt relieved and happy, and he felt justified, as though he had held a course with difficulty and at great cost to himself, and had gained a victory that was well deserved, although he had never dared hope for it. He felt better than he had felt for a long time, and he ate his breakfast with appetite.

He was still lighthearted that night when he came home. He let himself into the dim hall and hurried up the stairs without touching the banister, which creaked loudly in the silence of the night as it had done on the first day he and Delia walked into the house, when it was empty and full of hollow sounds. He was tired, and anxious for sleep. He was so sleepy that his mind was already sinking comfortably into the quiet, dark hours that waited for him. His thoughts floated drowsily ahead of him, drawing him into the room where he would rest, but when he opened the door and switched on the light he became wide awake. He looked at Delia's flowers, and he felt betrayed and shocked, as though she had set a trap for him. Whether she spoke or not and whether she was in the room or not she still managed to reproach him. There was no escaping her. And there was no contending with her. There was no way to deal with her. He had come to believe that she really did not know why she did the things she did. He thought of her standing in the room, and putting the flowers on the desk, and looking around her and walking out again, closing the door behind her so that the animals could not get in and annoy him, and all the time imagining that she was being "good." She never understood why she did anything, and she never admitted even to herself why she did anything. She didn't know, that was the real trouble. Where the rest of the world was concerned all she seemed able to understand was the necessity for obedience. She always did what she was told, and then she waited to be told what to do. She had no will of her own. Even to think about her irritated him. She was a great burden. It wasn't that she was lazy. She was always on the go, always doing something around the house or in the garden, and if she sat down even for a minute she had her knitting or her sewing or her mending in her hands. But the house and the garden and even the children were only a camouflage, and when all camouflage was gone and they were alone together Martin could not endure the sight of her passive face and passive hands, and her passive body. All he wanted was to get away from her. When they were alone together she seemed lifeless, and if there was a name for the expression on her face it was shame. Her shame

119

irritated him, because he felt it was artificial, and he thought she could have chosen another expression if she had wanted to—a more cheerful expression.

Now here were these flowers, put here to remind him, *too late,* of the wedding anniversary. And their beauty and innocence also called his angry attention to all the care she gave him. The room he was standing in spoke only of love. And it was her care for him that was driving him to despair—the ceaseless care that he understood, and could not return, and did not want, and could not avoid. He picked up the bowl of flowers so carelessly that some of the water splashed out, and he had to put his other hand to it to steady it. He would take the flowers downstairs and leave them somewhere, and in the morning he would not speak to her about them. And if she mentioned them he would simply say that he did not like flowers in the room. He had no choice. He had to get the flowers out of the room. They made him feel sick. As he turned from the desk the flowers all slipped sideways, and when he tried to right them the bowl fell from his hand to the floor and broke into large pieces, making very little noise on the rug. He bent and picked up two of the pieces and fitted them together, and then he bent again and collected all the pieces and the flowers and put the whole lot on top of the desk. Then he sat down on the chair and put his face in his hands. He wouldn't have had that happen for the world. He wouldn't for the world deprive her of anything, or hurt her. The poor thing, she had meant no harm. He could have left the flowers. It wouldn't have killed him, to have left them in the room for the one night.

He knew that what he had intended to do was far worse than what he had actually done. He was frightened now at the thought of what he had meant to do. He was more than frightened. He was terrified. What he had intended—to all intents and purposes he had done it. The breaking of the bowl had awakened him from a prophetic nightmare, and he knew that for the rest of his life he would be stealing down the stairs in this sleeping house with the bowl of flowers in his hands. Oh, yes, he would do it. Over and over again he would do it. He knew that. The temptation would always be too strong, the temptation or the provocation or whatever it was. His disappointment in her would always master him. He stood up. He was going to have to go downstairs now anyway to get a glass or something to put the flowers in, because without water they would be dead before morning.

Out on the landing he looked up the short flight of stairs, five steps, that led to the two bedrooms. The doors were closed, and behind them Delia and the children lay sleeping, dreaming, far away in themselves, not thinking of him. Their sound sleep turned the house into a refuge, and Martin thought, If this night could only last a week, or two weeks, I might have time to get everything straightened out in my head, and then I would know what to do. . . . If they would only sleep happily like that for a long time, he might find himself able to think again. But the coming of day, a few hours off, rose up in his mind like a towering wave that was all the more awful because it would be succeeded after twenty-four hours by another wave, and then by another. There was no end to the days ahead, and the ones farthest off, years from now, were gathering power while he stood waiting on the landing. It was a merciless prospect. There was no way out of this house, which now seemed to contain all of his future as well as a good part of his past.

And Delia knew nothing of this. She could never understand his suffering, even if he tried to speak to her about it. He was a lonely man. He had always been a lonely figure, more or less, but he was lonelier now than he had ever been. He was proud of his loneliness, and he understood it. He knew it was what set him apart. He was a solitary man, not an ordinary family man, not at all a domesticated sort of person. He believed his loneliness came from a deep source in his nature, and that it made him more sensitive than other men, and at the same time stronger—a visionary of a kind. He was hard to live with, perhaps, but Delia's trouble was not that he was hard to live with but that she did not appreciate him. Delia had no understanding whatever of him, and never would have. He had given up hoping for understanding from her. On she went, on and on, "improving" the house and working in the garden and saving for a new piece of linoleum or a new set of curtains, wasting her time for the most part, and yet at this moment, standing on the landing, Martin felt more like himself than he had for a long time, and he felt not only patience for Delia but pity, because she was so blind and so weak, living along like a little mole, with no idea of what life might be like beyond these four flimsy, commonplace walls.

He started down the stairs. Tomorrow morning was not going to be so difficult after all. When she came in with the tray he would show her the broken pieces and tell her he had only taken the flowers up to admire them when they fell from his hand. He would show her how he had saved the flowers for her in a glass of water, and he would promise to buy her a new cut-glass bowl. He would bring the new bowl home with him tomorrow night, and if it didn't cost too much he might even get her a smaller bowl of the same pattern as well. She liked things that matched. She wouldn't question him about what had really happened. She would be very pleased to hear he was going to go to the trouble of getting her a new bowl. She would tell him not to bother, but he would insist. She wouldn't mention the anniversary. There would be no awkwardness. Martin knew Delia was no more anxious for a scene than he was, and in any case they both had the children to consider.

The Carpet with
the Big Pink Roses on It

The beige carpet with the big pink roses on it had been taken up off the floor of the front sitting room and dragged through the hall and through the kitchen and out into the garden and laid on the grass, where it was now being beaten and brushed by a small woman whose face wore an unbecoming expression of severity. That was Mrs. Bagot. She thought it was funny that her two children, who ought to be getting fresh air, were in the house, while the carpet was out in the garden getting fresh air. The carpet owed its airing to the long dry spell. There had been no rain for almost two weeks and the grass was very dry. It needed water, and it would need it more than ever after having been crushed by the carpet. But because the grass was dry, the carpet was safe—there would be no damp spots on it. The carpet was safe, and the grass would be saved, although saved was too strong a word—there was no danger of the grass withering. The grass would be refreshed. And in the meantime the carpet looked beautiful, as though the true foundations of the garden had been uncovered and found to be full of pink roses.

Lily Bagot, who was seven, had the day off from school because one of the nuns had died. Lily wanted to come out into the garden and sit on the carpet and go away somewhere, but Mrs. Bagot had

The Carpet with the Big Pink Roses on It

said no. The carpet was in the garden to be beaten, not to be sat on or made into a playground. But to sit on the carpet and go away somewhere—Mrs. Bagot would have liked that, although she did not admit to Lily that she agreed with her. To get the two children and Bennie, the dog, settled on the carpet and then to vanish and go away somewhere even if it was only for the afternoon, or part of the afternoon. To disappear for a little while would do no harm to anyone, and it would be very restful to get away from the house without having to go out by the front door and endure the ceremony of walking down the street, where everybody could see you.

But all this dreaming was not getting the work done. It was a shame for Lily to be shut up in the house, but it couldn't be helped. As soon as the carpet was back on its floor again, Lily could come out, and in the meantime she was well occupied up in the bedroom with Margaret. Margaret, who was five, was in bed with a cold. Margaret had an inclination to get lonely when she was left by herself, and when she was lonely she screamed. She would not have a chance to scream with Lily there chattering and bullying her.

At Mrs. Bagot's back the laburnum tree was in perfect bloom. You would think, to look at it, that yellow was the only true color. Something—an overweight bee or an interfering insect—caused one of the yellow blossoms to fall, and it floated uncertainly down to the carpet, where it rested on the worn green stem of one of the central roses. Mrs. Bagot put her hand out to save the little victim from the dust and from her own violence. But then, instead, she stood up to rest her back. Oh, it was very gratifying to feel the pull on her back as she straightened up. She was tired. She knew it by the way her back felt. She was not imagining things. *She* might imagine things, but her back would tell the truth, and what her back said was that she was tired. It was very gratifying to feel her muscles sorting themselves out and trying to find their own shapes

124

again, and she paid attention to their complaints and pitied them vaguely. What she needed was a good stretch. She would like to stretch herself, stretch her arms up, stretch all the weariness out of her body, but she could hardly start stretching herself here in the garden. Mrs. Finn next door would think there was something the matter with her, and she would come to the wall that separated their gardens and start talking in a loud voice about illnesses and bad symptoms.

Mrs. Bagot knew that the thing to do was to go into the kitchen and sit down for a minute and then come straight back out and quickly finish with the carpet. But still she remained standing in the mild sunlight, with the laburnum making a dusky yellow shadow behind her head. The thought of stretching and resting had cleared her mind of all but the one word, sleep. Sleep—her mind was full of it, it was evaporating inside her head, clouding her thoughts, and she wondered how the one word, sleep, could be so distinct and at the same time so indistinct, like writing in the sky.

She went toward the house, only a few steps away. The cement patch between the grass and the stone wall of the house looked very swept and clean—she had done that herself, dragging the carpet across it. She hurried through the kitchen and straight through the hall. The children had been quiet too long. She was starting upstairs when she heard a sound from the front sitting room—Lily, of course, who would not do as she was told. Lily was lying face down on the bare wooden floor of the front sitting room. She was trying to see between the boards, focussing first with one eye and then with the other, and also trying to focus with her hands, which were bent into blinkers at each side of her face. She looked up at her mother, and her eyes showed that she was ready for the battle.

"Lily, I thought I left you upstairs," Mrs. Bagot said, and then she stopped. After all, it was not often Lily got a day off from school. "Never mind, Lily. I'm not angry, I'm not anything. It's only that I don't like you to be in here by yourself. And why are you trying to see through the floor?"

It was a very short story, quickly told. Lily had been given two pennies, which had been left in safety far out of her reach, on the mantelpiece in the back sitting room, but she had managed to reach them, and she had taken one of them and fitted it between the boards, and it had slipped, and was gone. And all she had been trying to do, all she wanted, was to see whether the penny would fit between the boards.

"I suppose it's my fault," Mrs. Bagot said. "I should have let you keep one of them in your hand. Then you wouldn't have been so curious. Well, you'll never see that penny again. It's gone for good. Never mind. It's happened before, and it will happen again. We were hardly in this house when I lost a sixpence. It fell out of my hand and rolled over there. I nearly had it and then it was gone, down under the house. The foundations of this house must be made of money."

"When will we get it?" Lily asked.

"Oh, how do I know? They would have to tear up the floor boards. You ask too many questions. Now, are you going to stay here, or will you come upstairs with me?"

"You ask too many questions," Lily said. "I'll come upstairs with you."

The window of the back bedroom, where Margaret was, looked out over the garden, and beyond the garden at the courts of the tennis club, and beyond that, but too far away to see, lay the Dublin hills. The carpet did a lot for the garden, Mrs. Bagot thought. The carpet and the laburnum together made a picture. She was sleepy again. It was really very silly. They might not have another day like this for a long time, and she could think only of wasting it in sleep. The carpet looked so inviting down there on the grass. It would be

The Carpet with the Big Pink Roses on It

just right, to lie there in the open air and dream, not sleep. She envied people who felt free to do as they liked, without feeling self-conscious or ashamed of themselves. There were a lot of women who would lie down on that grass, or on that carpet, and never think the less of themselves, and never wonder what other people thought of them. Mrs. Bagot wished she could be like that. They were lucky, those people.

She pulled down the blind, and the bright room became dim—a dim blue—and then she went back to the big brass bed that Lily and Margaret shared. The bed was covered by a red-white-and-pink patchwork quilt that hung down to the floor on each side. Margaret was sitting up, propped by pillows, and, alongside her, two cats, one orange and one black, had entrenched themselves in comfort. At her feet, the rough-haired white terrier, Bennie, lay on his side. Bennie prudently kept his arm over his eye, but he wagged his tail hopefully. The cats, open-eyed and wary, did not move. The big orange one, Sebastian, purred loudly and methodically. It was his only skill, and he was proud of it. He never stopped purring. He purred at friends, strangers, and furniture. Earlier in the day, he had draped himself, purring, along one of the thin branches of the laburnum, and he had continued to purr even when he lost his balance and was left hanging, like a fool, by his front paws, while he wondered whether to drop to the grass or try to scramble back to his perch. He purred for his life, and nobody knew whether he was truly stupid or truly amiable. Margaret had her hand on his ribs, where she could feel the purr working. Her other hand was on Minnie's thin black ribs. Minnie's purr was muted and premeditated. She only purred when she was happy. She was purring now, but only Margaret could be sure of that.

"Let them stay," Margaret said to her mother. "They are very good today."

"They can stay," Mrs. Bagot said. "If I put them downstairs, they'll go out and tear the roses off the carpet. And Bennie can stay, too. If he sees the carpet out there, he'll try to drag it back into the house. But you have to lie down and sleep now. You have to shut your eyes."

Lily laughed. "It would be worth anything to see Bennie bringing the carpet into the house," she said.

Margaret slept on the left-hand side of the bed. Lily's place was on the right, nearest the door. When Mrs. Bagot slipped the extra pillow from behind Margaret, she bent and kissed her, and then she kissed her again. Margaret stared up at her as though they were saying goodbye to one another. Margaret always fought sleep at the last minute, and she fought it in whispers, whispering her fears and longings, as though she hoped sleep would hear her and spare her because she was so interesting to listen to. She whispered now, and her voice barely rose above Sebastian's industrious purr. "Stay with me," she whispered. "Don't go away. Stay here with me."

Mrs. Bagot smiled at her, and then she looked up and smiled at Lily.

"Oh, she is full of tricks," Lily said. "Full of tricks, that's what she is."

"Margaret, I can't stay," Mrs. Bagot said. "I've got to get back down and finish the carpet." She walked around the bed and stood at the other side, near the open door. "Now, you will go to sleep," she said, "won't you?"

"Stay with me," Margaret whispered, "just for a minute, only a minute. Stay with me. Don't go away. Just a minute, stay with me. Then I'll go to sleep."

"Oh, Margaret," Mrs. Bagot said, and she leaned across the bed and smoothed the hair back from Margaret's forehead. Then she began to yawn, and she turned from the child and buried her face in Lily's pillow until the yawn was finished. The pillow was soft.

The Carpet with the Big Pink Roses on It

She pressed her face into it and drew her legs up on the bed and lay there. "Oh, this is very nice," she said, and she pushed off her shoes, first one and then the other. "Lift my shoes down onto the floor, Lily," she said, "and I'll just lie here for a minute, just until Margaret goes to sleep."

Lily took the shoes and put them on the floor, and then she stood looking down at her mother. "You're very flat in the bed," she said.

"Don't let me fall asleep, Lily," Mrs. Bagot said.

"Mother, could I ask you one more question?"

"What is it, Lily?"

"If the house blew up, then would we get the money?"

"What money? What are you talking about?"

"The money that's under the floor downstairs."

"The house isn't going to blow up. You shouldn't think things like that."

"But it might blow up, mightn't it? It might blow up."

"It might, but it can't. Will you stop talking and let Margaret go to sleep."

"Why can't it?"

"It—the house can't blow up because we are living in it. Now, stop it, Lily. I want Margaret to sleep."

"I have another question for when we go downstairs," Lily said.

Mrs. Bagot felt her arms and legs sinking down into the bed, as though they would hold her there, sinking slowly into soft ease, and then she felt her back sinking down, and then her shoulders began to rest, but she could not settle her head. Her hair was in the way, and she lifted her arm from across her eyes and pulled out the pins and pulled her hair over onto the pillow where it loosened out, tumbling sleepily to its full length.

The Carpet with the Big Pink Roses on It

"Oh, I hope nobody comes to the door," Mrs. Bagot said. "They will think I am a madwoman, with my hair down in the middle of the day."

"Maybe nobody will come," Lily said.

"Let me know when Margaret drops off," Mrs. Bagot said, "and then I'll get up. Don't let me go to sleep now, Lily."

Margaret had already dropped off. Margaret was fast asleep, and then Mrs. Bagot slept suddenly. Before she knew it, she was asleep. Margaret slept with her right arm lying alongside her orange favorite. Bennie slept. Minnie, sensing something unusual, crept across the bed and settled blissfully into Mrs. Bagot's long brown hair, the best nest she would ever know. They all slept safely. There wasn't a sound in the house. Nobody came to the door. Nobody saw them. There on the bed they might all have been invisible, or enchanted, or, as they were for that time, forgotten.

Down in the garden Lily sat on the carpet and travelled without delay to Paris. From Paris she went to Spain, where she hesitated, floating high in the air, trying to remember the name of Spain's capital city. The effort of remembering caused her to lie down, and as she lay there with her eyes closed the carpet turned around and sailed home, back to the garden, where it lay flat on the grass, looking again exactly as it had looked when the thought of sleep drew Mrs. Bagot gently into the house that might blow up but that would never blow up. Never, never. That house never blew up.

The Sofa

The new sofa was to be delivered today, Tuesday, but "sometime during the day;" no set time had been given by the people in the shop. Mrs. Bagot had been so pleased when they told her she would have the sofa for sure on Tuesday that she hadn't thought to ask if she should expect it in the morning or in the afternoon. She should have asked them to set a definite time, or at least to say whether the sofa would arrive in the early part of the day or later. As it was, she had spent the whole morning in waiting and it was now two o'clock in the afternoon. She had wasted the better part of the day wandering about the house and not doing much of anything, and yet you could hardly say wasted when she had really been waiting, and waiting for something worthwhile. The downstairs part of the house was going to be completely furnished at last. The sofa was going to make all the difference.

She was sitting on a low chair beside the fireplace in the back sitting room, where she and the children spent most of their time. The fire was laid—paper, sticks of wood, lumps of coal, all in neat bumpy layers, ready to blaze up and spit sparks at the touch of a match. The small hearth, of pale-greenish tiles, was washed and shone with a dull, clean glow. The hearthrug, thin and fringed, was woven in a dark Oriental pattern of red and green lines, circles, curlicues, and unfinished curves, and all it had in common with the linoleum that covered the floor was that both rug and linoleum were well taken care of. Rug and linoleum looked their best. The rug had been brushed until its worn spots looked hardly less rich than the rich design, and the diligently domestic red-green-and-brown fleur-de-lis pattern in the linoleum was clear as glass. And what it said was "I am a plain, inoffensive piece of linoleum, ready to last for years, even in a house where there are children." To the right of the fireplace, shelves fitted into a shallow alcove held Mr. Bagot's library, which included books by Sidney and Beatrice Webb, Darwin, Shakespeare, Turgenev, Edgar Wallace, Wolfe Tone, W. B. Yeats, James Joyce, Chekhov, Ibsen, Molière, Edgar Allan Poe, and others. The books were old for the most part, and well worn, but they were tidy, and at the moment they were nearly hidden from sight by the folding doors that opened the front sitting room and the back sitting room into one quite large room.

Mrs. Bagot had opened the doors back as far as they would go so that she could get an idea of how the front room was when it was empty, and it was nearly empty now, with the old piano gone that had taken up so much space and the sofa still to come. The sofa would be wonderful in that room. She had made a good choice. The carpet on the floor in there was beige with big pink roses on it and the sofa was fat and beige and had room enough for almost four people. The sofa would face the fireplace. The fireplace in there was the same as the one in the back room except that the tiles in the hearth were golden brown and the brass bars in the fender were flat instead of being round and had a panel of filigreed brass in between, so that the panel of brass ran all around the hearth, just as the Greek frieze ran all around the top of the wallpaper, just under the ceiling. It was clever of whoever had decorated the house to put that frieze around to break the hard line that might have showed where the painted ceiling joined the papered wall. The wallpaper was no longer in the best of shape. After all, it had been on the walls at least fifteen years, maybe longer. But even so, the room looked very nice. And what made Mrs. Bagot wonder was that the room looked quite furnished enough with just the carpet on the floor and the table of ferns there filling the bow window that looked out onto her small front garden and beyond the garden to the narrow Dublin street. The room looked very carefree with no furniture in it. The children had walked around in there this morning as though they had found themselves in a new house. They said they never saw a room with no furniture in it before. They walked on all the part of the carpet that had been hidden by the piano, and on all the part that would be hidden by the new sofa.

There were only two children—Lily, who was nine, and Margaret, who was seven. When they grew tired of walking around on the carpet they sat on it, and then they lay down. They were dressed for school and they had very little time to spare, but Mrs. Bagot could not bear to hurry them. By the time they came home from school in the afternoon, a good part of the carpet would be covered up by the sofa and they would never be able to play in the room like that again. She thought she had never seen them so completely before, except of course out in the open—in the garden, or on the street, somewhere like that. They were lying on the floor with their heads toward the windows and their feet toward where she was in the back sitting room, which they often called the dining room. They were on the carpet, and she was standing on the shiny linoleum that covered the dining-room floor. She could see the soles of their shoes, their knees, the hems of their dresses and of the coats that covered their dresses, and the palms of their hands—their hands were flung out, and she could see the insides of all their fingers. She could hardly bear it. They were just as they always were, but she put her hands together as though she was going to applaud them. She wanted to laugh out loud. She felt weak and silly with pride, with surprise and a joy that held no taint of fear. The children were safe. There was no one near to cut them down, or to put them in their place, or to look at them with the ugly eyes of suspicion and tell them they were too sure of themselves. There was no one to tell them to *stop*. Mrs. Bagot thought that the worst thing in the world was to be told to *stop* when you had no intention of doing anything and did not know that you had been doing something you should stop doing.

There was a solid bar of molding nailed across the floor under the folding doors. One of the doors could be bolted into the molding, and then when the doors were fastened together they stood firm as a wall and both the front and back rooms were sealed against drafts. Now that the doors were wide open, Mrs. Bagot could see how the edge of the rose-covered carpet lay neatly parallel with the molding and about two inches away from it. It needed only a row of footlights on this side of the molding to turn the carpet into a stage. It *was* a stage. She could see the children as though they were on a stage. The soles of their shoes, their knees, the palms of their hands, their necks and chins, their nostrils, their foreheads, and their straight hair—which spread out around their heads as though it was flying in the wind or with their movement, although they were motionless and there was no wind. They were watching her, looking at her and smiling. Their eyes were shining. They were waiting for her to tell them that they would be late for school, and she thought they might have been far above her on an important stage, dancing some wild, slow dance—something they made up as they went along. Bennie, the white terrier, brushed Mrs. Bagot's legs on his way into the room to investigate the children. There was plenty of space between the doors, and Mrs. Bagot was a very small woman, but Bennie must brush against her. Bennie must brush against her every chance he got, and he must put his nose against her hand when she sat in her chair, and he must follow her anxiously to the front door and stand anxiously wagging his tail while she talked to whoever was there, and all it was was that he must at all times know that she was still herself. Verification, ascertainment, recognition, and silence—Bennie lived in the blazing humility of perfect love. And Mrs. Bagot wanted to lie down on the floor with the children and embrace them both and press them *with her hands* into her memory so that she might always have them before her as she had them now—alive and confident in their independence, and seeing her. They saw her. She knew they did. Their smiles were happy and secretive. They were testing her. They were waiting for her to speak. She did not speak and she did not move. She kept smiling and she almost laughed with pleasure. She pressed her dry palms together and then she clasped her hands and let them fall down to arm's length in a gesture that seemed to say, "So this is the way it is." Bennie smelled each child's face and then he sat down between them. As soon as Bennie sat down, Lily jumped up.

"That's enough of this nonsense," Lily said. "We are going to be late for school."

"Nonsense yourself," Margaret said. But she jumped up, too, and pushed past Lily so as to get to the hall first. Bennie ran past both of them and began smelling their schoolbags, which were lying on the chair in the hall. The bags were particularly interesting to Bennie because each bag contained a wrapped lunch. Mrs. Bagot would not be bringing the children their lunch to school today. Today she had to stay close to the house and wait for the sofa. The children knew all about the sofa, and they were looking forward to its arrival just as much as she was. It was an important day in the house, and its importance had grown overnight, while they slept. Yesterday seemed a long way in the past, gone, quite gone. And tomorrow had a long way to travel before it would reach them. Tomorrow was still far away in the distant future. Mrs. Bagot could not think of tomorrow. In fact, she could not think of anything—the sofa kept getting in the way, and it was restless, as though it longed to be in the house and settled down so that ordinary life could begin again and everybody could go about their business as usual.

It was two o'clock and then it was past two. When Mrs. Bagot sat down and began watching the clock, she said to herself that when the hands marked two she would get up and find some little job to occupy her—something she could leave at a minute's notice. But two o'clock came and then one minute past two, and on, and still she sat, calmly doing nothing. That big clock was most dependable. It always kept perfect time. All the other clocks in the house were set by it, and it had ruled Mrs. Bagot's days and nights during all of her married life. Through the years she had watched it; she had looked at it in anxiety, excitement, apprehension, satisfaction, relief, and anticipation, and in disappointment, and in annoyance, and now she simply sat and looked at it as though she dared it to tell her to stand up and do something. But the clock, that had been so domineering all these years, had no power over her today, and as one wasted minute after another turned and vanished before her eyes she began to smile. She did not know she was giving the clock the same smile she used to give the children when they were babies and slept past their time and she smiled at them as though to say, "Sleep on, you will be awake soon enough." It was a secret smile, amused, absent, and speculative. When Mrs. Bagot smiled like that, her eyes reflected something she did not know about herself. She was in touch then with a spirit she did not know she possessed, and when she smiled her face was lighted by the faint and faraway glimmer of an assurance that was truly hers, but truly buried, buried deep down under the sound, useful earth of her thirty-two years of unquestioning, obedient life. She thought the clock was beginning to look quite friendly, and she also thought it had calmed down and was taking its time, just as she was.

The Sofa

She did not sleep, she did not even doze, but she must have been hypnotized by the clock's big innocent face, because when she heard the knock at the door she was terribly startled. She ran along the narrow hall to the front door, and as she ran she kept thinking that it was too soon; she was not quite ready for the sofa yet. But when she opened the door and saw the deliveryman actually standing there, she said, "Did you bring the sofa? I hope they sent the right one. I hope nobody has made a mistake." The man looked at her in surprise and said, "I just want to see how wide the hall is." He peered in past her and said, "We'll manage all right." And then he went down the tiled path to the miniature iron gate, which he had left standing open, and around to the back of the van, where two other men had opened the doors and were waiting for him without enthusiasm. Mrs. Bagot flew after him and around to the back of the van and looked in. Yes, it was her sofa.

The big man who had come to the door had already climbed into the van and was beginning to move the sofa out. She saw that he was grinning cheerfully at her, and she turned away in confusion and hurried back to stand at her front door. She felt she had made a fool of herself and shown herself to have no dignity, and she thought the men must be laughing at her for her eagerness. She made up her mind to look severely at the big man when he came into the house.

The sofa began to emerge, timidly, from the van, and as it did Lily and Margaret came into view, running up the street. Some other children from the houses around appeared and stood watching curiously. Lily and Margaret were quick to disassociate themselves from these unfortunate children who were not getting a new sofa, and they raced up the tiled path and stood beside their mother at the front door. She looked so serious and worried that they became serious, too, and worried. Getting a new sofa was not the simple matter they had imagined. The sofa was not just going to float into the house and take its place in the front sitting room. There might be difficulties. The sofa was all the way out of the van now and it looked huge and helpless, high and dry and stranded on the shoulders of two of the men, who did not seem to enjoy carrying it. "The legs on it are very small," Margaret said.

They were all afraid the men would drop the sofa and break its legs.

"I hope they don't drag it across the top of the railing and tear the underneath part," Mrs. Bagot said. She was trembling. "Listen to me," she said to the children. "We have to be very careful not to get in the men's way. When the sofa starts coming through the gate, you two run back and sit on the stairs, and I'll go back and stand at the head of the kitchen stairs. That way we'll leave the hall free and clear and there won't be any damage and the men will have room to move around. Now, are you listening to me—when they get it to the gate, we'll all go back."

With this strategy planned and agreed upon they were able to give their full attention to the sofa again. "They'll never get it through that little gate without destroying it," Mrs. Bagot said. But when the men got to the gate they lifted the sofa high in the air and carried it triumphantly and arrived so quickly at the front door that Mrs. Bagot and the children barely had time to rush back and take up their positions by the stairs. The sofa filled the hall for a minute and then it began to sidle into the front sitting room. Mrs. Bagot hurried into the back sitting room and stood where she had stood watching the children that morning. "Facing the fireplace, please," she said, which was unnecessary because there was no other way for the sofa to face.

The sofa looked very well in the room—much better even than she had expected. "It looks as though you had it made specially," the big man said, and she forgot to look at him severely.

She saw the men to the front door, and she watched the van

drive off, and then she went back to join Lily and Margaret in contemplating the sofa. They walked all around it, sat on it, stroked its back and sides, and said everything they could think of about it, and they continued to talk about it all through dinner, which they had in the kitchen as usual.

The Shadow of Kindness

Mrs. Bagot missed the children. They had been gone twenty-four hours. It was exactly that length of time since she had put them on the train, in the care of the guard, and sent them off to her sister and brother in the country, where they were going to spend a month. She wished the month was over. She didn't know what to do with herself when they were away. Without them the house had neither substance nor meaning. The house was lonely, that is what it amounted to, and Mrs. Bagot felt the house was making her lonely. But the house was going to look very nice when the children came back. She was already planning what she would do to welcome them. She was going to put flowers all around—she would cut all the flowers in the garden. And she was going to bake a cake and put both their names on it in icing: "Lily," "Margaret." And then there were other things she was going to do, but these preparations, which she had already memorized and timed to the minute, still left her with nothing to do for a month but look *forward,* and she knew a grown woman should have more life of her own. Even if she had children, a woman should have a life of her own that would stand up when the children were out of the house for any length of time. She knew that. It was not right to let yourself get so lost in your children that you could find no trace of yourself when they were gone. What would she do when they grew up? Of course, it was silly to think of it; not silly—morbid. She was letting her imagination run away with her. She would make herself a cup of tea and cheer herself up. The tea would cheer her up. Still, she did not move. She continued to stand by the big window looking out into her garden.

The big window was the window in the dining room. It was very big, a sash window, and almost square, and at the moment it was very bare, because she had taken the curtains down for washing. The garden was almost out of sight behind the rain. The yellow rosebush seemed far away, a steady blur of brightness, like a street lamp in the fog. And the other flowers, not as intimately massed around one center as the roses were, and not so strongly defined, seemed to be moving about by themselves, swimming slowly about in the wet gray air and arranging themselves in different patterns from the ones she had imagined and seen come to life as the summer wore on. This was the heaviest rain they had had for a long time and she was glad to see it—it was needed. And she was glad it had come today and not yesterday. The children would not have liked travelling in the rain. They had been looking forward to the view from the train windows. And then there would have been all that worry about damp feet and damp heads. Yes, it was fortunate the rain had held off until now.

Earlier in the day, in the morning, when she saw the rain getting heavier, she went out and cut all the full-blown and half-blown roses. She cut the white, the pink, and the red—all but the yellow. The yellow rosebush had been in the garden when she and Martin moved here, and she had a particular affection for it, because she felt it had encouraged her to set to work and make the lovely garden she had out there now. She seldom cut a yellow rose, and this year, as they bloomed, the roses on that bush had arranged themselves so marvellously that it was as though a great artist had made them grow in that certain way to match a picture he had in his mind. And so this morning she had left all the yellow roses to survive or fall together. As well as she could see, they were holding up, in a round shape that tapered slightly toward the top—a dense, delicate ball of yellow that was like a Christmas tree ornament or an Oriental roof. It was accidental, that grouping. It might never occur again. She was glad she had not disturbed them.

The white roses, and all the pinks and all the reds, made quite a big bunch. She had put them around in this room and in the front room and in the hall, and then, foolishly, she had put a small bunch in the children's room to make it seem less deserted. When she wrote to Lily and Margaret tonight she would tell them there were flowers waiting for them in their room, beside their window, on the little table that was all marked and stained with chalk and ink and putty and plasticine. The window in the children's room corresponded with this window where she stood—they had the back bedroom. The paper on the walls of that room was cream-colored and covered with miniature garlands of small blue flowers. The flowers were faded and as indistinct as the real flowers in her garden were today in the rain. It was old wallpaper and, like the yellow rosebush, it had been here when she and Martin moved in, years ago.

All the windows in the house were closed tight against the rain, but the damp had crept in anyway. Mrs. Bagot turned from the window. Her feet and legs were cold—that was how people got rheumatism. On a day as bad as this, if the children were here, she would have lighted the fire hours ago, even if it was an extravagance. There was no use risking colds and coughs. She took the box of matches from the mantelpiece and knelt down on the hearthrug. It was between two and three weeks since they had needed a fire, and the coals were nearly hidden under a litter of tiny balls of paper, thrown in there, she knew, by Lily. She hated to burn them up. She took one ball and smoothed it out and, as she expected, it was a code. Lily was always hoping to discover a code that would be easy to write and impossible for anybody except herself to understand. Mrs. Bagot thought of taking the others out, just to look at them, but then she thought better of it. If she continued to think like this about the children she would bring bad luck on them. She struck the match impatiently and touched it here and there to the newspaper at the bottom of the grate. There were tears in her eyes. She wanted the children to enjoy themselves, but she wondered if they thought of her at all when they were away from her. They would be falling in love with their aunt and with their uncles. They would come back at the end of the month pining for the farm and the animals and all the freedom they had down there. Well, it couldn't be helped. Maybe it was all for the best.

She started to stand up, when a warm body touched her leg. It was Bennie, the white terrier, who had come out of his sleep on the rug beside the folding doors to hear a match being struck and a fire beginning. He looked up at her. He had small brown poverty-stricken eyes and limp ears, but the line from his black nose to his chin was fine and square, and she often told the children Bennie had very good blood in him. She put her arm around him and felt how close his bones were to the flat white coils of his fur. She wondered how old he was. You never could tell with a stray, and poor Bennie had been on his last legs when she found him on the street one morning on her way from Mass and took him home. She might have been able to walk past him, but some young boys were tormenting him, and she knew she would never be able to look herself in the face again if she abandoned him to their cruelty. He had been in the house five years now. Sometimes he seemed like a puppy and sometimes he was a very thoughtful, grown-up dog. He was very faithful. He had never once snapped at the children. He had never even snapped at the cats, although Sebastian, the big orange one, was very greedy and often put his face into Bennie's food dish in the hope of finding a morsel there he might fancy for himself. "Good Bennie," Mrs. Bagot said, and pressed him closer to her side, and he stretched his neck up to her, and the storm of devotion in his eyes could never have found expression in speech. His silence burned with devotion, and so it would as long as he was alive.

She rubbed his shoulder and smiled at him and then she stood up. She moved easily, rising from her knees to stand with no effort, but when she was on her feet she felt dizzy. It was her own fault. She had not bothered to eat anything at breakfast time. She had had a cup of tea when she got up, and then, in the middle of the day, more tea, and that was all. She had felt angry with the children at breakfast time, because while she could feel angry she believed she did not miss them, and then, in the middle of the day, when her false anger, her pretense, had faded, she felt shame at the picture of herself going to trouble over food that the children would not be there to share.

Now then, she was going to have to stop thinking like that. She should know better by this time than to let herself fall into this train of thought. In the beginning, at the beginning of their marriage, Martin had warned her often enough against thinking, because thinking led to self-pity and there was enough of that in this world. What he had really told her was that she must stop forcing herself, stop *trying* to think, because her intelligence was not high and she must not put too much of a strain on it or she would make herself unhappy. "I don't want you to make yourself unhappy," he had said, and she remembered the nice tone his voice used to have when he spoke to her. Things had not been the same between them since Jimmy died. Jimmy would have been ten now —nearly two years older than Lily. Poor little mite, he had lived only three days, and she had not been herself for a long time afterward, and perhaps she had said things she shouldn't have said. She was sorry now for the things she shouldn't have said and that she couldn't clearly remember saying, but when she thought of that time, her mind turned to ether and she got all sleepy, and she knew it was unhealthy, not the right frame of mind for her to be in, and when the children were at home she was so busy with them that she had no time to let her thoughts go back. And she must always remember that Martin was very nice with Lily and Margaret, a very good father. He was very fond of them, and sometimes on Sunday afternoons he took them for a walk. He always asked Lily about her schoolwork, and took an interest in her. And he invented games for Margaret, to make her laugh. Lily took after him—she was very clever and always got good marks. Lily was a bit too sure of herself, perhaps, but she was a good child, and there would be a letter from her tomorrow, Mrs. Bagot was sure of that. Where the children were now, in the country, the postman went his rounds on a bicycle, and Lily would have been watching for him this afternoon.

It must be raining there, too, raining down on the trees and the fields and on the house where it stood at the end of the lane from the village. The lane was a mile long—a long ride for anyone on a bicycle—but the postman would have arrived, with the letter she had sent to them secretly the day before yesterday, when they were still here with her, and Lily would have been on the watch for him, to give him the letter for her mother. And the letter would come into Dublin on the night train, and it would be here in the morning. Well, Mrs. Bagot thought, with luck she would have it in the morning, but if it came in the morning post, she would have to give it to Martin—he would be sure to ask if there was a letter from Lily, so that he could take it along to the office to show his friends what a clever daughter he had. And then ten chances to one she would never see it again. It would stay there in the office and get mixed up in the papers on his desk and maybe be thrown out, unless someone took it. She would ask Martin to bring it back, and he would promise to bring it to her, but he would forget, and she might ask him the second time but not the third time—it was too much like nagging. And all this brought home to her how little she meant to anyone in the world except the children. And Bennie and the cats. Martin objected to the animals, and he had told her to get rid of them, but she refused to get rid of them. She had stood up to him there. Anyway, he hardly saw them. He woke up late, naturally enough, considering how late at night he had to work, and she brought him up his breakfast on a tray, and then he dressed himself and went off and came back in the early hours of the morning. He did not like her to wait up for him, and besides she couldn't and still get enough sleep to be able to give proper attention to the children. But she would always wait up for him if she thought that was what he wanted. But the times she had been up, when he got home at eleven o'clock, for example, instead of at one or two—at those times he had come in and hung his coat and hat in the hall and gone straight upstairs to his room without even saying good night to her. There were times when it seemed that he could not control his dislike of her, and yet she knew very well he did not dislike her. One night, not so very long ago, he had come into the front bedroom where she slept and waked her and asked her to heat up some milk for him, and when she brought him the milk he thanked her and told her he did not know what he would do without her. She had gone back to her own bed and lain there in an ecstasy of gratitude—a gratitude she did not understand and did not question. She knew positively that everything was going to be all right, and she was so sure of that—that everything was going to be all right— that she did not even wonder what she meant, or who or what it was she was thinking about. She only knew that her memory had lighted up and that all she remembered were times so happy that they must surely cast their radiance far into the future, over years so far ahead that she could not even dream of them.

146

The Shadow of Kindness

Once, shortly after she and Martin were married, shortly after they moved to Dublin, she had wanted to get material for curtains for the back bedroom, which was still unfurnished then, because there were only the two of them in the house. Martin said he had heard of a good shop, and he volunteered to go with her, and he said, she remembered very well, that he would take her there and see that she had someone to wait on her but that then he would have to leave her, because he had an appointment. But when they got to the shop, he didn't leave her. He stayed and watched while the man behind the counter showed her what they had in the way of cretonne. The man behind the counter gave Mrs. Bagot a chair, but Martin refused to sit down. "I feel like a bull in a china shop," he said, "but at least I needn't be a sitting bull." They all laughed, and a woman standing nearby waiting for her parcel to be wrapped laughed and smiled at Mrs. Bagot, and the man behind the counter winked at Mrs. Bagot and said, "That is a witty man you have there, Mrs. . . ." And she had said "Mrs. Bagot," in such a high voice that Martin burst out laughing and said to the man behind the counter, "She's still surprised at her new name." And then Martin said, "We're only four months married," and he spoke so proudly that even she could see his pride, and she couldn't take her eyes off him—she looked at him, she gave him the same devoted, desperate look that Bennie always gave to her.

Yes, that day had been wonderful. After they left the shop the day did not end; they did not part. She was certain when they walked out onto the street that he would hurry away, and she was ready for that—to turn and go her own way home alone—but Martin said, looking up and down the crowded, busy street, "I could stand a cup of tea. What about you, Delia? After all this exertion you'd like a nice cup of tea, wouldn't you?" He was grinning at her, and then he said in a false, funny voice, "A nice cup of tea for the lady of the house?" Two or three times over the years, she had gone back to that tearoom, but the tables were always full, and so she had never gone in there again. The tea had been very good, and the cakes, and the girl had given them special attention, just as the man in the shop had done. And after tea they had gone for a walk, strolling around, looking in the shopwindows, and when she reminded him of his appointment he said, "They can wait, I can see them any time. But when will I get another chance to show you off like this?" It was strange that at the start of that long-ago day, when she got out of bed in the morning, she had not had a hint that she was seeing the beginning of a day that would never cease to unfold in her memory and that would always be waiting there, undimmed and undamaged, providing her with a place where her mind could rest and find courage.

Martin had given up sleeping in the big front bedroom, because she and the children got up early and disturbed him, moving about, and now he slept in the small room next to the bathroom, on the landing halfway up the stairs. Lately she had been hoping he would say something to her that would give them both a chance of a talk, but he had said nothing. She knew things were not as they should be between them, but while the children were at home she did not want to say anything for fear of a row that might frighten the children, and now that the children were away she found she was afraid to speak for fear of disturbing a silence that might, if broken, reveal any number of things that she did not want to see and that she was sure he did not want to see. Or perhaps he saw them and kept silent out of charity, or out of despair, or out of a hope that they would vanish if no one paid any attention to them.

But here she was now, doing herself no good—it was only storing up trouble to let herself get weak with hunger simply because she longed for a *real* reason to feel sorry for herself. She would make the toast and have tea with it. But before she did anything she would open the folding doors into the front sitting room and let some of the warmth of the fire steal in there. The room where she stood was less a dining room than a back sitting room, because she and the children spent their time there when they weren't in the kitchen. The leaves of the big table had been let down and it stood flat against the wall, with a bowl of her roses on it from this morning. The floor was covered in linoleum, but the rug Bennie had been sleeping on before he crossed to lie in the warmth of the fire fitted very neatly under the folding doors, very much as though it had been specially made, and it gave the room a nice, well-furnished appearance. She opened the doors back carefully. The front room was dim. The curtains were still up on the windows in this room—long French windows that curved out into a bow—and the gray houses across the street were dark in the falling rain. Her own house, she supposed, looked dark to her neighbors over there. She saw that some of them had their lights on, although it was only five o'clock. There was an upright piano against the wall opposite the fireplace in this room. She had put a bowl of pink roses on the piano earlier in the day, and a small vase of them on the mantelpiece. She thought that what light there was in the room came from the roses and from the shining wood of the piano. Also, the fragrance of the roses was stronger in this room than in the back room where she had been standing for so long. Standing doing nothing, she thought. But instead of reproaching herself she went to the windows and looked out into the street, which was short and narrow and had two facing rows of houses, all identical with her own. She liked to watch people going up and down the street, and she sometimes came in here to attend to her collection of ferns so that she could watch what was going on outside without seeming curious.

The ferns, all of them tall and feathery and all in the same bright shade of green—bright moss green, grass green—were arranged on a table that stood inside the bow window. She had to leave a space between the two middle pots so that Minnie, the small black cat, could sleep there. Minnie's favorite spot was in the center of the table between the ferns, and if a suitable place was not left for her she would make one, squeezing herself in until the pots rattled dangerously. Minnie was there now, half asleep, and Mrs. Bagot stroked her and watched the street. The street was safe for the children to play in. It was a dead end, and there were no garages, and in any case very few of the people had cars. The milkman came early in the morning and the bread man at eleven, but otherwise Mrs. Bagot hardly ever had to open the front door, except for the children when they came home from school at half past three. At noon every day she walked to the school with the children's lunch.

The school was not far away—a short walk along the main road and then a longer walk down a side street that was wider and busier than this one, with much bigger houses, except at the end, where the houses were suddenly very small and close together. The school was across from the small houses, behind a high cement wall with a narrow iron gate in its center. The gate opened into a cement yard, where the children played at lunchtime, and the school building, gray and high, with a few large, oblong, institutional windows, fitted and matched the yard exactly, as though a child had drawn and colored it. The yard was completely closed in by high cement walls, and to the right, looking from the gate, there was a very long, low wooden bench where the smallest children sometimes sat in a row and did their lessons. There were children in the school who were no more than three years old, and some of them, Mrs. Bagot suspected, were only two. But they were able to walk—that was all the school required—and Mrs. Bagot would not have admitted to anyone that one of her reasons for going to the trouble of bringing Lily and Margaret their lunch every day was so that she could see the little boys and girls who were just able to walk. The little ones were let out to play before the rest of the school, and by the time she got to the gate they were generally running around, stumbling like moths from one side of the yard to the other and beating at the air with their hands, and looking up at their teacher as though they imagined she produced the light by which they played. There was no one to question Mrs. Bagot's right to stand and watch the children. If anyone questioned her she would simply say she had to bring Lily and Margaret their lunch. Well, there would be no bringing lunch for a while. It would be more than five weeks before they had to go back to school.

Mrs. Bagot turned from the street and from Minnie and from the ferns, and was surprised to see how like a mirror the big naked window in the back room was, but like a mirror that you could see through, a mirror that went both ways and showed both sides. It was like a painting. She saw the wet, reluctant daylight air out there in the garden, and the rain was falling so strong and straight that she was sure she could make out every separate driving line of it. Beyond and through the rain, as in a dream, there were the indistinct colors of the garden, and then, coming back through the glass to herself, she could see herself, with the folded-back door to her right, and behind her the wavering green heads of her ferns, and behind the ferns the starched white net curtains making a ghostly and final wall. She knew that what she saw was beautiful, and at the same moment she knew that she did not want to look anymore at the window or the garden or the ferns or anything. She was tired. She hurried out of the room and down to the kitchen, where she filled the kettle and put it on to boil for her tea. While the kettle was boiling she would wash her face and hands and straighten her hair. The cold water on her face would wake her up—she felt that she had been sleeping for hours, and not sleeping happily. She hurried upstairs. The narrow stairs from the hall had a wine-red runner that was held in place at each step by thin brass rods that she pulled out and polished every Monday. The rods shone more steadily in this evening's dimness than they ever shone on a sunny day, and the wooden banister glowed with the same warm and reverberating depth, as though the dying light called up sources of strength that went unnoticed in the self-sufficient daytime. The house was full of secret light that she never noticed when the children were at home.

After washing her hands, she hurried up the five top steps to the upper landing, where there were two doors opening into the front bedroom and into the smaller back room where the children slept. Both doors were closed, and instead of going into her own room, where her brush and comb were, she turned into the children's room and went across and looked into the small framed mirror that stood on their chest of drawers. She began to smooth her hair with her hands, but her reflection was so lost and pale that it frightened her, and she put on the light to reassure herself. She bent forward to the mirror again, and carefully pushed a loose strand into the neat bun at the back of her head, but as she moved, something moved with her, something much larger and even more silent than she was. Her shadow was on the wall to the side of the mirror and it was following her, and now it was bending with her, bending toward her, and she stared at it. The light in her own bedroom gave her no shadow that she had ever noticed. She paused and the shadow paused also, waiting for her as she waited for it. She looked closer and at that moment, as it bent its head, she knew what she was looking at. That was her mother's shadow there on the wall. There was no mistake about it; that was her mother.

Mrs. Bagot could not understand it. She and her mother had not looked alike. But there it was, her mother's shadow as she had often seen it—the thin line of the cheek, the indentation at the eye, the high curve of the forehead, and, above all, the little straying hairs that always escaped the brush to wave independently at the sides of her mother's forehead and at the back of her neck. The little stray hairs were never more than the length of a straight pin, and there were only a few of them. Mrs. Bagot thought she recognized every one of them, there in the shadow. She thought that if she put out her hand she would surely feel that hair again. She put out the light and then put it on again at once. There again was the neat, bent head, with the thin hairs making a frail pattern on the wall, a frail pattern that was more real at this moment than the pattern on the wallpaper, as the pencilled rain in a Chinese watercolor is more real than the strong and enduring landscape that lies beyond. It is my mother, Mrs. Bagot thought; there she is; how patient she is.

She sighed once and smiled at herself without looking at herself, and then she put out the light and went down to the kitchen, where she found the kettle boiling furiously.

The tea was soon made and so was the toast. She took down Martin's breakfast tray and set it carefully for herself, even putting a clean white cloth on it, but when everything was arranged, instead of carrying the tray up to the fireside, she pulled a chair up to the kitchen table and sat down and poured herself a cup of tea. She was too hungry and too thirsty. She could stand no further delay; she must have something to eat at once. She thought about the shadow that had been waiting for her up there in the children's room all these years and that had remained hidden from her until tonight. She had never seen it in any other room in the house and she did not think it was to be seen in any other room of the house.

She looked around her, but the shadow was not in the kitchen. Bennie was sitting on the tiled floor at her feet and she broke off a piece of toast and gave it to him. Sebastian and Minnie had suddenly appeared and were sitting thoughtfully beside their milk saucer near the door that led out into the garden. She got up and poured milk for the cats, and then she went back to the table and poured herself another cup of tea. She decided to make more toast, and to eat some of the chicken that was left over from the special dinner she had made for the children yesterday. She felt all different —not sad, not tired anymore. She felt very hopeful all of a sudden. It was wonderful how seeing that shadow had raised her spirits. It was wonderful knowing that shadow was upstairs and that it would never go away. It was almost like having somebody in the house.

The Eldest Child

Mrs. Bagot had lived in the house for fifteen years, ever since her marriage. Her three children had been born there, in the upstairs front bedroom, and she was glad of that, because her first child, her son, was dead, and it comforted her to think that she was still familiar with what had been his one glimpse of earth—he had died at three days. At the time he died she said to herself that she would never get used to it, and what she meant by that was that as long as she lived she would never accept what had happened in the mechanical subdued way that the rest of them accepted it. They carried on, they talked and moved about her room as though when they tidied the baby away they had really tidied him away, and it seemed to her that more than anything else they expressed the hope that nothing more would be said about him. They behaved as though what had happened was finished, as though some ordinary event had taken place and come to an end in a natural way. There had not been an ordinary event, and it had not come to an end.

Lying in her bed, Mrs. Bagot thought her husband and the rest of them seemed very strange, or else, she thought fearfully, perhaps it was she herself who was strange, delirious, or even a bit unbalanced. If she was unbalanced she wasn't going to let them know about it—not even Martin, who kept looking at her with frightened eyes and telling her she must try to rest. It might be better not to talk, yet she was very anxious to explain how she felt. Words did no good. Either they did not want to hear her, or they were not able to hear her. What she was trying to tell them seemed very simple to her. What had happened could not come to an end, that was all. It could not come to an end. Without a memory, how was the baby going to find his way? Mrs. Bagot would have liked to ask that question, but she wanted to express it properly, and she thought if she could just be left alone for a while she would be able to find the right words, so that she could make herself clearly understood—but they wouldn't leave her alone. They kept trying to rouse her, and yet when she spoke for any length of time they always silenced her by telling her it was God's will. She had accepted God's will all her life without argument, and she was not arguing now, but she knew that what had happened was not finished, and she was sure it was not God's will that she be left in this bewilderment. All she wanted was to say how she felt, but they mentioned God's will as though they were slamming a door between her and some territory that was forbidden to her. But only to her; everybody else knew all about it. She alone must lie quiet and silent under this semblance of ignorance that they wrapped about her like a shroud. They wanted her to be silent and not speak of this knowledge she had now, the knowledge that made her afraid. It was the same knowledge they all had, of course, but they did not want it spoken of. Everything about her seemed false, and Mrs. Bagot was tired of everything. She was tired of being told that she must do this for her own good and that she must do that for her own good, and it annoyed her when they said she was being brave—she was being what she had to be, she had no alternative. She felt very uncomfortable and out of place, and as though she had failed, but she did not know whether to push her failure away or comfort it, and in any case it seemed to have drifted out of reach.

She was not making sense. She could not get her thoughts

sorted out. Something was drifting away—that was as far as she could go in her mind. No wonder she couldn't talk properly. What she wanted to say was really quite simple. Two things. First, there was the failure that had emptied and darkened her mind until nothing remained now but a black wash. Second, there was something that drifted and dwindled, always dwindling, until it was now no more than a small shape, very small, not to be identified except as something lost. Mrs. Bagot thought she was the only one who could still identify that shape, and she was afraid to take her eyes off it, because it became constantly smaller, showing as it diminished the new horizons it was reaching, although it drifted so gently it seemed not to move at all. Mrs. Bagot would never have dreamed her mind could stretch so far, or that her thoughts could follow so faithfully, or that she could watch so steadily, without tears or sleep.

The fierce demands that had been made on her body and on her attention were finished. She could have met all those demands, and more. She could have moved mountains. She had found that the more the child demanded of her, the more she had to give. Her strength came up in waves that had their source in a sea of calm and unconquerable devotion. The child's holy trust made her open her eyes, and she took stock of herself and found that everything was all right, and that she could meet what challenges arose and meet them well, and that she had nothing to apologize for—on the contrary, she had every reason to rejoice. Her days took on an orderliness that introduced her to a sense of ease and confidence she had never been told about. The house became a kingdom, significant, private, and safe. She smiled often, a smile of innocent importance.

Perhaps she had let herself get too proud. She had seen at once that the child was unique. She had been thankful, but perhaps not thankful enough. The first minute she had held him in her arms, immediately after he was born, she had seen his friendliness. He was fine. There was nothing in the world the matter with him. She had remarked to herself that his tiny face had a very humorous expression, as though he already knew exactly what was going on. And he was determined to live. He was full of fight. She had felt him fight toward life with all her strength, and then again, with all her strength. In a little while, he would have recognized her.

What she watched now made no demands on anyone. There was no impatience there, and no impatience in her, either. She lay on her side, and her hand beat gently on the pillow in obedience to words, an old tune, that had been sounding in her head for some time, and that she now began to listen to. It was an old song, very slow, a tenor voice from long ago and far away. She listened idly.

> "Oft in the stilly night
> Ere slumber's chain hath bound me
> Fond memory brings the light
> Of other days around me."

Over and over and over again, the same words, the same kind, simple words. Mrs. Bagot thought she must have heard that song a hundred times or more.

> "Oft in the stilly night
> Ere slumber's chain hath bound me
> Fond memory brings the light
> Of other days around me."
> The smiles, the tears, of boyhood's years
> The words of love then spoken
> The eyes that shone, now dimmed and gone
> The cheerful hearts now broken."

It was a very kind song. She had never noticed the words before, even though she knew them well. Loving words, loving eyes, loving hearts. The faraway voice she listened to was joined by others, as the first bird of dawn is joined by other birds, all telling the same story, telling it over and over again, because it is the only story they know.

There was the song, and then, there was the small shape that drifted uncomplainingly from distant horizon to still more distant horizon. Mrs. Bagot closed her eyes. She felt herself being beckoned to a place where she could hide, for the time being.

For the past day or so, she had turned from everyone, even from Martin. He no longer attempted to touch her. He had not even touched her hand since the evening he knelt down beside the bed and tried to put his arms around her. She struggled so fiercely against him that he had to let her go, and he stood up and stepped away from her. It really seemed she might injure herself, fighting against him, and that she would rather injure herself than lie quietly against him, even for a minute. He could not understand her. It was his loss as much as hers, but she behaved as though it had to do only with her. She pushed him away, and then when she was free of him she turned her face away from him and began crying in a way that pleaded for attention and consolation from someone, but not from him—that was plain. But before that, when she was pushing him away, he had seen her face, and the expression on it was of hatred. She might have been a wild animal, for all the control he had over her then, but if so she was a wild animal in a trap, because she was too weak to go very far. He pitied her, and the thought sped through his mind that if she could get up and run, or fly, he would let her go as far as she wished, and hope she would come back to him in her own time, when her anger and grief were spent. But he forgot that thought immediately in his panic at her distress, and he called down to the woman who had come in to help around the house, and asked her to come up at once. She had heard the noise and was on her way up anyway, and she was in the room almost as soon as he called—Mrs. Knox, a small, red-faced, gray-haired woman who enjoyed the illusion that life had nothing to teach her.

"Oh, I've been afraid of this all day," she said confidently, and she began to lift Mrs. Bagot up so that she could straighten the pillows and prop her up for her tea. But Mrs. Bagot struck out at the woman and began crying, "Oh, leave me alone, leave me alone. Why can't the two of you leave me alone." Then she wailed, "Oh, leave me alone," in a high strange voice, an artificial voice, and at that moment Mr. Bagot became convinced that she was acting, and that the best thing to do was walk off and leave her there, whether that was what she really wanted or not. Oh, but he loved her. He stared at her, and said to himself that it would have given him the greatest joy to see her lying there with the baby in her arms, but although that was true, the reverse was not true—to see her lying there as she was did not cause him terrible grief or anything like it. He felt ashamed and lonely and impatient, and he longed to say to her, "Delia, stop all this nonsense and let me talk to you." He wanted to appear masterful and kind and understanding, but she drowned him out with her wails, and he made up his mind she was acting, because if she was not acting, and if the grief she felt was real, then it was excessive grief, and perhaps incurable. She was getting stronger every day, the doctor had said so, and she had better learn to control herself or she would be a nervous wreck. And it wasn't a bit like her, to have no thought for him, or for what he might be suffering. It wasn't like her at all. She was always kind. He began to fear she would never be the same. He would have liked to kneel down beside the bed and talk to her in a very quiet voice, and make her understand that he knew what she was going through, and that he was going through much the same thing himself, and to ask her not to shut him away from her. But he felt afraid of her, and in any case Mrs. Knox was in the room. He was helpless. He was trying to think of something to say, not to walk out in silence, when Mrs. Knox came around the end of the bed and touched his arm familiarly, as though they were conspirators.

"The poor child is upset," she said. "We'll leave her by herself awhile, and then I'll bring her up something to eat. Now, you go along down. I have your own tea all ready."

Delia turned her head on the pillow and looked at him. "Martin," she said, "I am not angry with you."

He would have gone to her then, but Mrs. Knox spoke at once. "We know you're not angry, Mrs. Bagot," she said. "Now, you rest yourself, and I'll be back in a minute with your tray." She gave Martin a little push to start him out of the room, and since Delia was already turning her face away, he walked out and down the stairs.

There seemed to be no end to the damage—even the house looked bleak and the furniture looked poor and cheap. It was only a year since they moved into the house, and it had all seemed lovely then. Only a year. He was beginning to fear that Delia had turned against him. He had visions of awful scenes and strains in the future, a miserable life. He wished they could go back to the beginning and start all over again, but the place where they had stood together, where they had been happy, was all trampled over and so spoiled that it seemed impossible ever to make it smooth again. And how could they even begin to make it smooth with this one memory, which they should have shared, standing like an enemy between them and making enemies out of them. He would not let himself think of the baby. He might never be able to forget the shape of the poor little defeated bundle he had carried out of the bedroom in his arms, and that he had cried over down here in the hall, but he was not going to let his mind dwell on it, not for one minute. He wanted Delia as she used to be. He wanted the girl who would never have struck out at him, or spoken roughly to him. He was beginning to see there were things about her that he had never guessed at and that he did not want to know about. He thought, Better let her rest, and let this fit work itself out. Maybe tomorrow she'll be herself again. He had a fancy that when he next approached Delia it would be on tiptoe, going very quietly, hardly breathing, moving into her presence without a sound that might startle her, or surprise her, or even wake her up, so that he might find her again as she had been the first time he saw her, quiet, untroubled, hardly speaking, alone, altogether alone and all his.

Mrs. Bagot was telling the truth when she told Martin she was not angry with him. It irritated her that he thought all he had to do was put his arms around her and all her sorrow would go away, but she wasn't really angry with him. What it was—he held her so tightly that she was afraid she might lose sight of the baby, and the fear made her frantic. The baby must not drift out of sight, that was her only thought, and that is why she struck out at Martin and begged to be left alone. As he walked out of the room, she turned her face away so that he would not see the tears beginning to pour down her face again. Then she slept. When Martin came up to the room next time, she was asleep, and not, as he suspected, pretending to be asleep, but he was grateful for the pretense, if that is what it was, and he crept away, back downstairs to his book.

Mrs. Bagot slept for a long time. When she woke up, the room was dark and the house was silent. Outside was silent too; she could hear nothing. This was the front bedroom, where she and Martin slept together, and she lay in their big bed. The room was made irregular by its windows—a bow window, and then, in the flat section of wall that faced the door, French windows. The French windows were partly open, and the long white net curtains that covered them moved gently in a breeze Mrs. Bagot could not feel. She had washed all the curtains last week, and starched them, getting the room ready for the baby. In the dim light of the street lamp, she could see the dark roof line of the row of houses across the street, and beyond the houses a very soft blackness, the sky. She was much calmer than she had been, and she no longer feared that she would lose sight of the small shape that had drifted, she noticed, much further away while she slept. He was travelling a long way, but she would watch him. She was his mother, and it was all she could do for him now. She could do it. She was weak, and the world was very shaky, but the light of other days shone steadily and showed the truth. She was no longer bewildered, and the next time Martin came to stand hopefully beside her bed she smiled at him and spoke to him in her ordinary voice.

Stories of Africa

A retired bishop of the South African Missions was coming for tea, and Mrs. Bagot and her two little girls were very busy getting ready for him. He was coming at four. The children weren't home from school until after three o'clock, and Mrs. Bagot had to get them to eat the sketchy dinner she had waiting for them, and then they had to get out of their school clothes and into their good dresses. Then she had to brush their hair and put on their new hair ribbons—wide ribbons of pale-blue satin. She dressed them alike, as though they were twins, although there was nearly three years between them. Lily was going on ten, and Margaret was seven. She had told them they were all going to hear great stories of Africa —strange tales of ostrich feathers, and monkeys, and cannibals, and big wild birds, and lions, and a sun so hot that people ran to get out of it.

"Is there no rain there, Mother?" Lily asked, and then she said, "When I'm a bit bigger I'll be able to look into your mirror while you brush my hair."

She was standing by the chest of drawers, which held a small standing mirror with the brushes and combs and ribbons arranged in front of it.

"When you're a bit bigger you'll brush your own hair," Margaret said quickly.

Margaret was sitting on the edge of her mother's big bed, waiting her turn. She was getting impatient. The Bishop would be here any minute. Lily and Mrs. Bagot were both silent after she spoke. Mrs. Bagot was silent because she was anxiously tying Lily's hair into the new ribbon, and trying to get it balanced so that each loop of the bow would be exactly the same size and would sit at exactly the same angle. And Lily was silent because she was always surprised when Margaret said anything that showed a capacity for thought. Margaret's words usually expressed desire, or protest, or affection. And Lily had another reason for silence. She could feel her mother's fingers struggling with the bow, and she knew that her whole appearance depended on the next minute or so, because if the bow went wrong the first time it would have to be untied and taken off, and the ribbon would be wrinkled, and there was no time to run the iron over it, and the chances of it going right the second time would be small. One word from her now might cause her mother's hand to slip, and so she was silent and tried to hold her breath.

They were in the front bedroom. The big brass bedstead was placed with its head against the wall. The end of the bed made a bright railing between Margaret and her mother and sister. She was sitting kicking her heels on the far side of the bed from where they stood, and watching herself in the long mirrored door of the wardrobe. The bed was covered from top to bottom with a patchwork quilt so large that it hung almost down to the floor on both sides. The quilt was very old, and it was precious to Mrs. Bagot, and she usually kept it folded away out of sight, but she had put it out today in honor of the Bishop's visit, and to satisfy the children, who had been pestering her to let them see it all spread out on a bed where they could really get a good look at the different patterns and colors. The Bishop would never see the quilt, of course, but it made the whole house better and richer just by being on the bed for the day. It was forbidden to sit on the quilt, and Margaret sat on it very lightly, hoping her mother wouldn't notice her. In the mirror she could see her own hands wandering around, touching the hard lines where the separate pieces, scraps of ancient dresses, were joined together in small, precise octagonals. This was disobedience, and she knew she would have to tell about it in confession. She had only lately made her first confession, and she thought her sins were like plums—bad plums that she plucked out of the air, which had formerly been clear and empty. Formerly, before she reached seven, the age of reason. And then, at the end of the week, she gave all the bad plums to the priest in the confession box. Always, at the last minute before she got into the box, she felt frightened, wondering what he might say to her, but he never said anything and always gave her a small penance. Now she sat on the quilt and looked at herself, sitting in sin. She watched herself thinking about confession and sin, and she felt she was in control of the situation and well able to manage for herself.

The chest of drawers was so tall and bulky that it spoiled the look of the bow window where it stood, but there was no place else in the room to put it. It nearly hid the middle part of the window but through the right-hand side pane Lily could see the narrow Dublin street outside, and the row of houses opposite, all exactly like her own. At the end of the street she saw the main road. A tram went by, coming out from town, and she hoped the Bishop had not been on it. There was still Margaret's hair to be done, and they would all want to be downstairs and ready before he knocked on the door. Then she felt a final, definite tug at her hair and her mother stood straight and stepped back, away from her.

"That's as good as I can get it," Mrs. Bagot said. "Turn around now till I take a look at you. And Margaret, get down off that quilt and come over here till I do your hair. It'll be a miracle if we're ready for the Bishop."

Margaret slid off the bed and came over to stand beside her mother. Her mother had known all the time that she was sitting on the quilt, and she had said nothing, because she wanted peace in the house when the Bishop arrived. Margaret would have liked to squeal with annoyance. Her mother had made a fool of her again. And Lily, who was standing rigid while her mother gave a final combing to the ends of her hair—Lily was watching her sideways to see if she would say something. She would have liked to push Lily, but more than that she wanted to say something to show her mother she was not a baby anymore. They treated her like a baby, letting her do wrong things and not saying anything, because they were afraid she'd make a scene. She wasn't going to make a scene with the Bishop coming. They didn't trust her any more than they would trust a tiny baby. Margaret wished she could say something clever that would put both of them in their place, but she could think of nothing. No words came to her and if they had come there would have been no room for them, because her head was full of tears that rushed forward, searching for her eyes. She was going to disgrace herself. She shut her eyes tightly but the tears burst out and she felt them beginning to pour down her face. She sobbed loudly. The first sob came out angrily, because she had tried to hold it back, and it left her helpless to resist the smaller sobs that drove up from her chest and straight into her brain, so that each time she opened her eyes to look at her mother she had to shut her eyes quickly again until the sob released her and left her longing not to make any more noise. The sound of the ugly sobs made her ashamed and made her feel dirty and sleepy. But she was helpless, and able only to stare at her mother with terrified eyes. She was adrift, tossing up and down on the awful tiny-baby fury that always seemed to be catching up with her, even out on the street in front of people. And the Bishop was coming. Margaret opened her mouth and screamed.

Stories of Africa

At the sound of the first sob, Mrs. Bagot lifted the comb from Lily's hair and hesitated before turning to look at Margaret. She could not face it this time. Margaret was having one of her crying fits and Mrs. Bagot could not face it, not with the Bishop coming. She felt she was very tired, and she thought resentfully that the Bishop could have chosen another day for his visit. It was always hard, dealing with these fits of Margaret's. It wasn't so much that it was hard as that it took time, first to calm her down and then to get her into bed so that she could sleep until her exhaustion lifted and she began to look like her normal self again, her normal pretty little self that everyone admired. Strangers in the street always glanced at Margaret, and when Mrs. Bagot took the children into town on the tram, the people sitting across from them always nodded and smiled at Margaret—at her pretty, anxious little face. Margaret had been a delicate baby and she was still delicate. She was born very thin and weak, and there had been doubt whether she would live until her first birthday. And now here she was sobbing her heart out in a fit of nerves that came only from her precarious health. School was a great strain for Margaret. She was always missing days at school, always having colds and coughs, and then she had a struggle catching up with the other children. And her balance was bad—she was always falling down and hurting herself. She was very small and light, not solid on the ground like Lily. This present outburst was the result of too much worry over the Bishop's visit. The thought of seeing a real bishop and speaking to him was too much for Margaret. Mrs. Bagot realized, too late, that she should have kept Margaret home from school today. Too late. But of course that is what she should have done. She should have kept Margaret at home and avoided all this last-minute rushing and fussing with their hair. In an instant of sickening panic Mrs. Bagot saw all the mistakes of her life rush together to congeal into the one fatal mistake that had made everything go wrong from the beginning. But the instant passed and with it her glimpse of that original mistake, the fatal one, which she could have named if it had only stayed before her eyes long enough to give her a chance to get a good look at it, so that she could see it and recognize it and call it by its name and know at last, once and for all, what it was she had done that separated her from the wisdom she knew other people possessed. She could not deal with anything, and in particular she could not deal with Margaret's crying fits. Well, the Bishop would be along any minute and there was nothing to be done now but reason with Margaret. By reasoning Mrs. Bagot meant that she would have to promise Margaret something, a treat. Mrs. Bagot knew perfectly well that it is wrong to bribe a child, but there was no time for anything now except a bribe. She would promise Margaret a day off from school tomorrow. Yes, she would keep her at home tomorrow and make a little bit of a fuss over her.

Then Margaret screamed. Mrs. Bagot bent quickly to put her arm around her. She was still holding the comb and Margaret slapped it out of her hand. Lily cried out and bent to pick up the comb but Mrs. Bagot gave her a little push and said, "Lily, run downstairs and go into the front room and stand at the window and watch for the Bishop. Call up to me when you see him coming, and then open the front door and leave it open, and go out and stand at the gate, and open the gate for him. Go on now this minute and call me when you see him."

As she went downstairs Lily heard her mother begin to speak in a very quiet voice that Lily associated with seriousness, and sadness, and patience, and weariness, as though she was trying to explain something that she could never explain, because it was beyond words.

Much earlier in the day, Mrs. Bagot had carried the alarm clock down from her bedroom and she now had clocks going in the kitchen, where there was always a clock, and in the back sitting room, where her best clock, the wedding-present one, had lived for years on the mantelpiece, *and* in the hall, on the hall table, where a clock had never been seen before. She had been watching one clock or another all day and all day she had felt she was losing time, but as she came downstairs now, holding Margaret's hand and moving carefully so that they took each step together, which was difficult because the stairs were narrow and Margaret was hesitant—as she came slowly and gratefully down the stairs she saw that the clock on the hall table said five minutes to four. After all, there was plenty of time.

The front sitting room was usually kept closed. Mrs. Bagot went in there every day to attend to her collection of ferns, which she kept on tables in the window. This morning she had cleared one table of its ferns, and this table stood transformed now, with a white lace-edged cloth covering it, and the white-china tea things shining in the light from the fire. The fire made the room very cosy. It was late May, a temperate day, but Mrs. Bagot knew that priests returning to Ireland from South Africa felt the change in the climate very much, and besides, the Bishop was a very old man. The Bishop and Mrs. Bagot's father had been the same age, and they had gone to school and grown up together on neighboring farms in Wexford. Mrs. Bagot's father had died when she was two years old, and she always felt her childhood had ended then, before it began. As far back as she could remember, she and her older sister and her brothers had been like little men and women, citizens of a republic where her mother was the stern, distant, and all-seeing head. It was said that Mrs. Kelly, Mrs. Bagot's mother, had never got over her husband's death. She was a silent, unsmiling widow, and the mantle of grief she drew about herself and her children became a substitute for the protection they had lost at his death, and, after that, it became a symbol of his will. Mrs. Kelly's children always did as they were told.

Mrs. Bagot wanted to ask the Bishop about her father. She wanted to hear someone tell her once again that she had been her father's favorite. She had heard it often enough, from her mother, and from her sister and her brothers. Mrs. Bagot had been told what a favorite she *used to be* all during the time when she was a child and when she was growing up, and she had got tired of hearing it, but all of a sudden she wanted to hear it said again. She hoped the Bishop would remember she had been her father's favorite, and that he would say so. But the Bishop was very old. He might have begun to forget.

She had bought a white iced cake for the tea, not trusting her own confectionery, and she had made bread, brown and white, and scones. And she had jam, and honey in the comb. She wished he would come. She was getting nervous waiting for him.

Lily turned from her vigil at the window when her mother and Margaret opened the door and peered in. The door had to be kept closed against the cats, to keep them away from the tea table, but Bennie, the old white terrier, lay on his side on the hearthrug pretending to be asleep but with his eyes wide open, waiting for the cake to be cut. Lily saw that her mother was smiling hopefully as she did when everything had gone wrong and was now on the mend, and that Margaret's face was shiny but calm.

"We're going to go down to the kitchen and get the kettle going," Mrs. Bagot said. "And you're not to take your eye off that window, do you hear me now, Lily?" As though it was *Lily* who had driven her mother to the limit of her patience. "Do you hear me now, Lily?" she said again, "I want to know the minute you see the Bishop."

Mrs. Bagot was no longer smiling, and as Lily looked at her

171

small face, pinched into severity and appeal, she felt a rush of impatience and misery. One way or another the day was sure to be spoiled. But there was no chance of saying anything because the two faces, Mrs. Bagot's and Margaret's, vanished, and the door closed. The little room was crowded, with the sofa and the chairs and the tea table and all the plants, and Lily could see nothing of Bennie except his back legs and his stubby tail, which now began to bang steadily against the hearthrug. Bennie had heard Mrs. Bagot's altered tone, and he was taking no chances. Good fortune had brought cake to the tea table, and Bennie wanted to be sure he would be allowed to stay in the same room with it.

"Cake, Bennie," Lily said, and the tail hesitated a minute and then began again, gently beating.

The front sitting room was smaller than the bedroom above it by the width of the hall that led to the front door, and the window where Lily stood watching for the Bishop corresponded with the window upstairs where she had stood while her mother combed her hair. There was no one coming up the street, no tall old man striding like a prophet toward the gate. The Bishop was late.

Just below the window was the curved flower bed Mrs. Bagot had cut out of the grass patch that was the front garden. The flower bed clung to the bow-window wall like a collar of daffodils, crocuses, and snowdrops. The grass, a tiny plot, was bright green and very trim. Mrs. Bagot had clipped it the night before, and this morning she had washed down the narrow red-tiled path that led to the front gate. The front garden was about the same size as the front sitting room, the red-tiled path was about the same width as the front hall, and its hat-and-coat rack and its table where the clock now stood at ten minutes past four.

The Bishop did not come hurrying around the corner from the main road and he did not come striding up the street. He arrived in a car, a big black car that rolled slowly up the street until it stopped before the house. It was a very important-looking car. Lily ran shrieking for her mother, and after that everything was all right. She got the front door open and was down the front path and had the gate open exactly at the moment when the chauffeur opened the rear door of the car and began helping out a large old man who was dressed all in black and wore a black hat. Lily had never been so close to a chauffeur before and she admired his puttees. Margaret pushed past her into the street and stood stiffly with her back pressed against the garden railing and her little face radiant with excitement. Mrs. Bagot stepped forward to offer her hand in help, although holy awe and superstition made her unwilling to touch the consecrated Bishop. She had been taught, and she had taught Lily and Margaret, that you never shake hands with a priest, and now, with the chauffeur's firm hands under his arm, the Bishop got out of the car and stood almost upright, leaning on his two sticks. He was a very shabby old man. Even Mrs. Bagot, standing in helpless veneration, could see that, and she also saw that his blue eyes were vague and distant, as though they had seen enough and could accept no more impressions, and were no longer inclined to make the effort to separate faces he had seen before from the faces of strangers. He put his sticks together and held out his hand to Mrs. Bagot with a humble and ministering forgiveness that was too calm to hold pity and too proud to hold reproach.

The captive monkey, reduced by grief and age to the lowest and furthest corner of her cage at the zoo, watches the crowd that stares at her with an acceptance so profound it shines like sympathy. All struggle had vanished from the old Bishop's eyes and Mrs. Bagot saw that he was close to death. She lifted her hands and gave him a smile of tremulous indignation, showing him how, one morning, she would face her own death.

"We have the tea all ready for you, Your Grace," she said.

173

"God bless you," he said, "but never mind 'Your Grace.' I'm a very plain priest. 'Father,' or 'Father Tom,' whichever you like. Delia, is it? Am I right? You're the image of your grandmother, Delia."

Mrs. Bagot was amazed by the Bishop's voice. She had expected smooth, sanctified tones, the voice of an ecclesiastical dignitary, and instead she heard the rough, warm, monotonous accents of home. Mrs. Bagot thought, He sounds like one of my own brothers. She moved alongside of him, keeping step with the chauffeur, who was on his other side, and together they guided him onto the narrow red path that had been washed twice that day, first by Mrs. Bagot and then by a soft shower of rain that still glistened in the grass and over the yellows, whites, and mauves in the flower bed.

The Bishop steadied himself against the railing that separated Mrs. Bagot's tiled path from her neighbor's.

"I'll be all right now," he said to the chauffeur. "Thanks very much."

"Mother, there's a lady in the car," Lily whispered.

"That's Mrs. Sheffield Smith," the Bishop said. "A very good woman. If it hadn't been for her I never would have managed to get here today."

Mrs. Bagot had never heard of her, and she began to think anxiously that she should run back and invite the stranger in for tea along with the Bishop, but she was busy guiding him into the house and into the sitting room and into the chair she had ready for him.

Mrs. Bagot did not doubt that Mrs. Sheffield Smith was a very good woman, but she thought she must be a very strange woman, and very self-important, that she did not even bother to look out at Margaret, who still stood with her back pressed against the railing, staring at the car. Mrs. Sheffield Smith must be very rich. The house she lived in must be very large, and no doubt there was a great deal that was beneath her notice. She had done them all a kindness by giving the Bishop a lift over, but it was a pity she couldn't have taken a minute to admire Margaret standing there in her best dress.

But when Mrs. Bagot had seen the Bishop into his chair she glanced out and saw to her surprise that the car was still outside, and at the same moment the chauffeur appeared in the doorway of the sitting room.

"I beg your pardon, Madam," he said, "but Mrs. Sheffield Smith wants to know if she can take the two children for a drive. We are going for a drive until it is time to call back for His Lordship."

Mrs. Bagot stared at him. Lily and Margaret were standing behind him. They were silent with longing.

"Oh, Mrs. Bagot," the chauffeur said, "I hope you'll let them come. It would be a great treat for Mrs. Sheffield Smith, and for me, too. She's not able to get out of the car, but she's waving at you, if you will just go to the window."

"Let the little ones go for the drive in the big car, Delia" the Bishop said.

"Yes," Mrs. Bagot said. "Yes, they can go. Get your coats, Lily."

She went to the window and looked and waved and smiled and nodded at the gray-gloved hand and the scrap of veiled face that appeared for a moment and then vanished as Mrs. Sheffield Smith sank back into her corner. The front door closed and the chauffeur and the two children hurried down the path and to the car. He lifted Margaret into the back, and then helped Lily scramble up into the front seat. The children had been silent as they put their coats on in the hall, and silent going out to the car. It was one of their ways of being good.

"They're gone," Mrs. Bagot said to the Bishop, or to herself, and she turned away from the window and took the chair opposite him.

"I can't get over how like your grandmother you are," the Bishop said. "You're the image of her. I knew I did the right thing to come here today. I'm glad to see you. Your grandmother was a sprite, like you. She was that supple"—the Bishop said "soople"—"that light on her feet, and small, but she was a very hard worker. And you take after her. I can see, just by looking around this room. It's a lovely place you have here."

He looked at Mrs. Bagot, at her plain navy-blue dress and her plain white blouse and her smooth brown hair, and he looked curiously around the small crowded sitting room, and rested his hands on the arms of his chair while he made a careful survey of the ceiling, and of the Greek frieze that ran all around the top edge of the wallpaper to make an ornamental border. He looked at the folding doors that closed off the back sitting room. Mrs. Bagot considered the back sitting room very ordinary, with its linoleum-covered floor and its gas fire and its big table where the children did their homework and where they all had their dinner on Sundays. The Bishop was very anxious to see what lay beyond the folding doors. He was full of curiosity about Mrs. Bagot. She had been born at Poulbwee, the farm he loved more than any other place on earth. His own family had all died out. There was not one left belonging to him around there, but he could still be sure of Poulbwee. He glanced from the folding doors to Mrs. Bagot and back to the folding doors again before he asked his first question.

"I suppose you have another room in there," he said reluctantly.

"Oh, the back sitting room," Mrs. Bagot said. "Or if you like you can call it the dining room. It's quite different from this room. The children do their lessons, their homework, on the big table in there, and I have the sewing machine, and we all have dinner in there on Sundays. Sometimes I open the folding doors back. I am keeping them closed today because of the draft. I don't want you catching a cold, Father."

The Bishop said nothing.

"Would you like to see in there?" she asked, in surprise, smiling at him.

"I wouldn't mind the draft," the Bishop said. "Anyway it's very sheltered here, beside the fire."

She stood up and opened the doors. She had cleaned the whole house in honor of the Bishop's visit, and now she was very glad she had polished this room. The smell of the wax and polish came to her, and the room seemed dim and rested in contrast with the commotion in the front room where there were the tea table and the ferns and the big Bishop. The Bishop leaned sideways in his armchair to try to see everything, and then he got to his feet and came very slowly over to where she stood, helping himself on the way with his hand on the back of the chair where she had been sitting. When he reached the edge of the linoleum floor he stood and supported himself with his hand against the folded door. Mrs. Bagot lifted one of the dining-room chairs over and he put both hands on the back of it and leaned on it as though it was a railing.

"Now I have a grandstand seat," he said, and from the slow, intent movement of his head and the delighted interest in his eyes you would have thought there were goldfishes swimming about in the air and in and out of the corners under the ceiling, or little birds flying busily around, some of them singing. "Oh, it's great!" he said. "You have a great sense of order, Delia. So did she, God rest her soul."

Mrs. Bagot understood that the Bishop was talking about her grandmother, Mrs. Kelly of Poulbwee. She had never known her grandmother.

"You have a gas fire in here," he said. "That's very handy. And that's your garden out there. I see a lot of yellow."

"That's the laburnum tree," Mrs. Bagot said. "And the side wall is covered with nasturtiums."

"And you have flowers there on the table. Your grandmother always kept the spring and summer flowers on the big round table in the parlor, even though nobody ever went in there. She had that Waterford-glass flower bowl that she was very proud of."

"Oh, the Waterford glass for flowers," Mrs. Bagot said. "It's still there at Poulbwee. It's like a fountain."

"Yes, a fountain," the Bishop said. "And it made a fountain out of the roses. They looked as though they had leaped up out of the glass. I never saw such colors. And they used to be reflected in the wood of the table the same way your flowers are reflected here in this table. I can see the yellow laburnum out there in the garden about as well as I can see the reflection in the table. My eyes are that bad."

He turned around and made his slow journey back to his place beside the fire, and Mrs. Bagot lifted the dining-room chair he had been leaning on back into its place at the table and came to sit opposite to him. She left the folding doors open behind her.

"Lately, more and more, I have been noticing what I can see and what I can't see," the Bishop said. "It's like going in and out of a dream, the way things, rooms, and faces fall away if I only take a few steps this way or that way. It is true that we walk this way only once. It is true. It is true. It is the truth. Indeed it is. It is the very truth. And the other truth is that all is vanity. Yes. . . . Those flowers you have in there on the table now, they are blurred to me as though they were only reflections of themselves. And the whole room in there is dim, very indistinct, but I know what it looks like, thanks to you. . . . I am very glad I managed to get over here today. If it had not been for Mrs. Sheffield Smith I never would have been able to come. They told me they had got a car to bring me and there she was. They are sending me to Parknasilla tomorrow or the next day. The Order has a house there for old fellows like me." Since his return from the Missions, the Bishop had been staying in a rest home at Clontarf. Parknasilla, in Kerry, in the west of Ireland, is a little pocket in the countryside where through some mysterious whim of nature the climate is semitropical, with warm, balmy air and plants and flowers, palm trees and bamboo and so on, that are not usual in other parts of Ireland. "They say the climate is like Spain, or the Riviera," the Bishop went on. "The Riviera! What do you think of that? They tell me about it as if they were sending me to Heaven."

He looked at Mrs. Bagot as though he had surprised himself by making a joke and wanted to be sure she had noticed.

"As though they were sending me to Heaven," he repeated.

But Mrs. Bagot did not want to see the Bishop's joke. She looked stern, and jumped up to take away his half-empty cup, and then she poured him a cup of hot tea and sat down again.

"I have been hearing of Parknasilla all my life," Mrs. Bagot said. "It's only a little place, but they have wonderful plants and flowers there."

"So they tell me," the Bishop said, but he had already lost interest in Parknasilla. "Well now, you have these two rooms here, and of course you have a kitchen."

Mrs. Bagot laughed. "Of course I have a kitchen," she said. "It is a very good little house, very well built. The kitchen is at the end of the hall outside where you came in. You go three steps down to the kitchen. Then there are the two rooms upstairs, over these two rooms, and partway up the stairs there is a half landing, with the bathroom, and next to the bathroom a very small room. We call it the boxroom. It has a nice window looking out on the garden."

Mrs. Bagot's husband slept alone in the boxroom but she wasn't going to tell that to the Bishop or to anybody else. The Bishop nodded at her, and then he asked the question he had been waiting to ask ever since he walked into the house. "You have the whole house to yourselves then?" he said, meaning that Mrs. Bagot was not obliged to share her house with lodgers.

"Oh, yes," she said, and then she said quickly, "We own the house outright. We have enough."

"It's what I thought," the Bishop said, "but I'm glad you tell me. You have a good man then, a good protector."

And having established that Mrs. Bagot's husband was able to provide for her and her children, and that they had, as she put it, enough, he proceeded to ask her a lot of questions, and she answered each question as easily and as proudly as though she was conducting him around her garden, or walking with him along a street in a country that was strange to him, although it had long been familiar to her. He asked her about her life, and as they spoke she had the feeling she was talking about someone who was very well known to her although they had never met. She was talking about herself, and she was amazed to find how much there was to be said about this person, herself, who had come into the conversation from nowhere and who was now becoming more real, although still invisible, with every word that was spoken. In response to the Bishop's trust in her she spoke as though in Braille, feeling her way eagerly and with confidence along a path that she found she knew by heart, every inch of it, even in the dark. And as she spoke, that path, her life, became visible—a natural path that was in harmony with the surrounding countryside. She saw that although she had walked the path without assurance, she had kept to her appointed direction, and she had not trespassed, and she had made no undue demands, and she had not spoiled anything along the way. Or at least this person, herself, who had come into being without warning and who was now so real in the room, this person, still unknown and yet well known, at least to the Bishop, who was so curious about her and so interested in her—this person,

Mrs. Bagot saw, had done nothing without good reason. Not only that, but this person the Bishop admired had done nothing wrong. In fact, it was all very interesting. Mrs. Bagot sighed deeply and then she looked horrified. She had forgotten herself before the Bishop. The Bishop was gazing at her with a timid smile, as though he had followed her thought. His smile was a crescent in his big oval face, which was very white, as though he had lost his color all at once, through illness. His lower lip was thick, and his upper lip was sharply pointed in the center so that it looked like a beak. They were lips that would have made a very resolute mouth when he was a young man. Mrs. Bagot looked devotedly at the old, ascetic, fleshy face, at the hooked nose, and at the faded blue eyes that watched her hopefully from far away, from Africa. The Bishop seemed to know that she was thinking of him now, because he began to speak again.

"You have the two little girls," he said, "lovely children. And what other children have you, Delia?"

"The eldest was a boy," she said. "The only boy. He would have been thirteen. He died at three days."

"Delia," the Bishop said. "My dear child. But it won't be long now. I'll see your son. I'll know him the minute I see him. We will have long talks. I will tell him all about this afternoon—all about his little sisters, and the old dog here, and all. By the grace of God, he is thirteen years ahead of me up there. Was he born in this house, Delia?"

Mrs. Bagot nodded *yes,* and then she said, "He was born and died in the front bedroom upstairs."

"In the front bedroom upstairs," the Bishop said, repeating her words carefully, as though he had been given information he had never hoped to get. "Oh, Delia, I am very fortunate that I came here today. I didn't know about your son. I came here to find you, and now I find him, too. He will show me the ropes. I hope I am able to walk better there than I am here. Please God I will. But I will see your son first thing. And perhaps, even before that, he will help me, at the last minute."

Mrs. Bagot smiled weakly, as though she was trying to show she appreciated a remark she did not really understand.

"At the last minute," she said, echoing his words but not his thought. Then she said, "There are a lot of last minutes."

"One for each of us," the Bishop said quickly. "Oh, it is another of the blessings Our Great Lord gives us, a last minute in addition to all the other minutes. A last minute. It fills me, the thought of it fills me with fear, and also with joy."

"Fear, Father?"

"My body is afraid, Delia, but my soul is filled with joy, and at this minute, when I am sitting here looking at you, and thinking of you and also of your grandmother, whose true daughter you are, I am all gratitude. I think of the days when I used to walk down the lane from the village of Oylegate to Poulbwee. It is a mile walk. You know it as well as I do. You must have walked that lane thousands of times. Oh, I can see you on that lane, walking along, admiring the scenery, missing nothing. That is why my soul is full of joy, when I think of the last minute that makes all the other minutes blaze up, and up, in praise of Almighty God and in recognition of ourselves and the way we are always reaching up, always being better than we are able to be. Your father and I used to walk along that lane from school every day, and then I would cut off across the fields to our place, Cooldearg. Cooldearg is gone; even the house is gone, torn down, and there is not one of my family left. But Poulbwee is still there the way it always was. Your father and I used to have great times. We were the best of friends from the time we were infants. We used to have great talks. I often think, if we could only call back into our minds the words we said when we were children, we would know a good deal about ourselves, and what we would know would be the best of ourselves. I used to watch the children out there in the mission—little small black children, very mysterious, very friendly and open. I used to watch them talking among themselves, and when I walked up to them they stopped talking, or if they went on talking it was with me in mind, and what they said was not the same. And it was the same with your father and me when we were children. Even with your grandmother, we watched ourselves. What we said when we were by ourselves was very different from what we said when there was a member of the older generation at hand. And so there is never anybody to remember what the children say, because the children vanish. Nobody ever knows what the children say."

"It seems a very long time from those days to now," Mrs. Bagot said, "and yet the lane is exactly the same. It's a full mile from the village of Oylegate to Poulbwee, and yet it never seemed like a mile. The lane is so nice, the way it turns around to suit the fields and then goes straight between the hedges when it gets a chance. And I used to like opening and shutting the gates as I went along. I never climbed over them. I always opened the gates and then shut them after me. And the last big turn you make, that brings you in sight of the house, the lane widens out and gets wider as you get nearer the house, and there are very high trees on each side along that last stretch. There was a place along there where I used to find white ivy."

Poulbwee is a very long two-story farmhouse with a deep thatched roof. The house is whitewashed and the front door is painted green. The front door stands open on a square hall that is only large enough to step into. To the right is the door leading into the parlor. That door is always kept closed. To the left is the kitchen, with the door always open. The inside wall facing you has a very small window in it so that anybody sitting at the kitchen hearth can peer out and see who is coming along the lane.

"Your grandmother used to watch for me," the Bishop said, "and the minute I came around the last turn she would appear out at the door and stand there waiting for me. I could feel her smiling as I came along down the lane. God bless her kind heart, she was never ashamed to show you that you were welcome, never ashamed, never afraid. She was very gentle. I could see that people with no sense and who did not know her very well might think little of her. . . . My first leave home from the Missions—my first and my last, because I never came home after that until now—I used to say Mass in the chapel in Oylegate every morning, and then I would walk down the lane to Poulbwee, and your grandmother would have breakfast waiting for me. I had been out of Ireland fourteen years. I went out to the Missions after I was ordained and I didn't see Ireland again for fourteen years. My mother was dead and there was only my brother at home. He never married and I suppose the loneliness got in on his mind. He lost heart. All the time I was there he kept talking about how he was going to sell up the place and go to America. He had already sold off all the stock and all the furniture out of the parlor, furniture that had belonged to our great-grandmother, and before that. I tried to persuade him to get a hold of himself and he said it was easy for me. I was always considered to be the scholar in the family, and he minded that. He said I was the favorite with my mother, and he may have been right, but she always intended the farm for him, although he was the younger. He was in a terrible way, catching a rabbit now and again for his dinner. He slept most of the day and most of the night. He was ashamed of sleeping so much and he didn't like anybody coming near the place and gradually they all began to stay away. I never knew a place could go down as fast as Cooldearg had gone down the last time I saw it. I had no warning. After the fourteen years away I made for Cooldearg as fast as my legs could carry me, and it was a great shock, to see it. A great shock and a great lesson to me, to curb my vanity that I did not know I had. The Devil is always waiting to catch us in our weak moments. My brother came out of the house and it was all I could do to keep myself from knocking him down. And yet the day I left he walked as far as Oylegate with me, where I got a lift into Wexford, and when we said goodbye I turned around and walked a bit back down the lane with him, and we shook hands and said goodbye again, and the tears were running down his face, and down my face, too. I watched him go. He never turned around until he reached the first turn and then he turned and lifted up his arm to me and then he was gone. I never saw him again. He sold up the place as he said he would and went to America. I never heard from him. But while I was there, that last time, I said Mass in Oylegate every morning and then I walked down the lane to have breakfast at Poulbwee. I could draw a map of that lane for you. I used to play a game with the children at the mission. 'Going to Poulbwee,' we called it. They got to know the lane nearly as well as I did, and every field along the way, and they were never tired of hearing about the house."

There was a time when the Bishop had looked on that lane from Oylegate to Poulbwee as the only path he knew through a maze that had no center and no form and no secret—worst of all, no secret. There was nothing secret and hidden that he could ferret out and destroy and punish himself for and do penance for. There was nothing. There was only the maze. As a young man, the Bishop had not understood that when he became a missionary priest he also became an exile, and the two words, "priest" and "exile," did not seem to him to be in accord, and he felt it was unsuitable and dangerous for a priest to know himself to be an exile. He felt his homesickness to be self-indulgence, but he was homesick all the same. He had doubts about his own worth but no doubt about the authority of his vocation. His only desire was to serve. To have faith and a chance to show it. The Bishop thanked God in deep humility for the chance that had been given to him. He had found, after leaving Oylegate, that he was not as great a scholar as they considered him to be at home. He felt himself to be a big clumsy fellow, more at home on the farm than he would ever be away from it, and yet when he put on his robes to say Mass he felt like a soldier in uniform on his way to fight for what he believed in. Even in his youth the Bishop never aspired to sainthood or martyrdom. To become, someday, a truly good and faithful servant of the One he loved—that was his highest hope.

When he was thirty-six years old, still plain Father Tom and nowhere near being a bishop, he reminded himself that we on earth are all exiles, exiled from the Presence of Almighty God. But the kind of exile he felt, living inside his own body and dragging along while the priest within him strode proudly, that was an entirely different kind of exile—somebody inconsolable and stubborn who was not intelligent enough to understand the earthly sameness between his own and other countries and who therefore in bewilderment tormented himself about the *difference*. Or you could say that an exile was a person who knew of a country that made all other countries seem strange. In that sense, the exile inside the priest, or living with the priest, hanging onto him, might be a helpful being, enabling the priest to dream sometimes and find a little respite in the tranquillity of memory and of familiar places. The Bishop, thirty-six years old, kneeling in meditation before his altar, arranged a sentence in his mind: *The strong resolute priest finds respite in the tranquil recollection of familiar places and in that respite gains the grace to be more humble and more watchful in his care of his flock.* . . . And then he ground his hands together in the impatience he had forbidden himself, the impatience that expressed a distress he feared because he understood it. What was he doing inventing and polishing and making phrases that said nothing at all? Anyone listening to him would imagine he thought Ireland to be a pretty little oasis of some kind or another, a kind of family paradise. He thought of his country, where terrible pride and terrible humility stand together, two noble creatures enslaved, enthralled, by what defines them, the bitter Irish appetite for humiliation. No, there was no complacency there, no complacency and no chance of any. He thought of his country and sighed in admiration, and grinned, although he knew he was being guilty of self-satisfaction. Then he took hold of his thoughts. He was barking up the wrong tree. What was bothering him and causing him all this weak misery was that he felt ill at ease, and clumsy, and confused, as though he moved through a maze that was formless until he made a mistake, and then in his mistake he touched something that made him draw back. Or to put it another way, in his mistake he touched something strong enough to prevent him from moving forward, something implacable. How could he have the temerity to expect to be able to help save the souls of the people around him when he had left his own brother to perish in a wasteland of bitterness?

Lily and Margaret were very much surprised that they had to ring the bell in order to be let into their own house. They thought surely their mother would have been waiting impatiently for their return, and perhaps a little angry with them for staying out so late. Mrs. Sheffield Smith had told them the Bishop would be late for his supper and that *she* would be blamed, but she smiled and they knew she was making a joke. They waited, looking up at the door as though their mother's face, when she appeared in answer to their ring, would be at least a foot higher than usual. They could not remember how tall she was, and they looked far up, like Bennie, bending their necks back. They each carried a very large box of chocolates with a picture on the lid of children in old-fashioned clothes.

When the door was opened, Bennie ran out excitedly and the children ran into the sitting room where the Bishop was standing up and arranging his sticks for his journey out to the car. Mrs. Bagot presented the children to the Bishop and then hurried out to greet Mrs. Sheffield Smith and thank her for taking the children driving.

Mrs. Bagot said, "It was a great occasion for them."

Mrs. Sheffield Smith said, "And for us, too, a great occasion. I hope you have no objection to chocolates. One at a time, I told them. They are charming little girls. At first they would not speak, and then they talked a good deal. You must be very proud of them."

"Oh, yes," Mrs. Bagot said. "And Mrs. Sheffield Smith, thank you for bringing the Bishop here today. It meant everything in the world to us, to have him in the house."

When Mrs. Bagot returned to the sitting room, the Bishop smiled at her before he spoke.

"Two great talkers you have here," he said. "I told them that on Mondays I saw more lions than monkeys, and on Thursdays I saw only giraffes."

Then he straightened himself and moved his sticks into his left hand. "And now," he said, "I will give you my blessing."

Mrs. Bagot and the children knelt down and Mrs. Bagot began to cry. The Bishop raised his right hand and raised his face, and blessed them, and then he looked down at them, and offered each of them his ring to kiss. He started across the room as they were getting to their feet, and they followed him out to the front door where the chauffeur stood waiting. The chauffeur and the old man went slowly down the red path, and when they reached the gate Mrs. Bagot and the children walked after them and stood in a row outside the railing while the Bishop was helped into the back seat. He sank back out of sight at once. The chauffeur turned and saluted smartly, with a wink for Margaret, before he climbed into his own place and the car started off up the street to where it would turn at the dead end. Mrs. Bagot and the children remained where they were, waiting for the car to come back. It came rolling down the street and slowed as it approached them, and then it stopped and the Bishop leaned forward and looked at them once again, and they looked at him. They waved and he nodded at them and then the car started off again and went on down the street and around the corner. The Bishop was gone.

Mrs. Bagot and the children went back into the sitting room and there was an argument about the chocolates, but finally both boxes were opened and Mrs. Bagot had first choice out of each box. Mrs. Bagot put her chocolates on the mantelpiece to save for later but the children ate three each and Bennie got cake.

TWO PEOPLE

A Young Girl Can Spoil Her Chances

Upstairs in the bedroom that he had shared with his wife for more than thirty years, Mr. Derdon stood erect before the chest of drawers that was his alone and worked placidly on the knot of his navy-blue bow tie. Mr. Derdon was wearing his waistcoat and his trousers. Both of these garments, which had been made for him at a discount by one of the tailors in the men's outfitting department of the shop where he worked, were of a smooth navy-blue wool material that had a faint gray line running through it. The coat of this suit hung ready to put on, over the back of a straight chair on his side of the bed. The companion chair stood on Mrs. Derdon's side of the bed, but there were no clothes hanging on it or laid across it. As usual, Mrs. Derdon had got up and dressed herself and got out of the room before her husband was properly awake.

If this was an ordinary morning, she would have finished her breakfast by this time. Already, on an ordinary morning, she would have begun on her housework, and when he arrived downstairs she would leave whatever it was she was doing and go back to the kitchen to wait on him while he had his breakfast. But this was not an ordinary morning. It was a nuisance of a morning. Today was the forty-third anniversary of Mrs. Derdon's father's death. She was having a Mass said for the repose of his soul, as she did every year, and, as she did every year on this day, she was going to attend the Mass, which meant that Mr. Derdon's morning was going to be upset—he had awakened annoyed, thinking about it—because she was not going to be on hand to give him his breakfast and see him off to work.

Mr. Derdon was taking his time over the arrangement of his tie. He was watching himself in the mirror that hung over his chest of drawers, but although his hands and his eyes were on his tie, his attention was downstairs in the hall, and he was listening for the sound of the front door closing, which would tell him that Mrs. Derdon had gone out of the house, and that he was alone and could go downstairs without fear of her seeing him. If she was going to go off like this, go off leaving him to have his breakfast alone, she was not going to have the satisfaction of seeing him settled at the kitchen table before she left. He had his mind made up. He was not going to go downstairs until he was sure she was out of the house. Time was on his side. He could hurry over his breakfast once he got down, but she should have been out of the house and gone minutes ago. She should have walked half of the way to the church by now, if she was to be kneeling in her place before the priest ascended the altar to start the Mass. He could afford to take his time. She would get tired of standing around down there waiting for him.

At last he heard the front door close. She was gone. Within the space of the minute that followed he had his tie right, and he had slipped into his coat, and he had put his glasses and his clean handkerchief and his change and his pen-and-pencil set and the other objects that lay through each night on top of his chest of drawers into his pockets, and he was standing at the head of the stairs that led down to their narrow hall.

It gave him a fright, to see her standing below him in the hall, dressed in her outdoor clothes, wearing her gray coat and her black Sunday shoes. Her head was bent, her face shadowed by the brim of her hat, and she was looking at something in her prayer book and standing very still, so that for an instant he thought he was seeing things, but she looked up at him and closed the prayer book.

"I thought you'd gone," he said.

"I had to come back. I forgot something," she said, and he continued on down the stairs and turned sharply at the foot and went straight down the three steps that led to the kitchen. She followed him. Of course, he knew very well what had happened. Trust her. Each of them had tried to play a trick on the other, and she had won. She had known all the last ten minutes what he was up to, delaying up there. She wouldn't call up to him, or come up, as another woman would have done. She would have called that "bothering" him. Doing the direct thing was "bothering" him. For some reason, she had been just as determined to see him as he had been not to see her.

"I suppose you know you're going to be late for Mass," he said, and he took the teapot off the stove and brought it to the table and sat down and reached for a piece of bread.

"I've left everything ready," she said.

She was standing uncertainly in the doorway. She even had her gloves on. In a minute she would have the gloves off and be fussing around putting more things on the table and asking him did he want anything.

"Are you going to Mass or not?" he said.

"Hubert," she said. "I thought of something very funny this morning. Do you know, I'm exactly the same age today that my mother was the day I was married."

"It was bound to happen sooner or later," Hubert said.

"Two days from today I'll be fifty-three, and it was two days before my mother's fifty-third birthday that I was married."

"I was married that day, too, you know," Hubert said. "She seemed a lot older than fifty-three," he added.

A Young Girl Can Spoil Her Chances

She hesitated, looking at his face, and at the table, and at his face again.

"Well, I just thought I'd tell you," she said. "It seems funny, when you think of it. I'm going now. Don't forget to give the front door a good bang. Be sure it shuts itself."

"All right, all right, all right," he said, but he heard the front door close, banging this time, and he didn't know whether or not she had heard him.

She had heard his voice, but not his words. She was satisfied. She had wanted to see him, and she had seen him. She didn't like to have to go off and leave him in the house by himself.

This day, the anniversary of her father's death, was always a queer day, and even now, after forty-three years, she was upset by it. Today it fell on a Tuesday. Tuesday, the ninth of September. He had died two days before her tenth birthday. Every year, when his anniversary came around, she was reminded that in two days it would be her birthday, and then, on her birthday, she would be reminded that on her tenth birthday he had been only two days dead. Not even two days, not officially, because he had died sometime between half past six and half past seven in the evening, and she had been born sometime after three in the morning. A few minutes after three, her mother had told her. So that at the moment when she became exactly ten years old, her father, not yet buried, was not quite two days dead.

Every year, on her birthday, she would count her own increasing years, and she would also think of the lengthening span of time that separated her from her father, but most of all she would think and think of those two incomplete days, and she always woke up on the morning of her birthday with a terrible feeling of apprehension, as though she had forgotten to do something important and was going to be found out. The feeling of apprehension that she had, at

A Young Girl Can Spoil Her Chances

the thought of the incompleteness of those two days, was terribly painful, and she could never get over the idea that something had been left undone in connection with her father's death—that he had failed to see somebody he might very much have wanted to see once again, or that there had been a carelessness about his wake or his funeral, or a lack of respect in the handling of his coffin or at his grave. She had been too small to see that everything was done the right way. She had been bundled next door to a neighbor's house with her little brother. From minute to minute she had not known what was happening to her father, or who was looking at him. But the neighbor's oldest girl had known; she had been watching, and when the coffin was carried in she had called to Rose to come and look at it.

Mrs. Derdon knew perfectly well that the incompleteness of the two days' interval between the hour of her father's death and the hour of her own birth was accident pure and simple and only accident, but there it was, the apprehension lived, and that—the sense of accident—was what it lived on.

But he need not have died. He had not been old and he had not been sick. He had been frail—he often lay down on the bed for a rest—but he had not been sick. If he had only managed to hold on for that little bit of time till he got to her birthday, he might not have died at all. He would have been safe. It would have been her birthday. It would have been the Big Day, and he would have been so watchful all day long, thinking about what an important day it was, that he might not have lain down for a rest when he came home in the evening, and if he had not lain down, he might not have died. They had both been so busy thinking of the Big Day, and talking about it, that they had paid no attention at all to the days that went before it, except to cross them off on the calendar with a pencil. The father had drawn a bright red star around the Big Day, but he had paid no attention at all to the days that went before it, and neither had she, except that they were both glad, every evening, that another day could be crossed off to show them that they were that much nearer to the day they were both looking forward to. All the days before her birthday had been ordinary days, dull workaday days, not to be valued but only to be pushed out of the way, and then one of the ordinary days had turned around and made itself into the most important day of all.

If he had been sitting with her that night in his old armchair in the kitchen, as he often was in the evenings, he would have caught back the breath he lost and then he would have been all right. She had often seen him catch back his breath. He always looked at her, and she would look at him, and see the tears come into his eyes while he caught his breath, and then they would both smile because he was himself again.

He used to hold her on his lap. That annoyed her mother. Her mother used to say that she was too big and heavy to hold, but he always said that she was no weight at all. When he went up to lie down on the bed, after he came in from work, Rose used to like to go up and lie down with him and talk to him until he was rested, but her mother put a stop to that.

He had come in from work as usual that evening, and Rose had stood beside him while he crossed off that day on the calendar. Then he had said, "Will I sit down there by the fire, or will I go up and take a little rest?"

Rose had said, "Whatever you like," and she couldn't help laughing when she looked at him, because she was always so glad to see him.

"Oh, I don't know, I think a little rest," he said, and he put his hand around the back of her neck, under her hair, and gave her a little shake. "Only one more day now, Rose," he said, "and then we'll see what we will see."

A Young Girl Can Spoil Her Chances

She was delighted, because she knew he was referring to the present he had promised her, which was to be a surprise. And Jimmy, who was only five then, was sitting by himself on the floor in front of the fire, and got up and came over to them, because he knew that there was to be something for him as well, even though it was Rose's birthday. And the father had bent down and said, "Yes, Jimmy, there'll be something nice for you, too." Then he had started up the stairs and she had stood at the bottom with Jimmy beside her, and watched him go up. He had not looked back, but then, of course, he had not known they had come to the foot of the stairs and were looking after him.

Her mother had not gone upstairs to see him as she usually did when she came back to the kitchen from the little shop that she kept in what had once been the front sitting room of the house. First the mother had been busy getting the tea, and then, when it was ready, she said she would let him sleep on awhile. And then the woman next door had come in and had begun talking. He had died alone. He must have been terribly frightened but he had been very brave. He had not cried out or called anybody's name. They had all been downstairs and they had heard nothing. But her mother and the woman next door had been laughing and talking. He could have called out and they might not have heard him. Maybe he had tried to call "Rose, Rosie!" "Rose" meant that he was calling her, and "Rosie" meant that he was smiling, calling her name for the second time. There had never been any need for him to call her twice. She had always run to the sound of his voice. He had always come into the house calling her.

She had been restless that night, sitting at the kitchen table with no one paying any attention to her. Her mother and the woman next door had been sitting facing each other across the fire. Jimmy was on his mother's lap and she was holding him close to her, with one arm along his leg and the other arm around him and around

his neck, her hand on his neck cuddling him while she talked over
the top of his head to the woman next door. Jimmy had been
wearing the short trousers that his mother had made for him from
an old skirt of her own, and the red jersey that his mother had
knitted for him. The mother had taken off his boots and stockings
when Rose brought him home from school, and his little feet shone
in the light from the fire.

Rose had sat there wanting to hold Jimmy but afraid to ask,
and at last she had said that she thought she would just run upstairs
and see how her daddy was. But her mother, who was different in
her ways when they had visitors, had given her a look that Rose
knew was put on for the benefit of the woman next door and had
said, "You stay where you are, Miss, and let your daddy have his
rest. I'll be the one to decide when it's time to wake him. Do you
hear me?" And the mother had given a significant nod at the
woman next door and said, "Rose is the greatest little busybody you
ever saw."

And the woman next door had smiled, not very nicely, and
said, "She's just looking for notice. Isn't that it, Rose?"

"Oh, she wants notice, all right," the mother had said. "But
sure, he spoils her. No matter what I say, he spoils her. And it's only
going to make it harder for her in the long run."

"Nothing worse than a spoiled child," the woman next door
had said, and then they had gone on to talk of something else, and
Rose had sat patiently on until her mother had seen fit to go upstairs to where the father lay.

Rose had never found out what it was her father had intended
to give her for her birthday, or what he had intended to give
Jimmy. There had been times—once or twice, anyway—that he had
made a deposit on whatever it was he wanted and then the people
in the shop would put the present, the toy or the doll, away until he
had the money to pay for it in full. Rose could not believe that he

A Young Girl Can Spoil Her Chances

had not put down a deposit on something for her someplace; not on the present for Jimmy, perhaps, because that would have been smaller, but on something for her. And she went in and out of Miss Greene's shop several times, and in and out of O'Malley's, loitering a minute and looking around and hoping that one or another of the people behind the counter would say to her that her father had made a deposit on something for her and that they had it there, keeping it for her, but nobody ever said anything to her about a deposit being made and she was afraid to ask.

But it was not the loss of the present or the loss of the birthday or even the loss of her father that afflicted Rose so much as the knowledge, which she alone possessed, of that lost fragment of time between the moment of his death and the moment that had marked her birth. A big piece of time had been broken off, and it had gone down, and maybe it had taken others besides him with it, but if it had she did not know of them. The terrible thing was that no one besides herself seemed to notice that a piece of time, a fragment, had been shattered off their lives, and that nothing had happened during that time—no minutes or hours or anything like that. It was on that uneven fragment of time that Rose concentrated her attention, trying to guess its shape (not exactly like a day, and not exactly like a night) and trying to imagine what accident had caused it to slip away when it might have held firm until she and her father had gained the safe ground of her birthday. It was her knowledge of the power of accident, and her natural, confused apprehension, as much as the desire to see that he got something to eat, that had caused her to trick Hubert into coming downstairs this morning, when she knew perfectly well that he was enjoying his sulk.

She was just in time for Mass. As she walked into the church she held herself very straight, and her face wore a self-conscious, almost disdainful look, the look of one who has found nothing to criticize so far but who fears that at any moment she may find herself among people who are beneath her and who will try to be too familiar with her.

Hubert knew that look. She only wore it outside the house. Hubert disliked having the order of his day disturbed. He didn't like to have his breakfast all topsy-turvy, and he didn't like seeing his wife running around the house at that early hour of a weekday morning with her hat and her gloves on, and her big bulging prayer book in her hand, but what he disliked most of all was to see her go out to face the world wearing the face that she showed to the world, the face that she imagined impressed people—as if anybody ever noticed her. Her pretensions, the pitiful air she wore of being a certain sort of person, irritated him so much that he could hardly bear to look at her on the rare occasions—rare these days, anyway—when they went out together. They had been living in Dublin for over thirty years and she was still the same simple girl from her simple country town, and that was all right, in its way, if she would be content with that, but the minute she got out of the house she started imagining things about herself, as though by imagining, and pretending, she could deceive people into thinking that she was the sort of woman she was not. And what was more, thinking that she could deceive people into thinking that she was a sort of woman that had never existed anywhere, any time, except in her head.

Hubert thought it was a very bad way to start the day, thinking about all that. But, once he started thinking about all that, he kept on thinking about it, and the end of it was that he arrived at work seven minutes later than usual, but still well ahead of most of the other men, and in a bad mood. He did not mention the dislocation of his morning to anyone. He did not like to give confidences, or to receive them, and he disliked being asked questions, and almost never asked anyone a question. His department, staffed all by men, was at the back of the big main floor of the shop, behind the wide, carpeted stairs that led up to the second floor. The ceiling of the main floor was over two stories high, and a balcony had been run around the walls of the men's outfitting department to create extra room for storing stock and for doing such work as making and checking sample books and checking orders. Today Hubert was to spend his time on the balcony, to begin checking the samples in the books against the amount of material they had in stock. The department did a lot of work with priests, and as he arranged what he wanted to get through in the course of the day, Hubert put clerical samples well out of his way, so that he might not come upon them until tomorrow, or even the day after tomorrow. Hubert's only son, his only child, was a priest, and Hubert disliked being reminded of the fact that John was now Father John Derdon.

He had been disappointed when John joined the priesthood, but, to tell the truth, at the same time he had been relieved. John was a poor example of a fellow, weak and timid and with no aptitude for anything and no inclination toward anything, and Hubert had never been able to imagine what he would do or could do with himself in the way of earning a living and making a life for himself. For a fellow like that, becoming a priest was as good an answer as any. He would be taken care of, and he would always be told what to do and what not to do. He would be safe all his life. In time, as he grew older, he would probably get to walking and talking with as much authority as any of them, in his black clothes. What had happened to John, his fate, could all be laid at Rose's door. She had ruined the boy. She had kept him all to herself all his life, and she had ended up by ruining him. It was a pity about John. Hubert did not like to think about John. There was something very meager and lost about him the last time he had come to see them, with his stiff new manners and his collar back to front and his carefulness about himself and about everything he said. Very uneasy

A Young Girl Can Spoil Her Chances

John was that day, as if he was trying to set a good example to himself, watching himself and then looking at his parents as if he was hoping they would tell him that everything was all right.

The morning that had begun badly for Hubert went on badly. The two boiled eggs that Rose had left ready for him, and that he had decided to swallow at the last minute, after having decided earlier to punish her by leaving them where they were, sat coldly on his stomach. He wanted nothing to eat when midday came, and he decided to take a stroll and maybe have a glass of milk or something.

It was a cool day with bright sun, but there had been showers in the morning and Hubert wore his raincoat when he left the shop.

He was an unremarkable, decent-looking man, not very tall. His face was pale and thin and he had blue eyes. He wore the expression of a friend, but of a friend who is making no promises. He walked as he worked, methodically, and made his way slowly along the narrow, crowded length of Grafton Street, sidestepping the prams and watching where he was going, not glancing in any of the shopwindows. Grafton Street was bedlam, he thought, and he was glad when he emerged into the wider and freer and quieter spaces of Stephen's Green. One of the high park gates, open, faced him diagonally across the green from the corner where he was standing.

It had been years since he was in the park, many years, but when he and Rose first came to Dublin it had been their favorite place, the favorite place of all. They were always in there on Sunday afternoons—they spent all their time there. They never minded the rain then, never minded anything; they walked through the park in all weathers. There was a hat Rose had then, a little hat with a brim, very like the hat she had worn this morning. She loved the park. She was always wanting to go in there. She used to like to feed the ducks, and she never was finished exclaiming over the beauty of the flowers, and over the ingenious arrangements of the flower beds, and over the convenience of the benches and chairs that were placed along the edges of the paths for people to sit on, and over the care that was taken of the grass and of the borders and of the shrubs. She was always in the park during those first weeks—months, it had been—before they found the house they could afford and moved out to Ranelagh.

During those first weeks together they lived in a house on Somerville Street, in two small rooms at the top of the house—a long walk up to get to them—and Rose had grown very fond of those rooms. The day they left Somerville Street, Rose cried. They were moving out into their own place and all she could do was cry. All she would say, when he asked her what was wrong with her, was, "Nothing. I can't help it. I can't help it."

She had seemed all pleased and contented with the house and he could not understand what had suddenly overcome her. He had been worried himself, worried about money, wondering if they were going to too much expense, and her tears had unnerved him.

Then, their first Sunday in the house, they were at their dinner, when she suddenly put her head down into her hand and began to cry again. "Oh, I wish we had stayed where we were. It was so nice there. I wish we could have stayed there."

He had lost his temper. He had said to her that there had been nothing but mistakes ever since their marriage and that maybe everything had been a mistake, the marriage, too, the marriage most of all, and what did she mean by saying that she wished they had stayed where they were, what was going on in her mind, she was better off now than she had ever been in her life before.

That was a miserable day, that first Sunday in the house. The place had looked so cold and bare and hard to deal with, even after they had the bedroom set arranged, and the rest of the furniture they had then—part of a sitting-room set and the yellow table and chairs in the kitchen. The place had still looked poor and bare, and even to him it had seemed a long and not a happy way from Stephen's Green. He had begun to wonder again if maybe they had gone in over their heads, but he had recovered himself, after his outburst, and when they were finished with the dinner, he had suggested that they get on the tram and take a ride into town to Stephen's Green, and walk in the park as they had been doing. But it was not the same thing at all, having to take the tram in and the tram back—it was as though they were now visitors in what had formerly belonged to them.

But the worst thing Hubert remembered about that unhappy day was the look of terror that had crossed Rose's face when he had spoken roughly to her. He had been shocked by the terror and hurt on her face. He had only struck out at her in natural annoyance and impatience—that is what he told himself—but the effect on her had been that she was trampled. It took nothing and she was beaten to her knees. Her plate was full in front of her but she ate only a little of it, bowed toward it all the time like a punished child or a punished, furtive dog. And then he left her to do the washing up, and when he came back down to the kitchen, having recovered his temper, to suggest that they go to the park, there she was standing by the sink finishing up what was left on her plate, and when he appeared in the door of the kitchen she had turned in a panic to hide the plate, to hide what she was eating, and he had turned and gone back upstairs, pretending that he had noticed nothing.

He never could understand her—her secrecy, her furtiveness, her way of stopping what she was doing and running to do something else the minute he came into the room, as though what she was doing was forbidden to her. She was afraid of him, and she never made any attempt to control the fear, no matter what he said to her. All he ever said to her was that she ought to try to take things easy, try to take life easier—things like that, that would reassure her. But she was afraid of him, and that was the whole of the difficulty, and that is what defeated him at every turn, and that is why he gradually, or finally—he could not have told how it happened—gave up any attempt to get on any kind of terms with her.

Anyone who saw them together could see that she was afraid of him—or Hubert thought he was justified in thinking that anyone who saw them together could see her fear—and it wasn't fair, because he wasn't the sort of man a person need be afraid of. She behaved sometimes like a person who was trapped in a place where she did not want to be, with a person she was deathly afraid of and who did not want her there. There were times when her face was not the face of a normal person. He shut it out of his mind after a time—her fear, or whatever it was that was the matter with her.

When the child was born she was much happier and she seemed easier in her mind, but then she became completely wrapped up in the child. It was unhealthy and wrong, the way she came to depend on John even before he was big enough to walk. Then she made John afraid of him, too. He would hear the two of them chattering away, but when he would open the door and go into the room where they were, they would both fall silent. He would catch them exchanging glances that excluded him. And when she wanted to reprove the child she made a habit of saying, "Your daddy doesn't like that, Johnny," or "Your father won't put up with that from you, Johnny." As though he, Hubert, the silent father, who never spoke an unkind word to the child, and who never had a chance to say much more than "Good morning" and "Good night" and "Happy Christmas"—as though *he* was the only one who didn't like what the child was doing.

Hubert had an idea that she knew perfectly well the power it gave her, her being afraid of him and his being always afraid that he was going to hurt her feelings, but he never went so far as to challenge her with that, with the power it gave her, or with his other suspicion, that she got a certain enjoyment out of irritating him. He never could bring himself to say, "You're afraid of me. I don't know why you're afraid of me. I think you ought to make an effort to get over it. It's not fair to me nor to yourself nor to the child. And I think you get a satisfaction out of being afraid of me. I think you know very well what you're doing—getting the child to side with you when there's no need for anybody to take sides at all. I don't like these games. I don't like them a bit. I wish you would make up your mind to stop all this nonsense. I wish you would stop it. All this cringing and running out of the room whenever I walk in will have to stop. It will have to stop. It will have to stop."

But when he got to that point in his thoughts Hubert would have to stop himself, because he would begin to feel his anger against her getting out of hand. The anger was dreadful because there seemed to be no way of working it off. It was an anger that called for pushing over high walls, or kicking over great towering, valuable things that would go down with a shocking crash. The thing he really wanted to smash was out of his reach and he did not even know what it was, but when he thought of things that were out of his reach but that he could smash if he could reach them, he felt better. But there was no way of talking to her. She took the least word as a rebuke, and when he made an attempt to talk to her, to talk sense to her, he only ended up feeling ashamed of himself and sick of himself and sick of her. But it was a long time now since he had made any effort to find out what was the matter with her or why she was so unhappy. Obedient, yielding, and gentle, she outwitted him at every turn. She gave in to him. She gave in to him on everything. It seemed there was no limit to her capacity to yield, and he thought there was no if or but about it—she would go on forever giving in, and make no move to assert herself. There was something

A Young Girl Can Spoil Her Chances

in her that he could not fight, or there was something in her that he could not find, and he did not know what it was or what was wrong.

It was her eyes that gave her away, or didn't give her away—whichever way you looked at it. She had her father's eyes and her father's features. That is what her mother had told him. The first time he saw Rose she was behind the counter, in the little bit of a shop her mother kept in what had been at one time the front sitting room of their house. You went in through the hall door and you turned right and you were in the shop. Rose was twenty years old then, and her hair was a very light, sunny brown. He noticed her hair that day, because she had her head bent over a scrap of crochet she was working on, and the sun shone directly on her hair through the square window behind her. Her hair was fastened back into a bun, in a style that was too old for her and that gave her a very plain, quiet look. She had a piece of cloth in her lap, a big handkerchief or a piece of a pillowcase or something like that, and when she saw him she dropped the crochet into the cloth and folded the cloth, making a little bag of it, and stood up and smiled at him, all at the one time. She seemed to be very glad to see him. He thought she was a nice-looking girl, very open-faced, like a child. With that open face and her obedient nature she should have had blue eyes, clear blue eyes, but her eyes were green, the color of seaweed, a deep green, not dark but full of clouds.

He asked her for a small packet of cigarettes. She reached to a shelf at her side and took them and put them on the counter, and then immediately she took them up again and opened the packet and counted the cigarettes inside. She counted under her breath and then "Six" she said, and showed him the open box.

"Isn't that what there usually is?" he said.

"I have to count them," she said apologetically, "or my mother will eat me. A man came in here the other day and took a packet of cigarettes like that, and the next thing I knew he was back complaining that there were only four cigarettes in the packet. And I didn't know what to do. I gave him another instead, and when I told my mother about it she was angry and she said he'd played a trick on me. So I have to count them now."

Hubert smiled at her but he was thinking that it was not surprising that someone had taken advantage of her. He was thinking of her as he walked down the street, when he heard her calling after him ("Wait a minute, wait a minute"), and by the time he turned she had already caught up with him, running after him.

"I only wanted to tell you that I have to open the cigarettes for everybody," she said, "not just you."

"I know that," he said. "You told me that."

"I was afraid I had hurt your feelings," she said.

"Oh, no, no. It's not that easy to hurt my feelings," he said, and he thought she seemed too excitable. He didn't like her running after him down the street like that, calling attention to him.

Rose and her mother and her little brother Jimmy spent their evenings in the room that was down the hall from the shop—a big dark kitchen that seemed to be all doors and that only had one window opening out onto their small, high-walled yard. The mother always sat in a wooden armchair beside the fire. Rose sat on a straight chair alongside a table in the center of the room, and Jimmy lounged on a wooden bench under the window. Jimmy was fifteen then, a silent boy who smiled every time you looked at him. Like Rose, he was constantly watching his mother. Rose used to sit there in that kitchen like a good child, hardly speaking. The night they decided to get married, he was sitting at the table across from Rose, and even then Rose hardly spoke, but she watched him. Even when she was pretending to look down at the table or at the fire, he knew she was watching him.

A Young Girl Can Spoil Her Chances

Rose's mother was a woman who knew what she was about. She knew the difference between right and wrong and she spoke her mind. She took no nonsense from anybody and when they were all there that night she said to him, "I hope you know what you're about, Hubert. It's no joke, getting married. It's not just a matter of putting the ring on a girl's finger. They say a young girl can spoil her chances, but a young man can spoil his chances just as easy and just as much. I don't know if you and Rose know each other well enough. You want to think a bit, you and Rose both. You want to wait a while and not rush in without thinking. You don't want to be in a hurry about this. You want to give youself time in case you want to change your mind. Better to change it now before it's too late. Rose is flighty. She changes her mind from minute to minute. She never knows what she thinks one minute to the next. She thinks according to whoever is talking to her. She's only a child. You want to be sure you're on firm ground before you take a long step. Now, I know what you're thinking, Rose. That I'm hard. I'm not hard at all. But I know you. You're a young fellow, Hubert, with no one to advise you and I'm older and wiser, and even if Rose is my daughter I want you to know that I have your welfare at heart just as much as I have hers. And she is changeable. She can't help that. It's her nature. I think you should think about this awhile."

"Oh, Mother, don't be talking like that to him," Rose cried. "It's not fair. You'll be giving him a bad picture of me. It's not a bit fair."

"I don't want any of your back answers, Rose," her mother said. "And now, to prove that I'm right, I'm going to give Hubert an example of what I mean."

"Oh, well, then, there's nothing I can do," Rose whispered.

"Here's what I mean," her mother went on. "And I'm telling you, Hubert, so that you'll know and so that nobody can be laughing at you behind your back. Do you know the lane that runs

A Young Girl Can Spoil Her Chances

alongside the Children's School over on Patrick Street? Well, you wouldn't know it, being a stranger here, but it's there, and there's nothing at the end of it but a disused stable with a broken door. The door got broken about a year ago when some young hooligans got in there one night, for what reason nobody knows and nobody likes to think, and they were never found, although we all have our ideas as to who they were. No decent girl would go down that lane by herself, and at night no girl would go down there with anybody if she had any respect at all for herself, but the tenth of June last, Rose slipped out of here when my back was turned and waited there at that stable for over two hours at night, from half past eight until nearly eleven, waiting for a young fellow down the street, a young fellow, a young rascal that's not good enough for Rose to wipe her boots on, or wasn't good enough until she let him wipe his boots on her."

"Oh, Mother!" Rose cried.

"That's what he did," the mother said. "And the reason she went there and waited was this. He came in here to the shop and told her he'd made a bet with some of his chums that she would meet him there, and he told her that if she didn't meet him he'd lose his week's wages and be a laughingstock besides. And, of course, without thinking twice or asking me, off she went in her best shoes and stood there for two hours. Stood there. Waiting for him. Any other girl in the world would have known what to do, but not this poor soft thing. So he won his bet and she'll never live it down. They broke their hearts laughing at her. And I'll never live it down, and poor Jimmy had his heart broken with the way they made fun of him in school. That's what she did. She did it out of softheartedness, and I know that, and I know she meant no harm, but it's not right for a girl to be so soft and so careless and to have that little respect for herself and her family. I've been meaning to tell you about this. I never intended to let her conceal it from you."

A Young Girl Can Spoil Her Chances

"There was no need for you to tell him, Mother," Rose said. She was crying quietly, with her head bent, and he wanted to reach across the table and take her hand, but he was afraid that her mother might guess that the touch of Rose's hand was already familiar to him. He was afraid of her mother.

"There was every need for me to tell him, Rose," her mother said. "And there is no need for you to cry like that. You're not a baby any more. You're talking about getting married, and you want to prove that you're sensible enough to get married. And that's why I say that you ought to think this over, both of you, a bit longer, before you make any promises. Think it over for a while. A month, or a week, maybe. Maybe it would be a good thing if you stayed away from here for a week or so, Hubert, and gave it thought. And Rose can be thinking, too."

"I'll be back in Dublin in a week," Hubert said.

Rose turned and looked at him and he looked across the table at her. He knew she wanted him to say that his mind was made up and that he would never change it. Her eyes were timid and afraid, but they met his eyes with certainty and she looked ready to smile. She was sure that he would say to her mother that his mind was made up and that the fellow who had played that trick on her deserved to be kicked, and that there was no doubt at all in his mind as to what he wanted to do and that they would go together to the priest at the first possible opportunity and arrange to be married as soon as possible. He couldn't be coming down here from Dublin all the time. And he wanted her, but Rose didn't expect him to say that out loud.

But Hubert was thinking that she was there for the taking. She would walk out of her mother's house with him, or she would stay there and wait for him. She would do whatever he said. No matter what he said or did, she would not complain against him or disagree with him. And there was time. And he wanted her mother to think him a responsible man who weighed and lived by reason and not by whim or impulse. He took his eyes from Rose and looked at her mother.

"Twenty-four hours," he said. "Either I'll come back tomorrow night or I won't. I'll sleep on it."

He looked then at Rose with a grin of complicity, but her face was not the same. It had been spoiled and blurred by astonishment and she looked stupid and cruel. She looked quickly at her mother, who regarded her with calm triumph.

"So be it," the mother said. "It's not long enough, but I can see that you know what you're doing. I was beside myself that night she went out, wondering what had become of her, and when she got back and I heard what she'd done I got onto her. I was ready to kill her. I finally asked her if there was any excuse she wanted to make for herself, and do you know what she said to me? She said, 'But, Ma,' she said, 'they would all have been laughing at him if I hadn't turned up.' Did you ever hear the like of that in your life? They would all have been laughing at *him,* and of course she couldn't have that, oh, no, they mustn't laugh at him, even though she hardly knew the fellow, except to say hello to, and so to save his face she must go and put herself in the way of being laughed at and worse—laughed at and talked about. I don't know what they didn't say about her. I had to force her out to Mass the next Sunday, and the Sunday after that. But she didn't want *him* to be laughed at. And she thought that was a good enough reason for what she did."

Stephen's Green Park is enclosed behind high iron railings and it is surrounded on all four sides by broad, busy streets. Mr. Derdon had walked along the west side of the green, keeping on the far side of the street from the park, and along the south side, past the massive-fronted city houses that had so impressed Rose when she first saw them. Now he made his way along the east side, past St. Vincent's Hospital and the college, and he found himself on the corner of Somerville Street. He stopped on the corner and gazed along the narrow, gray street, which was closed at its far end by three houses. It was in one of the houses along the side where he stood that Rose and he had had their first home. He couldn't remember the number of the house, and he was not inclined to walk along and look to see if he could remember the house when he came to it, but he knew it was one along toward the end of the row.

A friend of his, a man who had been a great friend of his at that time, had helped him to find the rooms. Frank Guiney, a very good-hearted fellow. He and Frank had been great chums, but Frank had gone to try his luck in England. Hubert wondered if Frank had ever come home again. There had never been any word from him after a couple of postcards in the weeks that followed his departure. Frank had been a great friend. The night Hubert and Rose arrived at Westland Row Station, Frank met them at the station and they all walked back to Somerville Street together, Hubert and Frank carrying the luggage and Rose carrying only a basket filled with bits of food—tea, sugar, things like that—that her mother had gone and got from the shop at the last minute before they left. There was even a bottle of milk, because the mother had said there would be no milk to compare with in Dublin. Rose hadn't wanted to take the basket of food. She had been embarrassed about carrying it, and in the train she had put her coat over it, covering the little bags and parcels it was filled with, but when they had left Westland Row and were walking along the street she carried it easily, smiling as she went along between himself and Frank. Frank complained that Hubert must have married an heiress, he had so much to carry. Frank was very funny that evening. He said the case he was carrying must be full of ornaments, it was so heavy.

"China ornaments," Frank cried. "China cats and china dogs

and great big china horses. What do you want with so many ornaments, Rose? Eh? Isn't Hubert ornament enough for you? Mind
you don't put him on the mantelpiece by mistake, now."

Rose had been all doubled up with giggling. Then when they
were along Somerville Street Rose said, "Which of the houses are
we going to live in?" And Frank gave a flourish of one of the
parcels he was carrying and nearly dropped everything with his
nonsense and he said, "The *best* house." When they came to the
house, stone steps in front and a dark-green door, scratched and
dented and with a crack in the fanlight, Frank put everything he
was carrying on the ground and stretched to rest himself before
starting the long climb to the top of the stairs.

Frank looked at Rose and he said, "She smiles and smiles and
smiles." Rose was obviously longing to go into the house and
straight up to see the rooms, but she stood obedient and pleased
while they both looked at her.

"She smiles and smiles and *smiles,*" Frank shouted, and then he
said to Hubert, "Does she never stop smiling?" And Hubert said,
"Never."

Now, as Hubert stood at the corner of Somerville Street, looking along the fronts of the houses to try to see which one might
have belonged to him and Rose, he was seeing the three of them as
they had stood there that evening, but the word in his mind was
agony. Agony agony agony was in his mind while he watched the
three figures that stood a few houses and over thirty years away
from him, and he watched until the vision dazzled and his eyes
filled with tears. He turned quickly away from Somerville Street
and continued along in the direction of the Shelbourne Hotel. Terrible the things you remember, he thought; it's a long time since I
have walked around here. It does no good to remember those times,
he thought, but at the same time he was thinking that it did no
harm to remember them. They had been blessed that evening, Rose

and himself, and Frank, too. They stood in the state of grace. And
then Frank had collected himself and his ornaments and the three
of them had marched into the house together and up the stairs with
all flags flying.

And today Rose was the same age as her mother had been on
that evening. Hubert glanced across at the park, and quickly
glanced again, with curiosity. How many years since he had been in
there? Ten, or more? He couldn't remember. He might go across
and go inside for a minute, find out if there were any changes. He
was enjoying his walk. The exercise was doing him good, but he
wished he had a newspaper to carry in one of his hands. Hands
always seemed to get in the way when they were empty. His hands
were in his pockets. He ought to have a stick, if he was going to
start walking as much as this. A stick was natural, if you were
walking. A stick or a newspaper. Anything more was a nuisance.

After John had gone away, left home, Rose had fallen into such
despair that one night he had bought a hyacinth and brought it
home to her in an attempt to distract her from herself, and he had
never felt so silly or so conspicuous in his life as he had felt walking
out of the shop and along the street with the plant between his
hands. They had wrapped it around with pink paper and folded the
paper into a high cone, making it look much bigger than it need
have looked, and much too festive. He had tried carrying it in one
hand but it wouldn't balance. He had chosen a blue hyacinth in full
bloom, and he was very anxious not to let it get bruised or broken.
He had an awkward time in the tram, with both hands on the
plant, and, as luck would have it, he had to stand the whole way
home that evening, of all evenings. By the time he got home he was
nearly angry. He had taken the pink paper off when he got into the
house, and he had put it standing in the middle of the dining-room
table where she would see it first thing when she came to the door
to call him to his tea. She had come in and he had pretended not to

notice that there was anything out of the way, and she had said, "What on earth?" and she had lifted the hyacinth off the table and put one arm around it to hold it while with her free hand she patted the spot on the table where the damp plant had been sitting all bare with no saucer under it. "Oh, Hubert," she said, "a lovely hyacinth. Isn't that a lovely color of blue. But it needs water. And I'll put it in a bigger pot. I have a big one out in the shed, the pot the poor rose geraniums died in. I'll get it out after tea. I'll have to find a good place for it, where it'll have all the sun." While she was talking, there was, in spite of the sadness that lived all over her face at that time, a little smile on her lips, a faint smile that was closed, secretive, half satisfied, you might almost say, and almost triumphant, as she talked about the hyacinth and what she would do for it. Then, of course, later on she had slipped back into the perpetual attention she paid to John's absence from their life. The fact that he had gone to serve the Church that she was so devoted to made no difference at all in her feelings, and did not console her.

Hubert wondered what had become of that blue hyacinth, whether it had flourished or withered away in the new pot she had put it in, if she had transplanted it into the garden later on, or what. He had seen hyacinths growing out in the open, he was sure of that. Perhaps that same hyacinth was in her front garden now, or in a sunny place at the back. If it was there, would it have grown bigger, and would it bloom every year, or what? He would ask her about the hyacinth tonight, just out of curiosity.

For a girl brought up in a town, Rose had an unusual interest in gardening and a great feeling for flowers. Her two gardens, the little one in the front of the house and the bigger one behind it, were always lovely. Even in the wintertime she managed to have something out there that would catch your attention. Even in the wintertime the beds had an appearance of order and form, and looked as though they were keeping to a pattern that had been devised for them, for those particular beds, and never for any other beds in any other garden. Rose had gone mad over the gardens in Stephen's Green Park. She said she had never imagined anything like the park. He had a memory of her walking there in a navy-blue skirt and a long-sleeved white blouse and no coat. It must have been a very warm day. The navy-blue skirt had a matching coat that went with it. She called this outfit her costume, and it had been her wedding dress.

The park was full of mothers and nursemaids and children that afternoon. The women sat along on the benches that lined the paths, and they talked to one another and watched the children and admired them and scolded them and called to them. The children were running all over the place. He and Rose strolled along. They were not yet used to being together.

Rose said, "I was just thinking, it's nice being married."

Hubert looked at her but she was not looking at him.

She said, "I can't see how a married person could ever commit a sin. I don't know what kind of a sin it would be that a married person could commit. There isn't a single thing I can think of that I would have to tell the priest if I went to confession this minute. Nothing is a sin any more. Isn't that funny?"

Hubert's eyes were on the path. Children's legs raced into his vision and disappeared as the small boys and girls chased one another across the path and around the benches. He dodged to avoid knocking down a very small girl in a white dress and white boots who stamped slowly and unsteadily along by herself and kept herself upright by embracing the empty air in front of her with open arms. As he stepped aside to avoid the child, Hubert saw Rose's skirt move as she walked along beside him. In the sunlight, in the navy-blue skirt, her slender hips appeared commanding and alien, and she was his, and if Hubert had been told at that moment that Helen of Troy had come back to earth and was called Rose he would not have denied it. Behind him a woman screamed, "Come back here, Paddy Mernagh, till I wring your neck!" Hubert thought of Rose and the future, and his thought was all of innocence and of the necessity of earning enough to enable them to hold their heads up and never have to give thanks to anybody for anything as long as they lived.

Hubert was approaching the corner of Grafton Street from which he had begun his walk around the square, and he thought that if he had time he might run across and take a look into the park to see what changes might have been made in there. All these years, and he had not been in there. He wondered why he had never taken John into the park when John was little. Maybe Rose had taken John in there. She might have, when they were in town to buy things. It would be a shame if John had never played there, and he was nearly certain that John never had. He wouldn't ask Rose about that. If John had never been taken to play in the park, Hubert didn't want to know of it. He was sorry now that he had made the effort to remember the exact number of years it had been since he had been in the park. It was thirty-three years since he had been in there. He had not been in there since the last Sunday he had gone there with Rose, their first Sunday in the house. It didn't seem possible that anyone could spend thirty years in Dublin without once going in and out of Stephen's Green Park, but he was a man of habit, and he always went straight home after work. Thirty-three years ago. He was twenty-eight then. He decided to cross the street at once and go into the park at the next entrance.

He paused at the curb to look up and down the street, and then he saw, at the far end of the square, a funeral approaching him on his side of the street. The hearse was drawn by two black horses that had black plumes on their heads, and he had the impression that the line of black mourning cars behind it would be a long one.

A Young Girl Can Spoil Her Chances

Hubert liked to follow the custom of paying respect to the dead by walking a few steps along with the funeral, even if it meant turning around and walking back a few steps. He had plenty of time to cross over to the park before the funeral drew alongside him, but he didn't mind the delay. He wanted to see the funeral pass and as soon as he had the chance he would look in the paper and guess which funeral it had been. The funeral was still a good distance away and he began to stroll idly toward it. He was measuring the distance between himself and the hearse, trying to guess the point where they would be abreast, and at the same time he saw, without looking, the figure of a woman who stood motionless in the gutter with her back to the street. She was there begging. He could tell that without looking at her. All his life he had denied beggars. He detested and despised them. He passed her by. The coffin was covered with rich wreaths of flowers, banked with flowers like an Easter altar. It was a coffin that spoke, even now, of the rewards of wealth and of the beauty and satisfaction of ceremony and order. Hubert turned to walk with it, and as he turned he admired it. He took one two three four steps, and five and six. Six steps were enough, and he had taken his eyes from the coffin and was about to glance discreetly into the first car of mourners when he found that his gesture of respect had brought him nearly face to face with the begging woman, and that she was looking at him and had pulled her hand out from under her shawl to take whatever he would give her. Her shawl was wrapped tightly around her shoulders and around the child she held, whose head was just visible against her shoulder, and it was the hand that supported the lower part of the child's back that was now extended to him, not in demand but expectantly, while she still kept her elbow close against the child, holding if safe. She thought he had passed her by and then changed his mind and turned back to her.

He turned his back on her and walked quickly away from her,

but not before he had seen her hand tighten and draw back to the child, and not before he had seen the look of expectancy on her face turn to a hatred so forlorn that for a moment it looked as though her face had been cut off. She thought he had done it on purpose. She thought he had turned back on purpose to disappoint her. But she must have known the funeral was passing. She had not been looking at the funeral at all. She had been looking at him and thinking of what she was going to get. She had seen him pass her and she had seen him turn back to her. She thought he would do a thing like that. She thought he was the sort of man who would do a thing like that. He thought he would turn back again, and this time quickly give her something, but shame kept him going and he walked more and more quickly away from her. A woman passing glanced at him and he realized he had been walking along muttering and rubbing his eyes, and what he had been saying was, "I wouldn't do the like of that. I wouldn't do the like of that." All the mourners must have seen him, hurrying along making faces like a lunatic. He wished he had given the woman something; it would have been easy enough, to give her something. There was no need for her to beg, there were plenty of places she could go to, where she would get help, but all the same she was pitiable standing there, and she had said nothing to him and she had not called names after him, as many others would have done in her place. But how could she think he was the kind of man who would play a trick like that? He should have explained to her that he was looking at the funeral, but she would still not have understood why he gave her nothing. To pass her by and not give her anything, all right, but to turn back to look at her and still give her nothing. It must have seemed that he was mocking her, or that he had something worse in mind. How could she have thought that of him? She held the child as if it was threatened. She had both arms around the child the way Rose used to hold John, as if there was nothing in the world but that one baby.

A Young Girl Can Spoil Her Chances

The way she held the child against her body was a reproach and a warning to everyone who came near it. Women like that were impossible to deal with. They would give themselves heart and soul to what they knew must go. There was no reasoning with them. All the mathematicians in the world could kill themselves working and those women would not even look over their shoulders to see what was happening. They would learn nothing and they would see nothing and they would care for nothing as long as they had the child. If you told them they were ignorant and reckless, risking themselves, they would not hear you. They would not be able to hear you. All the history and mathematics and architecture in the world were nothing to them alongside the history and the mathematics and the architecture of that one face. You could talk yourself black in the face and they would only wonder if it was time to change the baby. And they would be silent. You wouldn't get a direct answer out of them for love or money. You wouldn't get any kind of an answer out of them. They would not speak to tell the truth. The truth wasn't in them. You could walk away from them and leave them there and they would never call after you or say a word, but they would look at you until you remembered them and could not forget them and could not forget that they were looking after you the way that woman was looking after him now. How could she have thought he was the kind of a man who would do a thing like that?

He turned off onto a side street and made his way back to the shop by a roundabout way, and when he got there he went straightaway and washed his hands and face. Then he went to his table and began to work as best he could, but he felt there were eyes all over the place appraising him as she had appraised him and he could not stop thinking of himself and appraising himself as she had appraised him. Jack Minton came up from the workrooms to look for a bolt of gray tweed and when he was passing Hubert's table he stopped and looked at him and asked him if he was all right and if there was anything the matter. Hubert replied that everything was all right. Minton still hesitated by the table, looking down at him, but Hubert wouldn't look up and at last to make him go away Hubert said that he'd had a bit of a shock, nothing worth talking about, and he did not talk about it.

Late in the afternoon Rose came in from the garden where she had been working and sat down in her low chair near the fireplace and took a piece of gray-wool crochet from the old basket she kept always on the floor beside her. She had brought the basket from her mother's the day she was married and it had lasted as long as it had because it was too cumbersome for daily marketing and so she kept her work in it—her knitting and crocheting and the mending. She was making an afghan, square by square. As she worked, her lips moved, and every time she finished a row of stitches she lifted her head up as though she had suddenly come to a decision that had been difficult to reach but that was now pleasant to reach. From time to time she glanced appraisingly around the room and she watched the clock. The clock was mahogany and it had been a wedding present from an old friend of Hubert's, Frank Guiney, and it had a place of honor in the center of the mantelpiece. When she heard the boy leave the evening newspaper she got up and fetched the paper and sat down and began to read it, but when she heard Hubert's key in the lock she quickly closed the paper and folded it to look as though it had not been opened at all.

Hubert hung his raincoat and his hat in the hall and went up to the bedroom and changed his coat for an old three-button cardigan of tan wool. When he got down into the back sitting room Rose was sitting in her chair working on her crochet.

"I put the paper in your chair," she said.

A Young Girl Can Spoil Her Chances

"Is there anything in it?" he asked.

"No," she said doubtfully. "Oh, I don't know. Maybe there is."

He walked over to the window, where he stood looking out at her garden. It was only a patch of grass, edged with flower beds and bounded by gray cement walls that she had disguised with ivy and another creeper that had a red pointed leaf. It was just a patch, and she had spent a good part of her life trying to make it nice, and his son had spent his childhood in it, and he himself had spent all his summer holidays sitting out there in a deck chair. They never went away anywhere for a holiday because it cost money to go away, and in any case they did not like to leave the house alone.

"I'm going down to put the kettle on now," she said.

He turned and looked at her. She was getting up out of her chair. She did not get out of the chair gracefully but she got out of it easily, without helping herself with her hands, and when she stood up she stood up straight.

"Tell me something," he said. "You remember the hyacinth I brought you one time. What became of it?"

"The blue hyacinth," she said. "It did very well after I put it in the big pot. I showed it to you. It had a lovely bloom."

"And where is it now?" he asked. "Did you put it out in the garden?"

"Oh, no. Hyacinths *go*, Hubert. They only have one season. You have to get new bulbs every year."

"I'll get you another one," he said. "I'll get it for you tomorrow. I'll bring it home with me tomorrow night."

"Oh, you'd never find a hyacinth this time of the year," she said. "Only in the spring you get hyacinths, and this is September."

"Oh," he said. "I see. I forgot for a minute."

"I'm sorry, Hubert," she said.

A Young Girl Can Spoil Her Chances

He said, "It's all right."

"What put the hyacinth into your mind?" she asked.

"Nothing. I just happened to think of it," she said.

She went to the door.

"Will you light the fire for me?" she asked. "And I'll go on down." She hesitated, as though he might say no.

"I'll light it," he said. "Go on, go on, do whatever you have to do."

There was a box of wooden matches on the mantelpiece next to a framed photograph of John on the day of his ordination. Hubert avoided looking at the photograph. It was her morbid insistence on unhappiness that had caused her to put it there when she had another copy of it in a similar frame upstairs in the bedroom, and it wasn't a good likeness anyway and he intended one day to take it down and hide it. He struck a match and bent down and lighted the gas with great care and adjusted it by turning the tap slowly and pressing his lips together with the effort. Then he went to his chair and took up the newspaper and sat down. He did not open the newspaper. He sat quietly and watched the pale rose of warmth spread over the ashen grille in the grate. He sat like that until Rose called him to tea, and then he stood up out of his chair and buttoned his cardigan and pulled it down around his body and went to join her in the kitchen. As he went the words of their conversation about the hyacinth came back to him, and he smiled, thinking that in spite of the habitual apology in her voice she had been half smiling as she explained to him about the difficulty of getting spring flowers when it was not spring. Even poor Rose could not shoulder all the blame for the change in the seasons.

In the kitchen the tea was laid out on the table and Rose was standing up pouring the tea. He used to try to get her to leave the teapot on the table so that she wouldn't be jumping up and down every five minutes, but she insisted on leaving it on the stove where the tea would keep hot. He pulled out one of the old yellow chairs and sat down and in a minute she joined him, taking the chair across from him. In the middle of the meal he remembered the funeral and he told Rose about it, and she went up to the sitting room to get the newspaper to see if they could discover who it was had been buried with such pomp. While she was about it she collected the morning newspaper and the newspaper of the last three mornings in case they would have more information. She had a fairly good idea of whose funeral Hubert had seen—a wholesale grocer named Kinsella, whose father had come from Cork with nothing and built up a good business—but she didn't want to say the name aloud to Hubert until she was certain.

All the time she was going to get the papers and getting them, looking at the dates to be sure she had the right ones, and bringing them down to the kitchen, she was thinking how thoughtless Hubert was to bring up the subject of a funeral and not remember that this was the anniversary of her father's death. But she was interested herself and she stole a look at the papers while she was carrying them down and it was John Patrick Kinsella, it was his funeral Hubert had seen.

Rose left Hubert to read the full account of Mr. Kinsella's life and circumstances, which he had read earlier with less attention, because it had been in yesterday morning's news, and she herself looked idly through the back pages of the old Sunday paper, and found several items that she had missed on her first reading. When she remarked on this to Hubert he observed that she had never learned to read properly, that she was a careless reader who skipped too often and did not concentrate on what she was reading, and it was a pity because it was hard to form a good habit when you were older, and just as hard to break a bad habit once it had taken hold of you.

The Drowned Man

After his wife died, Mr. Derdon was very anxious to get into her bedroom, to have a look around on his own with the door closed and with no one there to watch him and wonder how he was feeling. It was not anxiety or grief or any painful sensation, not longing or yearning or anything like that, that drew him to the room, but curiosity. He wanted to look at it. The room, that had hardly existed for him while she was alive, and that he had seldom entered, although he had occasionally stood in the doorway or at least paused in the doorway to call something in to her on his way out of the house—the room now seemed mysterious to him the way an empty house will suddenly seem mysterious and even frightening to children who never noticed it when it was occupied, and the way a bird's nest lying empty on the ground after a summer storm will crowd the mind with thoughts that have nothing to do with wings and food and warmth and song: thoughts of vacancy, and thoughts of winter, and of winds that are too violent and nights that are too dark, and thoughts of stony solitude, endured in silence, and of landscapes that are too cold and flat and where no one cares to walk. The little nest, cast to the ground, contains an emptiness that is too big for us to understand. We cannot imagine how it must feel. It is a limitless emptiness, and beyond us, although we would like to be able to understand it, and examine it from all angles, and mark its

limits, and bring it under control, and then put it away in a comfortable place and forget about it. But the nest is nothing, no more
than a scrap. The empty nest is only a brazen image of the fear that
is so commonplace that we cannot merely walk through it every day
pretending we do not notice it but can walk through it and pretend
it is not there. As long as the nest is there empty, we look into it,
but then it is gone and we think no more about it.

As long as the door of his wife's bedroom, in which she had
died, remained closed and the room behind it empty, Mr. Derdon
thought of nothing else. The emptiness beyond the door excited
him, and he began to dream about it at night, and in his tired mind
the door was open to him, and then—mistake—it was not open to
him, and it expanded and contracted, being first a very big room
and then a very little room, but never its own size, and it developed
extra doors, strange doors that frightened him. And after these
dreams he awoke in the morning exhausted as though he suffered
nightmares, when all he had done was to dream of his wife's bedroom. His sister, his maiden sister, had come to Dublin to keep
house for him, and on the very few occasions when she went out the
woman who cleaned was there fussing around him and looking
after him. They felt he should not be left alone at this time. He
wondered what did they mean, "at this time." It was not a case of
this, that, or the other time. At the moment, it was simply *before*
Rose died and *after* Rose died, and when they said to him "at this
time," did they mean that he was never to be left a minute to himself for the rest of his life? They bothered him, always hovering
around him, and he wondered, in bewilderment, at all the freedom
he had had only a month, even ten days, ago, all the freedom he had
had and had not valued. Then, before, he had been immeasurably
free. He marveled at the freedom he had had. He wondered at it.
He had been free as a bird. Then, while Rose was alive, he could
have wandered up and down the hall in front of that closed door, if

he had wanted to. He could have walked up and down there all day long, passing up the hall, and passing back, and no questions would have been asked of him. *She* would never have thought of questioning him. He could have wandered there at will, for as long as he liked. Of course, he would probably have said something. He might have said, "I just thought I'd take a little exercise," or something like that. And then she would have said nothing. She might have smiled or nodded in that awkward way she had, as though her neck was not accustomed to little gracious gestures, as indeed it was not, but she would not have said anything. She would have gone on to do whatever she was doing and she wouldn't have asked him any questions. She might have said—there was just a chance she might have said—"Oh, exercising yourself, if that's what you want to do," meaning to sound casual and easy, and managing only to sound clumsy, like a shy child trying to be smart. But it was more than likely that she would have given him only a shamefaced smile, as though she had no right to see what he was doing at all, and gone away, off, on to whatever little job she had in hand. She would have gone and he would have been left with that silence of hers that gave him unlimited freedom, or what he knew now to be unlimited freedom, although then it had seemed to be only a burden, that burden of indefiniteness that left him always wondering what it was he had not done that he should have done, or had not said that he should have said. He never knew where he was with her. He never knew exactly what he had done or how he had spent his time, since there was no definite point where he could stop and measure what he had done, or how he had spent the time he had spent. Indefinite, now she made him indefinite to himself, and how could he mourn her, when there was hardly anything he could remember about her apart from the obvious facts that she had been gentle, quiet, uncomplaining, beautiful—or at least more or less beautiful in her youth—things like that. He literally could not remember very much about her. He began to believe that she had been invisible, but when he thought that, he felt that he might cry with fear, because how could he even think that, when *they* were there talking about his dead wife and he knew he had had a wife for more than forty years and they had had a son and the son had vanished into the priesthood, and here he was now and he could hardly remember one solitary thing about her and not really remember seeing her very much. And how could he grieve for what he could not define, or mourn for what had vanished without a trace. That was it—she had made no impression. Somehow or another, however she had done it, she had managed to live with a man, a sensitive, kindhearted man, for more than forty years without making the slightest impression on him. She had always been impossible. Several times, long ago, he had said as much to her. "You are impossible," he had said to her. And she had said *nothing*. She had said nothing and she had given him nothing, nothing to be angry about and nothing to be sad about and nothing to laugh at and nothing to wonder at and nothing at all to remember. She had given him nothing and she had left him nothing, and by leaving him nothing she had taken away from him the one thing that might have been a rock of strength to him now—that rock of grief where he might have rested in blessed isolation, not able to see or hear or speak or think with the sorrow that filled and destroyed him. But that monumental grief would now remain as it was, only a dream of grief that seemed from where he sat to be a dream of peace, because he knew that in that dreadful suffering he would find peace at last, and then he could rest himself, knowing he had done the right and proper thing, and had felt the right and proper emotions, those that represent the just tribute we must pay to death. But it was no use. He felt nothing. He could see and hear and so on, the same as usual, and he even had a little appetite for his food.

If they would only let him stand and watch her garden, he

might be able to see her there, she had spent so much time there. If
they would only let him stand at the back window and look at her
garden, and it was well worth looking at, he might be able to find
her there, and then he might be able to begin missing her—it was
the least he could do, to miss her. But he didn't miss her, he didn't
miss her at all; everything was just the same, he didn't miss her at
all, and if he tried to stand by the window looking out into her
garden, his sister or the other one would come clucking around,
trying to take him out of himself. Then, before, when he had his
freedom, he could have stood by that window forever without being
interfered with. Then, before, he could have sat all day long in his
armchair by the fire, dreaming about nothing, thinking peacefully
of nothing at all, immersed in memories so confused and so alike
that they were warmth to him; it was like thinking about warmth
to sit there like that doing nothing and remembering, really, nothing. Then, when she was alive and he didn't know the freedom he
had, he could have sat in his chair for as long as he liked, not
holding a book or a newspaper or anything, and no one would have
come up talking at him and telling him he mustn't be morbid and
that he must keep busy and interested. How could they know that
what was in his mind was morbid, when he did not really know
himself what was in his mind. They were training him as if he were
a dog, a poor unfortunate dog that had to do as he was told, and
not ask any questions, because he was a *dog* and for no other reason.
Poor dog. Poor animal. It made no sense. He had to move briskly or
they sighed. He had to talk distinctly and with some vivacity or
they gazed at him in worry and surmise. He had to take his walk
every day, not in the garden, because that was her garden and so
morbid, but out—he had to go out by the front for his walk. They
seemed to believe that there was no air at the back of the house any
more, but only in the front, beyond the front door, where the neighbors would come trotting up to him, people he only knew by sight,

and say things to him that he hardly understood and did not want to hear, although through some miracle he kept making the correct sorrowful responses to all their sorrowful platitudes. And he felt that every word he said was a lie, and when he returned to the house he returned worn out.

He would have loved to make a clean breast of things to his sister and the others. He would have liked to confess to them—he longed to confess to them—that he felt no grief. He wanted to tell the truth. He wanted them to know what a sham, what a sham he was, or at least show them that they were making him into a sham. But if he told them the truth they would think him a monster, and he would rather know he was a sham than be thought a monster. He was a man who could feel no grief, an empty man. Even so, he would have liked to be let do as he liked, but he hesitated to hurt their feelings. There were plenty of sharp remarks that came into his head, but he did not want to say them unless he was really pushed to the wall. He knew the women meant well. He could tell them to go, of course. They would protest, but they would go, and then he would be alone and then he could be quiet. If he ordered them out, and they saw he meant business, they would have to go. But he could not do that, when they meant so well, and then, it was something to keep in mind, that he could be rid of them in a minute, any minute. It was something to look forward to, the minute when he would order them out once and for all, and he did look forward to it. Once he made up his mind, they would go, and no ifs or buts. Once his mind was made up he would take no nonsense from them, but for the time being he let them have their way in the house and he did what they told him to do and he would go on doing as he was told for as long as it suited him and not one minute longer. But it was good to look forward to, the moment when he would turn them out. He would let them have their way, he would let them have their head, they would imagine themselves entrenched, and suddenly, all of a sudden, he would turn on them and show them who was master. The moment would come. He was sure of that. They would drive him too far. He was sure of that. He would turn when they least expected it, and he would blast them. He would send them packing. He had to smile, thinking of the surprise on their faces, and his sister caught him smiling, and he caught her catching him, with that sympathetic expression on her that meant she imagined he was thinking kind sweet gentle happy thoughts about his dearest departed, and he was so annoyed he could have hit her, and he turned down the corners of his mouth and began to look gloomy again.

They thought it was a sign of grief that he had ordered them to leave Rose's room as it was, but it was not a sign of grief at all. It had been an impulse that had made him tell them to shut that door and leave it shut. He had simply wanted to assert himself and to give a reasonable order and be obeyed, and they had obeyed him, but it had not been an important matter until all of a sudden, in some mysterious way, the closed door had become extremely important.

He thought that once he got into that empty room by himself with the door closed, he would be able to think more clearly and to know something that he did not now know. Once in there, he might be able to remember more of her than—as she was now in his mind—something humble and busy about the house. Once in there, he might be able to find more to think of than that eternal acquiescence. Even the very last word she had said to him was, "Yes." There was nothing strange about that, she had always said yes, but unbroken acquiescence had not been indefinite enough for her; she had always, until that last yes, had to qualify even her yes—"Yes, all right," "Yes, if you want to," "Yes, I don't mind, if you like. If you want to, I suppose so, yes." But that final "Yes," when he asked her should he send for the doctor, stood alone in his mind. He could hear her voice now, saying "Yes," and he recalled that even as troubled as he had been he felt surprised, and maybe even pleased, that she was definite. It had been as though he heard her voice once again after a very long time, when she said "Yes" like that to him.

As he looked forward to the day when he would order his sister and the other woman to leave his house, now he looked forward to the opportunity to slip into the empty room and be alone there, but without anybody knowing he was there. He waited for the chance when they would both be out of the house together. He schemed. He played up to them. He did not sit dreaming in his chair by the fire, but held his book in front of him and read it with attention. He asked them to bring him the evening paper, as though he was interested in what was in it. He did not look out of the back window into her garden. He ate what was put in front of him, and even suggested that if they both thought hard, and put all their brains together, they might be able to remember that he liked his eggs just lightly boiled, and that he liked them hot, because cold boiled eggs were bad for people, especially first thing in the morning. He grew bolder. He told them that when the conventional period of mourning was past they would all get dressed in their best clothes and go into town in a taxi and see a play or something. At that, they looked at him in astonishment, and then they turned their faces away, like disappointed cats who see that their prey has ceased to move and who hope that by pretending to remove their attention from it they will trick it into life again, and into movement again, and so find it still within their power. Mr. Derdon's sister and the lady who cleaned looked away, startled, and then they looked back again, but he knew their ways and he was still smiling. "We're not doing poor Rose any good, sitting around here with long faces," he said.

A couple of days after that, or it might even have been the very next day, through some miracle that was carefully explained to him, while he pretended to listen, he found himself alone in the house in the afternoon. He hesitated a short time before opening the door of Rose's room. He walked up and down the hall awhile as he had longed to do, and he thought about going into the room. He did not want to go blundering in. After all, once he had gone in, the emptiness that had been increasing in there since her death would be destroyed forever, and he was anxious to catch some impression of it while it still lingered. He walked up and down a few times, thinking intently and rubbing his hands together, and then without thinking any more about it he turned the knob and opened the door and went in and closed the door behind him. There was nothing. There was not even a perceptible emptiness. It was her room, or it had been her room, but she was not in it any more. The room said nothing. The emptiness, what emptiness he felt there, was not particular, and he could not pretend to himself that he could identify it as a special and individual emptiness that she had left and that she and she alone could have left. It was a general emptiness that filled her place—he might as well have been looking into a fallen nest to try to discover the nature of what was not. He grew tired trying to press himself into what was not there and therefore could not or would not resist him. There was no resistance in the room. There was nothing he could pit himself against. He felt let down, as he had when he was a child and Christmas was over, and at the same time he felt keyed up, as though he was going to have to face an examination, *take* an examination that he had not been warned about, that he had never known people had to take, that he was not prepared for and could not prepare for, since he had no idea of the nature of the questions that would be asked him or of the tests he might be called upon to perform. He had always felt uneasily that there was something other people knew, something everybody knew and took for granted, but that he did not know. He had sometimes hoped that he might come upon this bit of common knowledge, by luck, as he might come upon a touchstone that would guide him to the secret whose existence he felt, the secret that others had and that remained closed to him. What he had thought out loud in his own mind always was, "There must be more than this to life, there must be more to life than this." Oh, indeed indeed, yes, there must be more than this to it all, he used to think, and then, at such incredulous moments, he used to look into the faces of the people who passed him in the street, to try to read in their faces what he was sure they must know that kept them going every day—because it was not everybody that had his strength, and it was not everybody —there was hardly anybody who could have the fortitude to keep on going day in day out in the bewilderment in which he himself lived. It was not possible that others could go from day to day, as he did, for no real reason, or that others could put up the brave front that he put up, the brave, respectable front that was a front for nothing, and nothing but a front. At such moments, when he felt that he must make one more attempt to discover the secret, he used to glance, just glance, into Rose's face when he felt she would not notice him looking at her. He remembered that at such times, on those evenings, he used to hang his hat and coat in the hall as usual, and put his umbrella in the stand, and walk down the hall to where she sat, and he would sit down opposite to her and open his evening paper, but at such times he would use the evening paper only to camouflage himself as a reader while he watched her, not as a husband, not even as a man, but as a supplicant who hoped she might be able to tell him what had kept them together all these years, or what kept any two people together, or what kept people going and doing as they had been told they ought to do. When had all this obedience begun and who had marked out the appointed way where men and women walked without protest and most of the time without complaining? Most important of all, what reason had been given that guaranteed this obedience and why had the reason not been given to him as well as to everybody else? There was a common secret that he had not been allowed to share, and now it seemed that grief must also remain a secret to him, because even now, sitting in the room in which she had spent a good part of her time, and in which she had slept in her bed, he felt no grief. He was sitting on the straight chair she had kept handy to her sewing machine. The sewing machine was closed and made a flat smooth surface that was faintly marked by whitened circles, where she had kept some of her plants when the machine was not in use. She could have got herself a little plant table. He would not have minded the expense. He would have given her the money for a table, if she had asked him for it, but she had not asked. She had preferred to play the martyr and so, contemptuously and in despair of ever coming to any terms with her, he had ignored her or, as you might put it, let her have her way. She had preferred to clear the top of her chest of drawers when she wanted to do any sewing on the machine. Then to the top of the chest of drawers she would lift the plants, some of them big and heavy, and when they were all safely arranged she would open the sewing machine and go to work, bending very close to it. And with the work finished, she would go through the whole laborious process of transferring the plants back to the machine again. The machine was a makeshift plant table for her, as much in her life had been makeshift. Take, for example, that arrangement of old chocolate boxes on the blanket chest under the shelf where she had kept her few books. You would think, to see those chocolate boxes, and to note the careful order in which they were arranged, by size and also by shape, a rectangular one set straight and centered on top of a larger rectangle, the square ones built up like child's blocks on top of the squares, and the two long equal ones set apart from the rest, completing the design of even lines and sharp angles, all of it speaking of neatness and care and of an overpowering concern with order—you would think, looking at such an arrangement, that the boxes contained something of interest or of value. And what did they contain? Old bills marked paid thirty years before. Receipts for dinners she had never cooked, dinners so elaborate that she must have been dreaming of a visit from the king and queen of England when she cut the menus out of the magazines in which she had found them. Directions for making dresses that she would never in her life have had occasion to wear—there was a whole pamphlet that gave instructions, measurements, etc., for the construction of a satin ball gown. It would have been laughable if it was not so pathetic. One box contained cards of tailors' samples—bits of tweed, bits of serge, bits of velvet, bits of suiting and coat materials. He knew how she had come by those cards. She had never told him, but he had known her so well that he knew very well how she had come by those cards. He could see her now, standing in front of the tailor's window, one tailor one time, another tailor another time, admiring the bolts of cloth in the window and the pictures displayed of suits and coats, and imagining to herself that she would order something, a costume, as she would have called it, and making up her mind how she would like it made and out of what material. He could see her making up her mind, and opening the door of the shop, and going inside with that timid air of consequence that she affected in public and that had nearly driven him mad with irritation. And he could see her approaching the tailor, and speaking in the accents of a lady who may or may not bestow her custom here, and discussing with the tailor the cut and style of this coat or skirt or whatever it was she imagined she was going to buy for herself. And he could see her, in all her seriousness, taking the card of samples from the tailor and bringing it home and sitting down by herself in the afternoon to dream over it, carrying it to the window so that she could look at the scraps of fabric in a better light, and only lifting her eyes from it to look at the flowers in her garden, and all the time dreaming,

dreaming, dreaming, always dreaming, and what was it that she had dreamed about, all her life? She had never said. She had never even admitted how she dreamed her time away. If you had asked her what she was "thinking" about, she would have said, "Oh, nothing," and then quickly turned her hands to something to divert attention from herself. Or she might have replied, in answer to any question at all, "There is a bad scratch on the linoleum near the door there. I was wondering what I could do to cover it." She was all indirection.

The contents of the chocolate boxes revealed a mind given over entirely to trivialities and makeshift, always makeshift, making do, making last, putting to use somehow, wasting nothing except her time and her life and his time and his life. Even so, those times when he watched her secretly, he had had hopes that she possessed and would reveal to him the common secret that had been given to everybody except him. She had been weak, and it was simply impossible that she had lived along like that unless she was held by something, some truth, or some belief, some magic word, some comfort that she might have shared with him, if she had been willing to speak and able to speak. But the times grew rarer when he was able to watch her, because as he grew older he grew less and less able to bear the uneasiness that trembled all over her face when she felt his eyes on her. She would be sitting there knitting or sewing or mending or looking through one of the household magazines she loved, her face all intent on what was in her hands, and in the space of an instant she would become aware that he was looking at her, and the change in her expression would be terrible to see. Her face would become destroyed with shame and apprehension. And what it all amounted to, the beginning and the end of it, was that she was afraid of him. Once long ago he had been driven to challenge her. "Am I a monster or something?" he had shouted at her. "What's the matter with you? What's wrong with you? Why are you afraid to look at me? Am I a monster?" But she had trembled so violently that he had left her alone. She was afraid of questions. He left her alone. But it was no use going over all that again, no use thinking about it, better to put it out of his mind.

Still, he could not believe that even a human being as ineffectual as she had been could vanish from life without leaving any trace of herself at all. Any trace would be a sign that might guide him to the grief he wanted to suffer for her. But there was no sign.

He got up from the chair and went and stood by her bed. It was narrow. He stood there as he had stood on her last morning. Of course, looking at her that morning, he had had no idea how bad she was. He had gone into her room when she had not turned up as usual at nine o'clock sharp with his breakfast tray, which he liked to have in his own room, by himself. He went into her room in his dressing gown and slippers, and she was lying there in bed doing nothing, not even looking, although her eyes were open, and he was so surprised to see her, it had been so long since he had seen her lying in bed, that he said, "What are you doing in bed, Rose?" And she said, "Nothing." Her voice had been perfectly normal. He started to make some little joke that would lead him around to reminding her of the breakfast tray, when she said, in the same perfectly normal voice, "I have a terrible pain in my chest." And the minute she had said those words he felt the pain in his own chest, but with him it was not new but too familiar. He had often told her that pain was familiar to him, and here it was now again, his message from that treacherous old heart of his that was going to be the death of him someday, and he put his hand up to his own chest and said, "Will I call the doctor? He can have a look at me too as long as he's here." But Rose had not answered him. Instead, she began looking at him, and her eyes that he had always considered frightened and not direct, even furtive, preoccupied and worried—

those shaded green eyes suddenly seemed to belong to her, as though she had taken command of them for the first time, and was asserting her right to see for herself, and to look, and not to look at just anything but to look at everything, and then to choose what she really wanted; not that she would not see all the rest, but that she would look at and possess what responded to her, and if what responded was joy she would look at joy, and if what responded was pain, then she would look at pain, and if what responded was cruelty she would look at cruelty, until cruelty, like pain and joy, turned again and turned again and turned at last to show her what she had chosen to see in the first place, a face that was disposed to smile on her, eyes that seemed to recognize her, a heart that was inclined to value her, and hands that knew her but that wanted her just the same, just as she was, whatever she was.

She had lain there looking at him like that, and still she had not answered his question, and he said again, still stroking his dressing gown over his heart to signify his pain, "Will I call the doctor then, or not? I think I'll call him anyway, for myself. Do you want me to call him?" And Rose had said, "Yes." "Yes," she said, and the one word came out quickly, like a sigh or a laugh, like a sound of recognition and acceptance and mockery. "Yes," she said, but only once, as though she was finally giving in to something and accepting something that she had not wanted to give in to or accept yet.

He had gone then and called the doctor, and he had sat down in the sitting room to wait, and he had wished there was someone to bring him a cup of tea, and of course, when the doctor arrived and went into the room, all there was left to say was that it was over for Rose.

Now, Mr. Derdon thought, there was no use staying in that room any longer. There was nothing to be found there. He opened the door and went out into the hall and he left the door open behind him. His sister and the woman who cleaned could go in there now and do what they liked in the way of tidying up and sorting out her clothes and the rest of it. He didn't care what they did. He went into the kitchen and looked around, and then he left the kitchen and stood in the hall a minute, and then he went into the sitting room and sat down in his chair by the fire. He was too tired to read, and too tired to think, but he could not stop himself thinking. It was all a mystery, where their life together had gone, or why they had come together in the first place. He remembered the night he asked her to marry him. They were standing together on a small stone bridge that overlooked a river outside the town where she lived. He had not intended to ask her that night—he had meant to keep her wondering a little longer, not to let her get too sure of herself—but all of a sudden he turned to her and said, "I thought we might get married." She continued looking down into the flowing water and she did not answer him. He said, "I was wondering if you had thought of me at all." Still she said nothing and had not raised her head. Then he said, "Rose, please, for God's sake, will you marry me?" And she raised her head and looked at him—her eyes were still clear in those days—and she said, "Yes," and that was all she said. "Yes," she had said, in a voice that was definite and that at the same time seemed to have been forced out of her, as though she had wanted to say yes, and expected to say yes, but at the same time would have liked to put off saying yes for just a little while longer, just a little while. Her face, turned up to him that night, had been the face of one who finds herself fallen into the middle of a deep lake, and who does not know how to swim, but would rather hope for help than scream for it. "It was careless of me to fall into this deep water," her face seemed to say, "and I am all to blame for not having learned to swim, but even though I was stupid, not learning to swim, and even though the water is deep, I do not want to drown." And he had put his arms around her and told her he would always take care of her. Sitting by the fire now, thinking of that night, he found he could see her face quite clearly, as she had looked then. He could see her face, and in her face all the promises that her face had shown him, the promises that had not been fulfilled. Her walk, her step, had been brave and free and definite, and it occurred to him now, as it had before, that he had fallen in love with her for the exact qualities that were not hers at all. It was not Rose's fault that he had been mistaken in her. She had shone at a distance, but close to she had ceased to shine. Still, she was gone, she had been good, and he wished he could miss her.

When his sister returned home and found the door of Rose's room standing open, she hurried into the sitting room and confronted Mr. Derdon where he sat before the fire.

"I see the door of the room is open," she said.

"I thought it had been closed long enough," he said. "We can't make a shrine out of her room."

"Did you go into the room?" she asked.

"Yes," he said. "I went in there."

He looked up at her.

"There's nothing in there," he said, and he put his hands up in front of his face and started to cry. His sister started to cry, too, and she went out of the room and was back in a minute with a cup of tea for him. He refused the tea, and when she suggested calling the doctor he refused to see the doctor. He would not take his hands from his face and he would not get up and go into his bedroom and lie down and he would not do anything except cry. The tears hurt him. They hurt his chest and his eyes and they seemed to be tracing sticky wooden lines all over his face and neck and they hurt his brain and made it ache. The tears did not run down his face and away. They poured all over him and stayed on him and encased him, and when he tried to stop crying, because he was afraid he might smother in them, imprisoned in them, they poured out all the more and there seemed to be no end to them. The tears had him in a strait jacket, and he could not speak. Now that he could not speak, he wished he could speak, because he longed now to tell his sister the truth and have the matter cleared up once and for all. The tears hurt him and covered him with a pain that seemed to grow more unbearable every minute, but what hurt most of all was his inability to tell his sister that he was not crying for Rose, because he really and truly felt no grief for Rose, but that he was crying for the lack of grief, because surely poor Rose had deserved more than a casual dismissal from life, and that most of all he was crying simply and solely because he was sad. He was sad and he was crying, and that is all there was to it. But he could not speak to tell his sister that, and she continued to watch him, helpless with tears herself and murmuring about how happy Rose was in Heaven, and he could not speak to her to tell her that it was all only a masquerade and that he was only a sham of a man, and after a long time, when he finally got command of himself, it no longer seemed worthwhile to tell her, and the way it worked out he never told her, and never told anybody.

A Free Choice

Rose stood waiting for the dance, a waltz, to end. She felt ill at ease, being stranded like this without a partner. She wondered why Hubert Derdon had not come in search of her, to ask her for a dance, or to ask her if she would like to go into the dining room and find something to eat. A lot of them were in there in the dining room, she knew, but she did not want to go in there alone. She would rather have been sitting down, more out of sight, but there were no chairs along the sides of the room but only at the ends. Mrs. Ramsay's drawing room, cleared for dancing, seemed enormous, and from where Rose stood the ends of the room seemed not only far away but impassable, with sofas and chairs crowded together and people sitting there together, people who knew each other well but who did not know her very well, and she was younger than any of them and anxious not to appear to push herself upon them. Her mother had warned her not to be forward. It was only an accident that she was at the party at all. Father Kane had arranged for her to be there. The party was being given for the people who worked at Ramsay's shop, where Rose's father had worked before his death. Father Kane was very good. He had even arranged for Rose to get a ride in the car that brought a crowd of the girls from Ramsay's.

Rose thought the room was lovely. She was standing in front of long sweeping curtains of blue velvet. The blue of the curtains put the blue of her dress in the shade, and her dress was velvet, too. Rose felt that the dress she had made for herself, that had seemed so grand at home, could never compete with the splendor of the curtains, and since she was not competing with the curtains, she felt that they protected her, falling from the top of the tall windows to the floor behind her as they might well have fallen in front of her. She had been looking forward to seeing this room, which was famous in the town, although not many people had had the privilege of visiting the house and seeing it for themselves. She recognized the velvet curtains the minute she walked into the room, and she turned at once to speak to Hubert Derdon about them, but just as she turned, Mr. Lord, who had been a very old friend of her father's, came up and asked her for a dance, and she danced off with him, feeling very nervous and shy, and when the dance was over, Hubert had disappeared, and she had not had the chance since to speak to him and tell him what she knew about the curtains.

She had first glimpsed the curtains as she walked through the front door into the big hall outside, and she had been astonished, as though she had caught a glimpse of an old friend from long ago, someone she had worshipped and had never dreamed of seeing again. There were the curtains her father had told her about, and they were exactly as he had told her they would be. And he had never seen them finished. During the months before his death Rose's life had been full of talk about velvet, and he had brought home bits of velvet to show her—rose velvet and red velvet, several different colors of green velvet, a yellow velvet that was called amber but that he said was old gold, mouse-colored velvet and orange velvet and blue, his favorite color, every shade of it. Many of the other men and women who had been working in Ramsay's a long time had been delegated to do this or that job in connection with the decoration of Mrs. Ramsay's house, and to Rose's father she had given the task of finding the velvet for the curtains. He had to find the right weight of velvet and the right color to go with the wallpaper, which had been chosen from an English firm that supplied the best houses in London, Mrs. Ramsay had told Rose's father. He brought a scrap of the paper home to show to Rose, and the samples of velvet that he had collected, and they went over them together every evening, and in the morning he took them back to the shop. He wasn't able to bring all the samples to show to Rose—there were some, made in Italy, that he dared not risk losing—but those he could not bring home he described to her. He said that Rose had a very unusual sense of color, and he was proud when, after he had the samples all arranged on the kitchen table, she put her finger on the colors she favored, and they were always the colors he favored, too.

She was only nine then, and now she was nearly twenty, and there were the curtains, as new-looking now, she was sure, as the day they had been put up. Mrs. Ramsay had been inclined to pick a blue red but Rose's father had had his heart set on a real blue, and he had brought Mrs. Ramsay around to his way of thinking. He was very proud of his victory. He and Rose rejoiced over it. He promised Rose that when the curtains were put up he would some- how get Rose into the house to see them. He wanted Rose to see the big dining room, too, and the big wide front hall that had a fire- place in it. He had not been upstairs, but he told Rose he could imagine the rooms up there—how nice they must be, all fully fur- nished.

He had seen a glass dressing table go up the stairs—Mrs. Ram- say's new dressing table. He said to Rose, "I never saw the like of it. I think she must have gone to fairyland to find it. It was in a big wooden box out on the lawn in front of the house and the two men who had brought it began to take it out of its box. They walked all around the box, looking at it and tapping it before they found the right place where they would begin to open it. They didn't take the top off the box and lift the table out, they took the box away from the table a bit at a time. First they took the top off and laid it on the grass and then they pried the sides off and the way they worked at it you'd think they were afraid of it. Then the table was out in the open and they cut away the paper it was wrapped in and you should have seen it there, all glass with the sun shining down on it. She has an arch there over the path, covered with roses, and the table caught the roses and made the most of them. A looking-glass table, that's what it is. Mrs. Ramsay will be able to see all around herself but I wish you could have seen the way the roses looked in it. It sparkled in the sun and all the roses sparkled. It made a fairyland out of the garden. I felt that I was dreaming. I looked up. The sky was blue. It was a lovely day. Rose, you should have been there. I was standing in the drawing room, no curtains on the windows and no carpet on the floor yet, all bare, but I like the wood under my feet, the bare wood—the floors are lovely in that house—and I was looking through the window at the table standing there in the sun and I was thinking about you and making wishes for you. I was wishing . . . I don't know what I didn't wish for. Then they picked the table up and began carrying it into the house. They set it down for a minute in the hall and it looked as if the sun was still shining on it. Then they began carrying it up the stairs. They watched each other's feet and they never spoke a word all the time they were going up the stairs and they went very slowly, one step at a time. The table tilted a bit and I could see myself in it, all different ways. There is a prism in the Protestant Library—I will take you there to see it. I won't tell you what it is—it is called a prism, prism—and then you won't know what to expect and you will be surprised. And Mrs. Ramsay has a big diamond that she wears on her marriage finger. There are a lot of things that catch the light. I watched myself all the way up the stairs. That is a very big enormous square hall she has there, with as many windows in it as if it was a room, but I was standing as quiet as if the table depended on me as much as on the two that were carrying it and I began to feel as if I was at the bottom of a well watching myself go away from myself. I was standing there looking up. It is very funny to see yourself looking up the stairs. I suppose that is the way we appear to God—always looking up when we want something. Then they got up on the landing and the table went away out of my sight. I suppose I won't see it again."

The curtains comforted Rose because, although she had not remembered them all these years, she recognized them the minute she saw them. All these years they had been here, looking just as he had imagined them and as he had described them. The curtains had been here, looking like this, on the day she had not come with her father—on all the days she had not come here with him, or gone anywhere with him, days and weeks and months that had followed him into eternity. She began to believe that she had been remembered at some time far back, at some moment when she had thought herself down and out and forgotten and derided. It had all been only in her imagination, that she had been forgotten. She had not been forgotten at all. She felt she had as much right in the room as any of the others who were dancing around and talking together in little familiar groups. Even though she had no job at Ramsay's—they were hiring very up-and-coming girls there now, one or two even from Dublin—she had been in on the plans for this room, she had known as much about it as anybody, long ago; before the wallpaper was on the walls, she had known about this room, the furniture that was waiting to go into it and the carpets that had been bought for it. The two little marble-topped tables near the fireplace there—she remembered them now, although she had never seen them before. And the big sofa was against the end wall, under the landscape picture from France, as he had told her it would be. It was all as he had told her it would be. They had rejoiced together over the beautiful room that was growing in their minds. There were two small white plaster portraits on the wall, one on each side of the door that led into the dining room, and he had never been able to remember the names of the people they represented. He called them "masks." Rose looked at them now, and thought them very dull, very religious-looking, very out of place in this brilliant rich room. She thought of her father looking at them and wondering who they were. He could have asked, but everybody seemed to know, and he had not wanted to appear less well informed than the rest of them.

He had been very pleased that Mrs. Ramsay had called him in on the planning of the house, and that she had trusted him to find the right stuff for the curtains. She had asked his advice on other matters connected with the decorating and painting, and even on the placing of the pictures. He told Rose that this extra work provided him with a great chance, the first real chance he had ever had, and that it might mean great things for him. He and Rose both knew that he was fitted for something better than unrolling and rolling bolts of linen and cotton and serge over the counter all day long. He told Rose that miracles would never cease, because it was just at the moment when he was feeling himself to be of no importance to anybody at all in the world that Mrs. Ramsay had sent for him and started to talk to him about the way she wanted her new house to be.

It got on her mother's nerves, the way they covered the kitchen table with scraps of velvet every evening and sat there together going over the scraps as though they were counting gold and diamonds. Her mother said it was getting to be too much of a good thing and that it was bad for Rose to sit there dreaming over things she could never have. Rose and her father were like two misers sitting at the table over their treasure while her mother stood and confronted them. At that time of the evening, after tea, Rose and her father generally had the kitchen to themselves. They had a small

A Free Choice

shop in what had once been a front sitting room, and Rose's mother went in there after tea and sat there talking with anyone who cared to drop in and occasionally selling something—bread or cigarettes. She became more and more annoyed about the samples as the weeks wore on and still the color of the curtains had not been settled on by Mrs. Ramsay and still Rose's father talked about them and about what Mrs. Ramsay had said to him.

"Mrs. Ramsay is making a fool of you and picking your brains for nothing," Rose's mother said. "And you are making a fool out of the child, giving her notions about herself and what she knows. What does that child know and what good would it do her if she did know anything? What chance has she got, and why can't you leave her alone and let her learn her lessons? She has a bag of homework there, hasn't she? She won't thank you later on in life. Giving her ideas is all you are doing."

When she spoke like that, Rose's father used to take his hands off the table and put them in his lap and stare down at them and say nothing. When she left them and went back to the shop he always sighed, but he did not look at Rose, and then he always said, without raising his head, "No use provoking her. Let her have her say. She means no harm."

Rose looked at the masks, and pretended to be so interested in them, far away as they were, that she could not look into the faces of any of the dancers as they went by. She felt that she had been stranded there in front of everybody. She blamed Jim Nolan, who had been her partner in the last dance. He had given her to understand that he would be back, and so she had waited for him and he had not come back at all. At first she imagined he had been delayed but now she realized he had never had the slightest intention of coming back. If she had only known, she could have found her way out of the room and then she would not be standing here making a show of herself. It was not fair. There was a chance he might have been annoyed at what she said to him, but he had not seemed annoyed, and he must have known she meant no harm.

She had been delighted when Jim asked her for a dance. He had worked at the same counter with her father years ago, but he was not more than ten years older than she was, and he was very handsome and tall. The other men who had asked her to dance were quite old men, all of them married and old enough to be her father. She was surprised that Jim took any notice at all of her, because he was popular and she knew that every girl in the room was watching him. He had a lovely friendly smile. She had always seen him, all her life, in Ramsay's, and around the town, walking with somebody, usually a man; he was great with the girls but the women laughed when his name came up and said he would be hard to catch. He was different from the other men, very dark; there was something foreign about him, like an actor.

Before dancing with Jim, Rose had believed that she was having a lovely time at the party. All of her father's old friends had come one by one to ask her for a dance and one time there were two men competing for her hand—Mr. Cleary, who was fat and nearly bald, and Mr. Fagan, who was thin and always smiling—and they asked her to choose between them, and she could not, and they all stood there laughing and she felt very much at home. Mrs. Cleary came up to them and took Rose's hand and asked her how had she learned to be such a good dancer, and she told them about the way her father used to always dance her around and make her keep time, and Mr. Cleary said, "Your father was a great dancer. I can see him now." And Mr. Fagan said, "When he danced, he was enjoying himself. You could see that." Then Mrs. Cleary squeezed Rose's hand and said she was a good girl and that it was a pity her mother hadn't come tonight, to see how popular she was.

But when Jim asked her to dance—from the moment when he

appeared before her to her astonishment—she remained in astonishment. The brilliance of that moment when she had first looked into his face and said she was free remained around them, and made them both free from the rest of the people in the room so that she understood at once that it was not the velvet curtains or the masks that had made the room familiar to her but the impression that remained on it of her father's hand. Somehow, however he had done it, her father had managed to make the room ready for this moment when she and Jim would dance together. Her father had loved her. This room could never have been his. And as it was now, he had only dreamed it. He had never seen it at all, but he had known how it was going to be.

She looked up at Jim and told him it was her first big party. He said nothing, but he smiled down into her eyes as though he knew what it was she really meant to say. How could Jim know what she really meant to say, when she did not know it herself? She was filled with gratitude, and with the assurance that whatever she said next did not matter very much, because she was saying it to him, and he would not mind what she said, because it was Rose who was speaking. "I am afraid I am not a very good dancer," she said. The truth was that she felt she was dancing quite well—splendidly, in fact, although she was a little worried for fear she might not be able to stop gracefully at the end. But Jim continued to smile at her and seemed to hold her more closely to him, and he told her she was much lighter than a feather, lighter than a swan's feather, lighter even than a thrush's feather. Then he began laughing and he asked her if she had ever danced with a feather bed, and without giving her time to say no he told her to look over her shoulder and she found herself staring straight at Mrs. Fleming, who was in charge of the hat counter, and whose extravagantly towering hair arrangement was designed to draw attention away from her fatness, which was alarming, seeming to flow solidly not down to the floor but away from her and around in all directions, as though she grew larger while you watched. But Mrs. Fleming had been on the floor all evening. She had not missed a step, dancing around like a young girl with all the younger men, smiling brightly on everyone, like an empress.

Now when Rose found that Jim was inviting her to laugh with him at Mrs. Fleming she was exhilarated, as though she had won a great trophy she had not known existed. She felt that her new dress was as good as any dress in the room, and that she was a natural dancer and could dance with anyone. There was no doubt about it, people would say that she and Jim were meant for each other. He had only been acting with all those other girls. He had only been playing for time. He had not been himself, and it was perfectly possible that he had never been himself all his life until this moment. She would be a very good influence in his life. He would see that her heart was true and that she was not like the other girls, who were only out for a husband.

It was clear to her, as she laughed up at him, that all the stories she had heard about him were lies, or at least that he was misunderstood by those who envied him. He was not wild and a flirt and a drinker and a loud talker, as people said—he was not any of those things, he was something else entirely, and she wanted to confide her understanding to him and to show him that he could trust her, but he was making it obvious that he could trust her, and they were dancing too fast for conversation, so she contented herself with saying to him, boldly, that she thought he was a funny man. He looked at her sharply and he looked very pleased, so that for a moment she thought he was going to stop right there on the floor, and he squeezed her hand tightly—that is why she thought they had stopped dancing—and he said, "You're going to have some explaining to do, young lady. You're going to have to explain that remark."

And then they seemed to dance faster than ever, and when the dance ended he swung her around in a half circle so that for the moment she lost her balance, and when she righted herself she laughed very loudly, taking it all in her stride, as though she were accustomed to occasions like this and to the world, and some of the older women nearby turned and glanced at her and then at Jim, and looked away. She knew they thought she was making a show of herself but she did not care. She turned smiling to Jim, thinking he would take her arm and lead her off to sit down where they could have their talk, but instead he smiled affectionately at her and thanked her and walked quickly away. He would be back, she knew, and she began to wait for him. Mr. Lord, with whom she had had the first dance, came up and asked her to be his partner again now, but she told him she was engaged and he smiled and said, "Oh, so that's the way it is, is it?" and went away.

That was the moment, if she had only known it, when she could have made her way out of the room and to a place where she would not have been so conspicuous. But how could she go, when there was a chance that Jim might come back? And now she had been standing here for a long while, hardly noticing the time, and she would have to go on standing until the dance was over. If she walked in one direction, to the dining room, and made her way through the crowd of people gathered at the end of the room, all of them talking together, sitting and standing, all familiar together, she might find Hubert Derdon among them and he would imagine she had come looking for him. And then again, in the opposite direction, toward the hall and the stairs that led up to the ladies' cloakroom, she might find him in that crowd there at the end of the room or in the hall itself, and she did not want to find him.

Not for one minute would she want Hubert Derdon to think she, Rose, would try to find him or that she would ask him for anything or expect anything from him. Only last night he had asked her if he might see her home from this party. She had been very pleased. That was only last night. She had thought of him all day and of the way he had looked at her when he turned at her door and spoke about the party. And here she was, and except for that one minute when she had seen him in the hall, just after she arrived with the other girls, he had not spoken to her. It was a shame. She had imagined herself walking around here with him, and that everyone would see them together. She could have told him about the velvet curtains and all the rest. There was a lot to tell him that she had imagined he would like to hear. She and Hubert had never been alone together. Her mother had always come in and sat in the kitchen with them when he came to visit, and then her mother had done nearly all the talking, with Hubert occasionally making a sharp remark. That was one of the things Rose had against him—his tongue was too sharp. He was too sure of himself. But he was very nice, or at least he had seemed to be nice until tonight.

Perhaps Hubert had found one of those smart girls from Ramsay's; Father Kane would have introduced him around. This was Hubert's first visit to Wexford. He had come down from Dublin on a holiday with a nephew of Father Kane's, and Father Kane had been taking the two of them, Hubert and the nephew, all around everywhere in his car and showing them all the sights. But Hubert was a quiet sort, and he liked to walk by himself and to look around by himself, and one afternoon, walking like that, he had come into the shop and Rose had been behind the counter and so they had met each other, and for the last week he had been dropping in for an hour or so every evening. He was a stranger still, and it was clear now that he would always be a stranger. There was no use hoping for anything from anybody. She wondered if by chance Father Kane had said anything against her. Father Kane might have said that she was not quite good enough or something like that.

A Free Choice

Father Kane was fond of her and he had arranged for her to come to this party, but perhaps he had his doubts about her. There was no way of telling. And Hubert might have changed his mind about seeing her home. Perhaps Hubert was reluctant to be seen in public with her. And there was always the chance Jim Nolan might ask to see her home, and if he did, she wanted to be free to go with him. Hubert was a stranger and he would be going away soon and she could never feel as much at home with someone like him as she could with someone like Jim Nolan. She wished she was whirling around the floor with him again, being told that she was as light as a feather and that she was going to have to explain herself because she was so interesting. She should have offered to go with him when he walked away from her. It was what any of the other girls would have done.

She wondered where the music was coming from. She knew it was coming out of a piano, but she was certain she remembered hearing a violin during the time she had been dancing with Jim Nolan. She had wanted to ask some of the other men she was dancing with where the music was coming from, but she had not wanted to betray her ignorance of a house like this. In a house like this there would be a special room for the music, she was sure of that, although she did not know what the room might be called, or where it might be placed in the house. She had heard there was a cellar here with wine in it, but perhaps that was only a story.

People were always talking about the Ramsay family, and everyone had been surprised when Mrs. Ramsay invited all the ordinary people who worked in the shop to a party. It was nice of Mrs. Ramsay, but it was not like her to be all that familiar with those who worked for her. Mrs. Ramsay was very stately. She had been standing in the drawing room here holding court when Rose had arrived, and Rose had wondered if she should go up and greet her, but she had decided not to call attention to herself, and then the music had started, and the dancing. Father Kane had been standing at Mrs. Ramsay's elbow then, and he had waved at Rose but he had not beckoned to her to come and be introduced. Even so, Rose had hoped that Mrs. Ramsay would notice her, but Mrs. Ramsay had not noticed her. Mrs. Ramsay's youngest daughter had just come home from a year at school in Paris. Everyone said that the Ramsay girls were spoiled but that the youngest was the worst of the lot and that she had to have her own way in everything. Her name was Iris. Iris Ramsay. There was no sign of Iris Ramsay here tonight, but then it was not likely that she would bother with an affair like this when she had seen so much of the world and knew what was what.

Now she was sure that the music was coming from the dining room and she looked in that direction and there was Jim Nolan walking out of the dining room and toward the dancers in the company of two women Rose did not know except by sight—they both worked at Ramsay's. They were much older than Rose and she had admired their dresses earlier—they were both very smart. Jim had not so much as looked in her direction, although he must have known she was still standing there and that she was waiting for him. All the time she had been standing here he had been in the dining room talking with his real friends. Rose began to tremble.

The people dancing around on the floor seemed very noisy all of a sudden, and very much occupied with themselves, and selfish, and their talk and laughter sounded ill-humored and at the same time intimate, as though they rejoiced in a private joke at the expense of some person who might, at any moment, be at their mercy. Surely someone had turned up the lights; the room was too bright, and in the brightness, which was hard on her eyes, Rose felt that her face was burning, and her body felt confined and tired in the dress she had made for herself. She believed that she had made the dress well, and that she had even made it very well. She had dreamed that Mrs. Ramsay might notice her appearance, and might compliment her, and then she would be able to tell Mrs. Ramsay that she had made the dress herself, and from a pattern bought at Ramsay's, but that the choice of velvet had been her own—the pattern-maker had recommended taffeta. She had even gone so far as to imagine that she had made the dress better than she knew, and that Mrs. Ramsay, with her practiced eye for style, would notice how nicely it was cut, and that she would recognize in Rose what she had recognized years ago in Rose's father—the extra touch of imagination that she had told him he possessed, and the unusual instinct for color.

The room was too hot. She felt in the short sleeve of her dress for her lace handkerchief, so that she could pat her forehead with it, but the handkerchief was not there. She remembered taking it out of her raincoat pocket out there in the hall and fitting it carefully, all folded into a triangle as it was, into the sleeve, but now it was gone. But it couldn't be gone. It was real Irish linen, edged with real lace, and it had been a present from her mother four Christmases ago, and from the day she received it until tonight it had lain in its tissue paper in its original complicated pointed folds. She had never so much as shaken it out. She had barely touched it. It had stayed in its box, lying like a treasure at the bottom of the drawer where she kept her clothes, until tonight. It couldn't be gone, but it was gone. It must have slipped from her sleeve when she was dancing around so gaily, making a show of herself. If she hadn't been so taken with herself she might have felt it go. Now it was down there on the floor under someone's feet. It would be a rag by this time. Even if it was a rag, she would be glad to have it back. Her mother had hesitated a long time before buying it, and then she had asked that it be wrapped in white paper, because it was a present, and she had carried it home and walked in smiling and saying to Rose, "I have something lovely for you." It was the best handkerchief money could buy. Her mother had gone out to buy a woolen vest for herself, and she had seen the handkerchief, and instead of buying the vest for herself she had bought the handkerchief for Rose. The lace on it was real and there was a great deal of lace on it. When Rose first opened the box and lifted up the handkerchief, she and her mother looked at it very carefully, tracing the shells and roses and daisies and shamrocks and ivy leaves that covered it like the ornamentation on a wedding cake; and not funereal anyway, because they were so small and so white—not a cold or an icy white but a radiant white, like rose petals.

Rose knew that when a thing is gone it is gone. She tried not to think about the handkerchief, but she could not forget that it had been, was being, kicked around the room like a rag. There was no use thinking about it, and there was no use wondering who those plaster casts that he had called masks represented, or what names those faces had been called by when they were alive. If he were alive now, she would ask the names and tell him when she went home tonight. She would not mind asking. He had always said that she was very brave. But if he were alive now, he would be here tonight with all the rest of them and her mother would be here and the three of them would be the center of attention, because her father would have got along so fast and gone so high in Ramsay's after the curtains were up.

Rose had carefully not been staring at the dancers as they went by, but now she looked and saw, quite close, a tall dark girl with a pearly forehead. The girl was Dr. Malloy's wife, his bride, and she was dancing with her husband. They had been dancing together during most of the evening and once Rose had seen them talking and laughing with Mrs. Ramsay. They had not been married long. They had met in Dublin and been married there and Mrs. Malloy was still very much of a stranger. Rose had heard her mother say

261

that they were only children. And the woman next door had said they were children who did not know how well off they were and that some people went through life being spoiled. The woman next door had gone on to say that it was only an accident they had married at all, because Dr. Malloy had been interested in another girl altogether, and he had only married this one on the rebound. Rose's mother had said, "Oh, everyone knows she was not his first choice, and she knows it, too, poor girl." The Malloys were dancing smoothly in time with the music, which had grown faster, but they were not smiling or talking. They were looking at each other and their faces reflected a common memory that was still too new to be familiar and too brilliant to be believed in. Rose thought, They cannot take their eyes off each other.

Oh, why could everything not have been different? She looked away from the Malloys and tried to measure the distance, the great distance, between her and the door that would provide her with escape. Why could everything not have been different, but if everything had been different, everything would still have seemed exactly as strange to her. Her mother said, "Rose simply does not know the difference." Another time, her mother said, "Rose, you don't know the difference and you will not learn." But why could everything not have been different? Why could Hubert Derdon not have asked her to dance at least once? From time to time during the evening, she had seen him watching her and she thought he had even nodded at her once in a while as she danced around, but he had never made a move to come near her and now there was no sign of him at all. Why had Jim Nolan asked her to dance if he was only going to make a fool of her? Why had Mrs. Ramsay not made some sign of recognition, and why had Father Kane not even taken the trouble to speak to her? Why were the ceilings so high in this house, and why were all the girls so sure of themselves, and why had nobody taken the trouble to see that she, Rose, got something to eat, or a glass of lemonade at least? She was not going to walk into that dining room by herself and walk up to the table, or tables, or whatever they had, and ask for something as if she was a beggar.

The only thing to do now was to get out of the room as quickly as she could. It did not matter who saw her or what they said about her. It could not be helped if Hubert was around the hall and saw her. She did not care what he thought or what anybody thought. She longed to be at home and out of sight. She would make her way out of the room and go upstairs and take her raincoat off the big rack that was set along on the landing up there. Then she would slip out of the house and go home by herself. It was a very long way and she was afraid of the dark but she had to get home. Her mother would want to know what sort of a feast Mrs. Ramsay had provided and she would not be able to tell her. And where was the music coming from? She knew nothing. She felt she knew nothing.

She hurried toward the end of the room, keeping so carefully out of the way of the dancers that she scraped the shoulder of her dress twice against the wall. Her dress would be marked from the wall, but that did not matter now. And after all, it turned out to be quite easy to make her way through the throng that was collected at the end of the room. None of them looked at her, and no one seemed to think that there was anything at all remarkable in her appearance, alone and hurrying as she was. She need never have feared that they would imagine she was trying to push herself upon them.

The big square hall was deserted but someone had opened the front door to let the cold air in and Rose began to shiver as she ran up the stairs. It would serve them all right if she caught a bad cold. One blessing—the landing was deserted, and the bathroom door by the coat rack was open to show, in the wall inside, a square window of red-and-green glass. It would be very dark out. She turned to the big rack that was crowded with ladies' coats and scarves and began to rummage for her raincoat. A sound from the long dim hall behind her made her turn and she saw a girl in a bright-blue uniform coming out of one of the rooms. It was Mary Lacey, who had gone to school with her.

"Oh, Mary," Rose said, "I never saw you in your uniform before."

"And you in your silks and satins," Mary said, in a disagreeable tone, but her face was forlorn.

"Oh, Mary, I made it myself, every stitch," Rose said, "and it's only the cheapest velvet—nothing like as good as the curtains on the windows downstairs. I bet your uniform cost a lot more than this, Mary, and better made, too."

"Oh, the same old Rose," Mary said. "You haven't changed a bit. I remember the day after your poor father's funeral. You came to school, we were at our desks waiting for the nun to come in, and you said to me, 'Oh, Mary,' you said, 'it was a lovely funeral, only for the coffin.'"

She opened her hand and they both looked at the key that lay there on her palm.

"I had to lock all the rooms up here earlier, before anybody got here," she said. "She's that afraid somebody might try to steal something from her. And then she told me to come from time to time and see if everything was all right. I don't mind. I'm glad enough to get out of the kitchen. They left the door open between the kitchen and the pantry, and every time the dining-room door opened I kept looking along to see what I could see. I couldn't help myself."

"I'd forgotten about the coffin," Rose said. "My mother said, 'It's time to close the coffin.'"

"With all they have in this house," Mary said, "all their belongings and all their money and all, you'd think they'd have different keys for the rooms, but no, it's the same key for all the rooms. The kitchen used to be in the basement but they brought it upstairs. They can do anything they like."

"Is it very hard work, Mary?" Rose asked.

"Oh, it's more tedious than anything," Mary said. "Not hard. But look, there's someone on the stairs. Come on back in here with me."

She pushed open the door of the room she had just left and went in there, with Rose following her, and closed the door softly behind them. The room was dark except for the faint red light cast by an altar lamp that burned low under a large picture of the Sacred Heart. The picture was hung between two windows and the lamp was set on top of a glass-fronted cabinet that stood against the wall there. Rose could see the shine of the glass panels and through the glass small white shapes, of little ornaments, perhaps, precious china ornaments that were too good to be left out where they might be touched. The curtains were drawn across the windows; she could see only tall dark forms where the light would enter in the daytime. And where the darkness became impenetrable she knew the bed was, by the outline and the bulk she sensed there. But Mary was pulling her by the arm.

"Look, Rose. Look at that. Did you ever see the like of that? It's her dressing table. I'll never forget the first time I saw it. It's all glass. Even the little knobs on the drawers are glass. Only the legs are wooden. Isn't it lovely?"

"It's lovely," Rose said, and as she approached it, walking only a few steps to it, she began to see her own shadow and then her face in the large oval mirror that made its center, and then she saw Mary, who was standing behind her, and the two girls stood and watched themselves.

A Free Choice

"We look very mysterious," Mary said. "Don't you think we look mysterious—as if we weren't here at all. I wish I looked like this always. I'm fatter than you are."

"It's the uniform," Rose said. "It's too big for you."

Mary giggled. "I knew you'd say that," she said. "The minute you said it, before you said it, I knew that was what you'd say. I wish I could always look mysterious, this way. I don't look like myself at all. I could float up and down the main street and I wouldn't care what anyone said about me. I'd go to Dublin and then to London and I wouldn't say anything to anybody. And if anybody said anything to me I'd say, 'I'm Miss Iris Ramsay and I don't like *anything*.' . . . She makes me sick, that one, the way she goes around the house pretending to talk French. And there's nothing anybody can do to please her. Her mother is going to do the whole house over for her. That's why she's having this party, to get all the good they can out of the place before they start to do it up. They would have had to move everything anyway—the carpets and the furniture and everything. They're going to get all new curtains and new paint and new wallpaper everywhere, and a new carpet for Miss Iris's room."

"They're going to take down all the curtains?" Rose said.

"All the curtains, downstairs and up here. She says the place is too heavy and old-fashioned. She wants all light colors. And she wants this dressing table for herself. She says it's not suitable for an older lady. She says it's suitable for *her* room. She's to have it. She means to have it and she will have it. When could I ever put out my hand and see a thing I wanted and say that it was mine? Oh, what difference does it make to me? I have to laugh. What difference does it make where it is? Not a particle of difference. What do I care what room it's in? Whatever room it's in, it's still not mine. This room or that room or her room or some other room, I'll see it just as much and want it just as much. Tell me something, Rose. I want to know— Is Jim Nolan down there?"

"Yes. I saw him. He's down there," Rose said.

"I thought I heard him," Mary said. "First I thought I heard him talking and then I thought I heard him laughing and then—I was in the kitchen; he must have come into the dining room—and just before I came up here I heard him again."

"I saw him," Rose said. "Here and there. He was talking to two women from Ramsay's—Miss Martin, I think her name is, and another one."

"I knew he'd be here," Mary said. "Oh, what's the use. I knew he was here. He always goes around with the same gang of fellows, and when I saw one of them, Tommy Rice, I knew he was here."

"He fancies himself," Rose said angrily.

"You're right there," Mary said. "He fancies himself. Oh, yes, he fancies himself. No doubt about that. He fancies himself. More and more he fancies himself. But I knew that."

(These were the words she said, but her voice, helpless, went on its own way. *He is perfect,* her voice said. *He is perfect. He is perfect. Yes, he is. Perfect.*)

"I was great with him once," she said. "Well, I suppose I can say I was great with him. It was only for a couple of weeks, a little over two weeks, last summer. He thought I was great. I believed him. It must have been a poor sort of greatness that I had, but I didn't know the difference then. Oh, I don't care. It's over and done with. When a person doesn't want you he doesn't want you. Oh, I wish I could go away. Even a few miles, but I wish I could go to Dublin."

"Oh, Mary, I wish there was something I could say to you," Rose said. "I would like to kill him. He is not good enough for you. It's awful. Everything is all wrong. You are worth ten of him."

A Free Choice

Mary looked at her as though she might say something, and then she looked as though she had decided not to say what she really wanted to say but to say something else instead. "Oh, it doesn't matter," she said. She sat down in the easy chair that stood not far from the dressing table and she put her head back and sighed.

Rose took a step toward her and would have touched her, but she was afraid of making the pain worse. She tried to think of the word that would mean comfort to Mary, but either she could think of no words at all or all the words she thought of were wrong. It was useless. "When a person does not want you, he does not want you." That is what Mary had said, and Rose knew it for the truth, but how she knew she did not know.

She thought of Hubert Derdon, and of how he had looked at her last night, when he had asked to see her home, and of how he had looked at her tonight, when he had not asked her to dance. She felt she was between the devil and the deep blue sea. The last few evenings, when Hubert had been coming to the house every evening, she had been glad to see him walk in, and happy and excited as long as he was there, but every evening, the minute he stood up to leave, she had wanted to tell him not to bother to come back again, and to tell him that she was not depending on his visits. Every time he walked out away from her into the night, without even a hint that he might come back, she felt like telling him that it meant nothing to her whether he came back or not; but he always went without a word, smiling at her but never giving her a chance to tell him that if he never appeared in the house again she did not care, and that she would rather he never came back at all than to come back and go off again leaving her with what was worse than emptiness.

She would rather have no hope at all, and know there was no chance for her, than to have to contend with this little hope she had, that she was ashamed of, because it was so little and so timid. She felt that Hubert knew about this hope—that it was little and that it was timid—and that he was amused by it and that he was playing with her and hoping she would betray herself and then, for some reason unknown to anyone, he would laugh at her. And her mother would laugh, too. And her mother's reason for laughter was not unknown to her but familiar. Her mother would laugh out of despair, because once again Rose had let the side down. Her mother would laugh because her mother knew that sooner or later somebody would let the side down, because that is the way it was in their family. It was bad enough to be not good enough, but to invite laughter was a crime against the family. And everybody outside the house was ready to laugh. Her mother had told her again and again that they were all only waiting to see somebody make a false step.

Rose did not want to turn away from Hubert, because to turn away would be to admit that she had been turned toward him and had been disappointed. It was very important to keep hope secret, because then the disappointment that followed would also be secret. A girl who let herself in for being laughed at deserved what she got. Rose did not want to turn away from Hubert and tell him never to darken her door again, but she wanted to turn away from him before he had the chance to turn away from her. But she did not really want to turn away from him at all, because without him before her eyes she would have to look again at what did not exist—except in darkness, where it could not be seen, although she knew it saw, and in sleep, where it could not be heard, although she knew it cried out to her. She did not want her father to see her sad.

The red flame under the picture of the Sacred Heart flickered wildly, and sank, and went out. Rose put her hands to her face to keep herself quiet and then she put both hands out and caught

A Free Choice

Mary by the shoulder and felt her start from sleep to wakefulness. "Oh, Mary," she said, "wake up quick! The Sacred Heart lamp has gone out! Please wake up."

Mary sighed, and then she jumped to her feet. "Oh, Rose," she said. "How long was I asleep? Was it long?"

"Only two or three minutes, Mary. I wouldn't have wakened you only that the lights—the light in the lamp there went out. I'd better be getting on downstairs. I shouldn't be in this room at all."

"You'd better be getting downstairs and I'd better get back down to the kitchen. I'll get another light for the lamp. I'm going to open the door now, Rose, but don't you go out till I see if there's anyone on the landing."

There was no one on the landing, and as Mary bent to lock the door behind her she smiled up at Rose. "I don't know what's the matter with me, falling asleep," she said. "I keep falling asleep. Every time I sit down, I fall asleep."

She walked quickly away from Rose toward the back stairs and she must have heard Rose call her name but she did not turn around or look back. Even after she had disappeared Rose continued to look after her. She had remembered a hundred things to say to Mary, but she had not been able to remember the right thing to say. She knew that if she had been able to take away all the wrong words she would certainly have found, underneath them all, the one word that would kill pain, and kill it, and make it never come back anymore. There was such a word. She had known it once, and she knew it still, but she could not translate it for Mary. *Father.*

What Rose wanted was a word for Father. She wanted a word that she could *say*. There was a simpler word for Father now, but she did not know what it was. In his new form, he was formless, and would not answer to Father. There was a word for him now, as he was now, but she did not know what it was, only that it was a common word, and that she ought to know it so that she could say it to herself in a whisper. Once, he took her to the abandoned quarry outside the town, and they stood together near the edge, and saw the glitter of water on the bottom far below them, and he had thrown a penny in, and they had watched it drop down, and he had told her that the penny would fall forever and that it would never stop falling, because the quarry was bottomless and the water they could see was only the beginning of a drop so deep that no man could imagine it. He said that for all he knew, and for all anyone knew, the penny might continue to fall through all eternity. And then he had laughed at her and told her that if she wanted to save money she should throw it in the quarry, because no one would ever find it there, and only she would know where it was. Only she, and only he.

In the hall below, Hubert waited alone and watched for Rose to come down the stairs. He held her lace handkerchief in his hand. He had seen it slip from her sleeve as she entered the drawing room, and he had picked it up and put it in his pocket to keep for her. He would have told her he had it, but she had given him no chance to speak to her. She had danced off, and then she had gone on dancing, round and round the room, and finally she had begun dancing with that Nolan fellow, and he had gone off in a rage to the dining room and eaten ham sandwiches one after another so that he would not have to watch her smiling in the arms of that glorified corner boy, that ladies' delight, that actor at love.

Hubert was angry and anxious. She had slipped away. He had lost her forever. He was sure of it. He had looked for her everywhere. He did not want to ask one of the girls to go up and find out if she was all right. He did not know Rose very well and he did not want to annoy her. And he did not want to ask anyone to go up anyway, for fear that she might not be up there at all. All these past nights it had been the same thing every night. Every night he had gone to her house to make sure she was still there and had not vanished, and every night, when she saw him to the door, she turned that face to him that said she was seeing him for the last time, and did not care—that face of indifference and of downright cruelty. Because she knew very well why he came back, night after night, without being asked, and without any hope of being asked, apparently. She must have known why he continued to appear at her door, making a fool of himself, and not caring that he was making a fool of himself. And he didn't care that he was making a fool of himself now, standing right out in the middle of the hall with her little handkerchief in his hand. He had begun his vigil by leaning carelessly over there against the open front door, with his hand and her handkerchief in his pocket, and a careless eye on the stairs, but his anxiety had got the better of him and he had moved near and nearer to the foot of the stairs until now it was all he could do to restrain himself from going up the stairs two at a time and calling out to her to come to him and stop her nonsense. But what if she wasn't up there? She might have vanished, flown, slipped away home by herself. It was only to be expected. She would do whatever came into her head. She had no sense. She was like a child. She often appeared to him like a child who walks through a madhouse and is not afraid because she does not know the difference between inside and out. But she had every right to be afraid. Anything might happen to her. What if she had taken it into her head to go off home alone? He might never see her again, because she was as good as invisible with that mother of hers always there in the kitchen with them every night, always there and always talking.

Then Rose appeared, coming around the curve of the banisters from the landing above. Hubert thought, Lord, what a beautiful house this is. Look at the wonderful staircase they have. And he

watched Rose. He thought, She is immortal, with that fair hair. . . .
She made him think of the Forest of Arden. She had her coat over
her arm and she was coming down slowly one step at a time, like a
child. He thought she looked discontented, but then she glanced up
and saw him watching her and she gave him a conspiratorial smile,
as though he had seen her at a disadvantage and she did not mind.
He thought, She is not very big, and he wondered admiringly what
size shoe she wore. When she reached the third step from the
bottom she stood still and looked at him.

"I am afraid of the stairs," she said, and then she said, "You
look very polite, standing there."

"I was thinking I would like to take a bite out of you," he said,
and he grinned foolishly as she stepped down three more times and
came to stand before him.

He gave her the handkerchief, relinquishing it as though he
were giving up his passport, or his ticket of passage, or, as it was, his
one and only hope of refuge in her country. She took the handkerchief without surprise, but he saw how her fingers closed around it
once she had it in her hand. She looked at him and he thought, She
is the only one in the world who can see me. . . . Her eyes were
green, the color of seaweed, and in their depths he found the light
that would define him and enclose him in constancy. He thought,
She is my own true self, and he wanted to tell her all his troubles.

"I can't dance," he said. "I would have told you before, but I
was ashamed."

"Hubert," she said, "there were a whole lot of things I wanted
to tell you. I wanted to tell you about my handkerchief, that it was
lost, but it wasn't lost at all, but I didn't know that. There were a
whole lot of other things I wanted to tell you about, about the
curtains and so on—a whole lot of things. But first I want to know
—there is no one else I can ask, but please don't laugh at me—I've
been wanting to know, where is the music coming from?"

A Free Choice

"Oh, wait till I show you," he said. "It's as good as an orchestra. You'd never find it unless you were looking for it. The house is bigger than you would think. We have to go through the drawing room. Wait till you see. I'd never have found it only that I was looking for you."

He took her coat and folded it over the back of a chair. "That will be safe there," he said.

He took her hand and led her toward the drawing room as though they were about to dance, like the others. At the entrance he felt her hesitate before the confusion in the room, and he smiled at her to encourage her.

"Come along now, Rose," he said, "chin up and step together. If we're not careful some of these lunatics will trample us under."